TROUBLE AT BUZZARD PASS

ALSO BY JOHNNY GUNN

Western Short Story Showcase

Brookside, Oregon Territory Series
Ezekiel's Journey Series
Jack Slater Series
Slim Calhoun, Bull Morrison Westerns
Snake and the Dog-Man Classic Westerns
Terrence Corcoran Series

TROUBLE AT BUZZARD PASS

SNAKE AND THE DOG-MAN
BOOK 4

JOHNNY GUNN

WOLFPACK
PUBLISHING
— EST 2013 —

Trouble at Buzzard Pass
Paperback Edition
Copyright © 2023 Johnny Gunn

Wolfpack Publishing
9850 S. Maryland Parkway, Suite A-5 #323
Las Vegas, Nevada 89183

wolfpackpublishing.com

Paperback ISBN 978-1-63977-873-7
eBook ISBN 978-1-63977-181-3
LCCN 2023948609

TROUBLE AT BUZZARD PASS

"THIS AIN'T what I had in mind, boys. Five scrawny cows?" Joshua Baker pulled his Winchester up to his shoulder and killed two of the cows with two fast shots. He levered a third round home and spun on the three outlaws standing off to the side. "Ain't even worth skinnin' 'em out more or less sellin' 'em."

"There weren't any better than these, boss," Adrian Nestor almost whined out. "Somebody gave you some bad information. There weren't no more than twenty cows in the whole damn range. Sure weren't no good-looking steers."

Baker was closing in on twenty-five years, had already spent four of those in prison, and carried anger close to the surface daily. He got the information from Claudio Valenzuela that there would be a thousand or more steers, ready for market, on the east range of the Lazy R ranch, fifty miles west of Lane's Crossing.

"Get rid of these stinking pieces of crap," Baker said. "I'll be back. Sanchez, ride with me."

Victorio Sanchez was a twenty-year-old charro

straight out of the mountains of northern Mexico. His English was good, his horsemanship was better, and he was more cow savvy than most. He also had learned the art of the running iron early in life. He could turn almost any brand into whatever it was you wanted. Juan Vasquez, the fourth member of the gang, was also an expert with the running brand.

Baker's gang had been raiding ranches in and around the large San Bernardino County for two years, and a lack of law enforcement was almost an active partner. Running off to Mexico with small numbers of large herds kept the gang in money, food, and liquor. Many of the large ranchers didn't get along with each other, hadn't formed cooperatives for protection, and Baker used that to his benefit.

It was coming fall, time to bring the herds down from the high mountains and get them ready for the markets. There were several packing facilities that in turn served the large Los Angeles basin and south into the growing San Diego areas.

"Where we goin', boss?"

"To kill a man, Sanchez. To kill the man gave me some wrong information. A liar." Baker could almost hear Valenzuela's laughter when he found out that Baker swiped five dry cows instead of fifty or more fat steers. "We're gonna kill the man that told me about them steers you boys couldn't find."

"You sure you want to ride into Lane's Crossing? That sheriff don't much like you, and he promised to kill me on sight. You sure about this, boss?"

"I ain't never been more sure of something in my life, Victorio. We're gonna ride in, find that lying bastard, fill him with half a pound of lead or more, and ride out. Mallory won't even know we've been there."

2

"Claudio's still working at the Desert Rat Saloon and that's across the street from the sheriff's office. I'm with you, boss, but we better be muy careful, eh?"

"Take us the rest of the day and into the night to make the ride, Sanchez. We'll walk in the back door of that saloon, up to the bar, kill that lying fool, and walk right back out. If Mallory's having his after supper cordial"—Baker snickered at his joke—"we'll kill him too. Let's ride."

"ONE OF THESE mornings it ain't gonna be there and I'm gonna know I'm dead." Snake had a cup of coffee in hand as he walked out the front door of his house, high in the San Bernardino Mountains of Southern California. He watched the sun make its appearance, casting brilliant light all across the dreaded Mojave Desert, lighting rimrock ridges, cascading into meadows just below the porch he was standing on.

Those meadows were home to a large herd of cattle and a smaller herd of horses. "Don't know just what it is that I've done to deserve all this, but it must have been sumpin' fierce." He looked around and realized he was alone on the porch and just kept right on talking anyway. Texans, he told people, always talked to themselves. *A great mind enjoying a great mind.*

Andalusian mares and foals were prancing and dancing in the nearest pasture as Snake settled down into a chair to enjoy his morning coffee. "Ain't been but a few years ago and old Dog-man and I got ourselves run right out of Deadwood. Best thing that ever happened to this old boy."

He laughed thinking about him and Dog-man trying

to sell maps to gold mines that weren't really for sale. "Chased us off, that sheriff did, and we stumbled into some fine pay-dirt somewhere in Mexico. And now look at us, sittin' on some fine ground in California."

They named their ranch the Rocking Snake, and that was also the brand. The blacksmith in Lane's Crossing is still cursing them out. Those branding irons were more than difficult to fabricate and probably impossible to alter into something else.

Far out to the west, dimly lit by the early sun, he watched two men on horseback move some cattle from one one-hundred-acre pasture into another, both deep green with rich grasses. "Gotta be taking them critters to market soon. We are talking prime critters, too."

Snake is about thirty, lean to skinny, smart-ass from the word go. Has a head full of blondish hair that is always in need of a comb or scissors, and like most mornings, he hasn't quite got his shirt tucked in yet. He and his trail partner, Dog-man, have spent the last few years dodging the law a few times, working with the law a time or two, finding a prosperous gold mine, making friends and enemies from Deadwood to El Paso and from Las Cruces to San Bernardino.

They have settled in these beautiful mountains just outside Lane's Crossing, a major stop for those traveling across the Mojave Desert. Lane's Crossing is near the headwaters of the Mojave River, a long ribbon of water that runs mostly underground. Where it surfaces, there are water hole stops that are the lifeblood of the desert. The trail is becoming more and more necessary as development in Arizona Territory needs what's available in Southern California.

Lane's Crossing is in the San Gabriel Mountains, home to ranches, a few mines, and a few outlaws. Snake could look west across a vast valley or unusually wide and deep canyon, toward the San Bernardinos. That area has been known as the Cajon Pass since the early days of Spanish exploration and the ranches there are from early land grants issued by the King of Spain.

Lush grasses, rolling hills, ancient hardwood forests of oak, live oak, and the softer woods of pine and cedar, make for raising exceptional cattle herds. Exceptional cattle herds are magnets for banditos, rustlers, con-men, and card sharps.

The road from the coast of California to the blistering deserts of Arizona Territory come right through Cajon Canyon and Lane's Crossing. Supplies are moved by way of express companies, herds are moved to market, and outlaws feel right at home.

Snake heard some noises inside the log home he built and slowly eased himself all the way up and ambled inside. "Up with the sun, are we? Good morning, my darling," he said, gathering Louise, better known as Lion Killer in his long arms. "Got us another beautiful morning out there."

"We need to take a long ride through those wild hills out there and figure out what kind of herd we'll put together for the market. Ain't never been on a cattle drive, Snake. It's all I can think about."

Memories of April and her children, of driving those cattle through Arizona's terrible desert, flashed through Snake's head and he had to shake them back into the shadows. Before they left, though, he wondered how she was holding up with her new husband. How were those little scamps he came to love.

He held her back at arm's length and enjoyed the view. Louise was tall and thin, her hair hung in long waves and curls, and her eyes were as bright as the

5

morning sun. "Don't rightly know why you like me, girl, but I surely do know why I like you. Let's make that ride today. Bring a couple of the boys along to keep a good tally."

"Bring Pedro, too. He's getting so big and strong, Snake. You saved his life and brought him home as a little Mexican orphan. We'll never let him go. He follows you around, tries to walk like you, tries to talk like you. You're something, cowboy."

Snake found Louise on his and Dog-man's trek across the Mojave Desert, a waif of a girl, badly injured and alone. She and her father were skin and hide hunters, and while she was out lion hunting Indians attacked and killed her father. She and Snake locked eyes and soon locked up in marriage.

It was a rocky start, getting their ranch put together, fighting off outlaws, she finding herself pregnant and then being wounded in a fire-fight and losing the baby. It wasn't all bad for the couple. Snake saved the young Mexican boy, Pedro, and they adopted him. He's eight years old and idolizes Snake and Louise.

"He was skinny, weak, and afraid of his shadow just a year ago. Today, he's a fine horseman who wrestles with some of the charros who work the ranch. We'll have a quick breakfast and make that ride," Snake said. "Get Pedro up. He's wanted to do this for a week."

"When we run the cattle into market, will we bring the horses too?" Louise asked. "They are so beautiful."

"No, we take the cattle to meat market, not those horses. We'll have our own ranch sale next spring. Those horses, straight out of Spanish royal blood, trained by Mexican vaqueros, will sell at a high premium, pretty girl. It's a long line of horse tradition that goes all the way back to the Arabs and we're a part of it now."

2

DOG-MAN, ranch foreman Francisco Alvarado, and hired hand Wayne Nichols were standing at one of the corrals watching horses run, making dust when Snake and company arrived. "What's your plan, Snake?" Dog-man asked.

"Count some fat steers," he said. "Join us?"

"Love to, but today's mail day. Gonna ride into town and see if we got any word from

Gila Bend or Tucson. We've got money coming from both places, Snake and haven't heard a word from anyone for some time. We got some of the money from George Dawson for running those freight wagons through. I'm thinking he might have put the rest in our account. I'll check the bank, too."

Money from their gold mine in Mexico and from other activities has been in an account they've drawn on to buy the ranch, stock, and implements, and other expenses. Lane's Crossing gets mail and supplies from Arizona Territory once a week and from Southern California once a week. "Thought I'd take Juanito with me."

Dog-man looked at the skinny little charro and chuckled. "He can't count anyway."

Juanito used a couple of well-worn Mexican phrases that would have brought a blush to a whore house madam, and Louise laughed right out. "Ooh, you bad boy," she said. "You two are going to get in trouble, aren't you? That's the whole purpose of going to town."

"Not me, Señora Snake," Juanito said, but his eyes were dancing and he couldn't hide the grin. "Only have one, maybe two little tiny drinks of Mescal. No more."

"That's right, Juanito, we're going to town on business," Dog-man said. "This is serious business."

"While you're doing your serious business, order what supplies we'll need to move our cattle to market. The big stockyards are in San Bernardino, so we'll be on the trail for some time." Snake said. "We'll have a good count by the time you get back."

Along with cattle Snake and Dog-man were also in the horse business by way of their foreman, Alvarado. Breeding and training Spanish Andalusian horses in the Spanish and Mexican vaquero tradition will add to their ranches' viability. Snake comes from the Texas school of horsemanship and found himself adept at the vaquero methods which were similar.

Snake, Louise, and Pedro walked into the barn to tack out their horses and Dog-man and Juanito moved into the corral to find theirs. "Heard that Lucy Gonzalez has opened a new cantina, Juanito. Good place for us to have dinner after our business."

"Desert Rat Saloon is good place to find Mescal, Señor Dog-man. Pretty girls, too." He laughed.

IT WAS a quick five-mile ride into Lane's Crossing, a busy little desert community that thrived on people moving through, west to east, and east to west. Permanent population was under three hundred, many of whom were older men who had spent their years prospecting in that vast desert to the east.

One would find them on most lazy afternoons settled onto benches along the main road swapping stories, creating new stories, and watching all the traffic move through. From time to time one would get up, stretch, and wander into a drinking palace for a cold beer to cool off some, and then wander off to a different bench.

Dog-man nodded to many as he walked the street, and many went out of their way to ask about Lion Killer. They took that girl into their hearts because, as so many knew, she was one of them despite her young age. Her story, losing her father, being well known among the tribes of the desert, and helping Snake and Dog-man protect their ranch while being seriously wounded, was just what they loved talking about most.

There weren't that many men who made their living off the hides of wild animals and Louise was the only woman any of them knew about. The fact that wolves and lions didn't intimidate her in the least was only part of her story. Folk tales were spread wide about people like Lion Killer.

"Go to the general mercantile store, Juanito, and I'll meet you after I pick up the mail." The young charro, dressed for a day in town, not on the range, smiled and took off. His pants flared and showed color in the flair, his sombrero was canted at a roguish angle, and his spurs shone in the sunlight. He wore a blazing white shirt, a black horsehide vest, and carried a sidearm with the distinctive Colt name tucked in a black holster.

On the other side of the wide gun belt was a frontier-style knife that was honed to razor sharpness. The handle was hewn from an elk horn and fit the charro's hand perfectly. His young face shone in the hot sun telling anyone interested that he was in town to have a bit of fun.

Dog-man walked into the Wells Fargo office for his mail. "Got anything for us, Sam?"

"I just got it separated, Dog-man and there's a couple for you and Snake. Sheriff was in and said if I saw you, he wanted to have a chat." He handed a letter and a larger package to Dog-man and went back to his little desk.

The letter was from George Dawson as was the package and Dog-man made his way to the general mercantile store to meet Juanito. He stopped in the sheriff's office on the way and found Mallory at his desk. "You're looking fine, Sheriff. Been out in the sun, eh?"

"Morning, Dog-man. Sit down, have some coffee. Need to talk about a couple of things. I've got word that Josh Baker and his gang of rustlers are starting to make their moves on some of the cattle herds. Anything you or Snake have heard?"

"Getting ready to put our critters together and move 'em to market but haven't been off the place for some time. Baker? He's got a great need for killin', that man has. He runs off with some fine beef and runs 'em down to Mexico." Dog-man settled in with a cup of coffee. "We'll have all our hands and their guns moving our herd. He needs to be taken down hard."

"Your boys are good," Mallory said. "Word I got is that the big YR herd will be hit first. Their cattle are some of the finest in the canyon."

"Next to ours." Dog-man chuckled. "Baker needs to be taken out of business. Did the coach driver say anything about an attempt on him? He was sure upset on his last ride over."

"No, and after talking to him, I'm sure it was Baker who made that last attempt. Sloppy work for sure. He lost one man, Wells Fargo lost a messenger, but no passengers or mail was lost. Baker shows up around Lane's Crossing and I'll take him out."

Mallory, not too many years ago, had been a fine sheriff but the years have weighed him down. Years and a few bullets, a knife or two, and many, many fists and feet. Dog-man was looking at a tired old man sitting behind the desk and wondered whether Mallory had it in him to take on Joshua Baker and his gang.

"Let me know if you hear anything else about Baker. I'll pass all this on to Snake and our crew. We'll be leaving out in a week or two. Don't pass that on to anyone." He shook hands with the sheriff and made his way to the mercantile store. "Half the day is gone already," he muttered, angling off to the south for the big marketplace.

3

"GOT THAT LIST FIGURED OUT, JUANITO?" Dog-man nodded to George Peterson, the storekeeper and found a chair near the pot-belly stove that hadn't been lit once since March. *Just a normal thing to do, I guess. Plunk down near the stove even if it is ninety degrees outside.* He snickered at his thoughts and opened the letter from George Dawson. *Hope this is good news. Damn, I walked right by the bank. Well, this letter first.*

Juanito and Peterson were still going over the list Juanito brought in. "I think we've just about got it all," Peterson said. "They'll have that railroad through here one year soon and you won't be making trail rides anymore. I'm already planning for a stockyard right here in Lane's Crossing. Got the ground, got the contract for a siding right up to my place. Yes, sir, got that contract signed and sealed."

Peterson was the kind of businessman who was always looking ahead. He didn't deal in what was happening today, was far more interested in what was being planned for tomorrow. If tomorrow arrived,

Peterson would be there, a broad smile on his freckled face, to welcome it.

"That's mighty good news." Dog-man folded the letter and stood up. "Sheriff just told me that Joshua Baker's gang is on the move again. Railroad will put him out of business. If I send the wagon in tomorrow will you have all this put together?"

Peterson was among the first to settle in Lane's Crossing, built and leased out several of the buildings along the main road, including the big three-story hotel. "My boys will have it all ready for you, Dog-man. Mallory say anything about hiring a deputy or two? That man's in no shape to be sheriff. Should have retired a year or more ago. Some of us were serious when we wanted Snake to be our South County Sheriff. Sure wished he'd a taken us up on the offer."

"Can't run a ranch like ours and be a sheriff, too. Mr. Peterson." Dog-man smiled and nodded his head. "There are some hereabouts that want you to hold the job."

"And run this place, too?" Both men were laughing at the thought. "Seriously, though, we do need a new sheriff. Need to find a nice young man who ain't afraid of nothing. Keep your eyes out for one, eh?"

"Will do. Let's hit the bank, Juanito, and then grab something to eat. I'm starved." He looked at the store-keeper. "Where did Lucy Gonzalez open her new cantina?"

"One block over, Dog-man. Good food, too," Peterson said, pointing south.

DOG-MAN WAS SATISFIED with their account, heard more stories about an uptick in rustling and hits on stages, and he and Juanito headed for the cantina. "I'd rather not ride home in the dark, Juanito, but it looks like that might happen. We'll get some good food in us, have one drink at the Desert Rat Saloon, and leave out."

The day was rapidly coming to an end, men, women, and children were filling tables in the cantina when Dog-man and Juanito walked in. "Just in time, eh? Another ten minutes and this place would be filled." The cantina served all the old Mexican and Spanish dishes and the aroma spilled out onto the street all day long. There was never a time between five in the morning and eleven at night that someone wasn't at a table eating.

"You order, Juanito. My Spanish is horrible."

"I like the way Señor Snake speaks my language. It's funny to hear him talk. You talk good, Señor Dog-man." He and the lovely lady taking the order spent several moments flirting before Juanito made their order.

"Mighty pretty young girl, there. Be careful, Juanito."

The strong and good-looking charro smiled and would welcome the kind of danger Dog-man alluded to. "The danger of a beautiful young woman would be most welcome," he said. "Danger for some is bliss for others, señor."

———

"WE AIN'T but an hour out of Lane's Crossing, Sanchez. We'll ride in on the back street and go in the back door at the saloon. Most important that I kill Valenzuela. If we run into that old sheriff, we kill him, too."

As they approached the village, dusk was changing to night, and they rode at a quiet walk down one of the side streets and turned toward the main road and the Desert Rat Saloon. It was mid-week and far from any paydays at ranches or mines, and the two men eased their way into a mostly empty saloon by way of the back door. Some called it the privy door as it led to the outside necessary.

Four men were standing at the long bar, a couple of tables were occupied by some of the old prospectors, still telling wild tales, and Sweet Sue from Saint Lou was at the piano slinging words and notes in all directions. Manuel Valenzuela was behind the bar polishing a glass and listening to some of the men talking.

Valenzuela was in his forties, wore his black hair slicked back, had a thin, pencil mustache and long flowing sideburns. His white shirt was starched as was his white half-apron.

"There's that sumbitch, Sanchez. Let's just walk right up to the end of the bar. It's open there and when he comes down, we'll sink our knives as deep as they'll go."

"That man with those two, over there," and Sanchez nodded to three men in the middle of the bar, "is the sheriff." Sanchez had a worried look on his face. "Can we take both Valenzuela and Mallory out at the same time?"

"Your take out, Manuel. I'll take out the sheriff. Make it quick and quiet and run like hell for the horses," Baker said. "I've wanted the sheriff for a long time."

———

"WE'VE GOT TROUBLE, SHERIFF," Dog-man said. He nodded without looking directly out to the side. "Baker and one of his guns just came in the back door. They're behind you." Dog-man nodded to Juanito. "Watch out for that feller with Baker."

Dog-man and Juanito hadn't even had time to sip their first beer when Baker came in. Dog-man spotted the sheriff when they came in and joined his table. He wanted to ask some of the questions that Peterson had brought up, such as hiring deputies or even giving consideration to retiring.

Mallory used the mirror behind the bar to watch Baker move toward him. "Coming right at me," he muttered. Juanito saw Sanchez move toward the end of the bar and drifted that way while Dog-man never took his eyes off Baker. Whether Baker saw that or not, isn't known, but he kept the sheriff between himself and Dog-man thinking that Dog-man had no play.

"He's got a knife," Dog-man said, pulling his weapon, finding the sheriff blocking any shot he might take. The sheriff was too late trying to turn and pull his side piece, felt the knife drive deep into his chest, felt his knees go limp. Sheriff Mallory was all but dead as he crashed to the floor.

Baker pulled the long blade, spun and ran as hard as he could for the back door. Dog-man had his Remington out and got two shots off before Baker was out of the building. Sanchez saw the sheriff go down, Valenzuela was still too far away and ran hard for the back door. Dog-man shot him dead before he reached the door.

"Make sure he's dead," Dog-man yelled out and knelt next to Sheriff Mallory. Mallory bled out before anyone could do anything to help him. Dog-man looked into the sad old face, now with a rather calm and peaceful look to it and stood up. "Too late for the doc," Dog-man said. "How's that idiot?"

Juanito stood up. "One dead idiot, boss," Juanito said. "I think you might have hit Baker. I'll go check."

"Wait, we'll both go." Juanito was young, aggressive, and willing to do anything Snake or Dog-man asked of him, but he had to be slowed down once in a while.

"Gotta think. Baker might be down but holding a big weapon waiting for you to go boiling out that door."

"Aaii. Not good for my health."

They opened the back door slowly, well back on each side and when there were no shots, they stepped out. Sanchez's horse stood at the rail, alone. Dog-man shook his head. "Happened so fast. Snake would have killed him."

"You hit him," Juanito said. He was on his knees looking at a splotch of blood on the dirt. "Hard enough to make the man bleed hard. You got him good, Señor Dog-man."

It was hours before they were able to make the ride back to the ranch. Getting the bodies taken care of and notifying county officials about the death of the sheriff took a lot of time. Dog-man turned down the offer of the badge three times before they finally started the ride back to the home ranch.

The night was warm and as dark as sin with only starlight to help them stay on the trail. There was no moon. "They're gonna have a hard time finding someone to take that job, I'm afraid," Dog-man said. "Did you talk with the barman? Why was Sanchez walking to the end of the bar? Surely wasn't to rob the joint."

"No. Not to rob, to kill. Did you see me talking with that other feeler? He's the range rider from Cajon Pass. He'll be at the ranch tomorrow. Anyway, he said Claudio Valenzuela, the barman, also has a gang of rustlers and was going to try to put Baker out of business. Sanchez was going to kill him."

"Range Rider? Slim Ferguson was hired to keep the lion and wolf population under control? He calls himself a range rider. I guess that's what he would be. I doubt if he and Louise should get along." Dog-man snickered thinking about it. Ferguson was all show with beads and feathers, wolf skin hats, and trying to look like some kind of make-believe Indian.

Dog-man rode quiet, letting his mind work over what just happened. A beautiful little valley like this and there are fine ranches raising the best cattle and horses, and then comes the filth, he thought. He and Snake had seen it all across Colorado, Arizona Territory, New Mexico Territory, even during their time in Mexico.

Build something nice and there's sure to be somebody willing to tear it down. We've got grass belly high to a steer and two gangs of thieves now planning to take what we have. This'll get Snake all riled for sure.

4

"STARTING TO GET WORRIED THERE, PARTNER," Snake said as Dog-man and Juanito rode in. "Have some trouble?"

"We had trouble and it's gonna be with us for some time, I'm afraid." Dog-man stepped down from his horse and started undressing him, talking the entire time. "We've lost the sheriff. Josh Baker took him out. Juanito thinks I hit him during the shooting, but I'm not sure. Did kill one of his gang though."

Snake chuckled. "Two years ago those men would have been safe as all get out, Dog. You been practicing?"

"Don't start." He tried to hide a wry grin knowing how right Snake was. And, yes, he thought, he had been practicing. Dog-man was an excellent shot with a rifle, but Snake used to tell him he couldn't hit the barn from ten feet away with a handgun.

He set his saddle on the rack, slipped the headstall from the horse, and tried to hide a little smile. "It was Victorio Sanchez that was killed. Do you remember the bartender Valenzuela?" Snake nodded. "Juanito said that Slim Ferguson told him that Valenzuela has put together a gang of rustlers as well. When we move our steers, we're gonna want just about every one of us on that ride.

"Oh, and Ferguson now calls himself a range rider and will be here to see us tomorrow sometime."

"Sounds like trouble brewing. What are they gonna do for a sheriff? Mallory was old but he did good for many years. Word gets out they ain't no law in Lane's Crossing we'll see a lot of ugly visitors."

"Pressed me for the job. They'll be after you come sunrise," Dog-man said. "Mallory never even had a deputy. South County's gonna get interesting."

Snake gave a long look at his partner, scraped his boot through the dirt, and looked up into the sky. "I wonder what it is that would make a man want to be an outlaw? Ever thought about that, Dog? Just how much trouble is it to be a cattle rustler?"

"What brought that on?" Dog-man remembered back when more than one lawman considered the two of them outlaws. "We been called outlaws, you might remember."

"Yeah, but we wasn't, was we," Snake drawled out. "Well, we spend a lot of time raising cattle and horses but when you think about it, we really don't have much to do with their bein' raised. They do a pretty good job of raising themselves. All we do is try to offer good feed, safe area to live, and doctoring if necessary. But an outlaw, well, he has to spend most of his time worrying about bein' caught or bein' shot during the crime. He has to spend even more time plannin' the crime.

"Seems to me that bein' an outlaw is a tiresome job. Sure more so than bein' a cattle and horse rancher."

Dog-man gave his partner a long look, smiled, and decided not to get in the conversation too deep. "Spent some time thinking about all that, Snake?"

"Watching them young steers grow gives me time to think about things like this. It'd be a wonder if Josh Baker spent much time thinking about life and its little problems, eh? The funny thing is, it's far more work being an outlaw than it is being a rancher, but I bet men like Baker don't even see something as simple as that. They work harder than we do, Dog."

"Let's go have some coffee, Snake."

LIFE on the ranch was busy for most of those living there but Louise found she wasn't really a part of the organization. Several weeks ago she and Snake had a long talk about it. "I ain't a cowboy, Snake, I ain't much of a cook, and I need to keep a whole lot more busy than I've been."

"Don't need to, you know that."

"Ain't a question of doing work that needs to be done. It's all being done. I ain't contributing, Snake, just sitting around getting in everybody's way."

"I got a job for you, pretty lady, and one you are most qualified for. We've lost a few calves, some sheep, had a horse or two attacked. You know what I'm talking about?"

Louise jumped up from the table and ran around to wrap her arms around Snake. "Oh, I do," she said. "You don't know it but I've built all new hide stretchers, got my knives and guns in perfect order. I'll be in buckskins from now on, Snake. Why didn't I think of that?"

She and Snake were always up well before sunrise and after a quick breakfast, she would be off and into the mountains surrounding the large ranch. She worked a trap line and did some trailing as well. Losses, particularly of sheep dropped almost immediately and hides of wolves, coyotes, and lions were being stretched and prepared for market, taken care of daily.

Lion Killer was back on the job. She sent notices to some of the men who used to buy her hides when she and her father were in business and they promised to drop by the ranch to buy what she was producing.

Rain was falling hard as the two walked out on the porch, hoping to watch the sunrise. "Don't look like we'll have that pleasure today," Snake said.

"Dog-man didn't get back until late last night, Snake. Something bad happen?"

"Did," he said. He spent the next few minutes bringing her up to date. "We'll have a visitor later today. Slim Ferguson. You know the name?"

"I know him." She almost growled it out and the look on her face told Snake this wouldn't be a pleasant little get-together. "He calls himself a fur and hide trapper. He don't take very good care of his hides, though. Mine have always outsold his. He's big and proud, Snake, but ain't much good at taking care of his hides. Do you know what he does? He sets out poisons, Snake. He kills as many good critters as he does the varmints. Poisons, Snake."

"He'd best not set out poisons around the Rocking Snake. I'll have his hide," Snake said. He gave Louise a long look and knew she'd probably get him first. "He's been working the Cajon Pass Ranch, calling himself a range rider. Knows something about the gangs of rustlers working this area."

"Well, with this rain, the wolves and lions won't be hunting hard. Maybe I'll just stick around the ranch today and chat with Ferguson. He don't think a woman should be a hunter. Don't much care for me. I'll just stick by your side and chat the old boy up some."

Snake chuckled as she went inside wondering what kind of show he was in for. *That woman don't much care for Ferguson. I know I don't ever want to be in her sights.*

She walked back into the house for more coffee and Snake watched each step she took. Not very tall, thin and leggy, she was the most wonderful sight he could wish for. *Them buckskins are about as tight as they could get. Damn me, but I could watch her walk all day long.*

Young Pedro broke the reverie as he came out onto the porch. Just nine, the boy had already put on several pounds and loved Snake and Louise almost as much as they loved him.

"Hi, Papa," he said, wrapping his arms around the tall thin Texan. "Are we going to work some horses today?"

"Don't think so, son. Ain't a good idea to work them colts in the mud. Besides, I can hear thunder out there, too. Sit on top of a horse and you're a lightning rod. Maybe we'll just get that checkerboard out and you can beat me again."

Pedro laughed and ran back into the house. "Maybe," he said. "I think Mama wants to teach me more about taking care of hides the way she does. Did you see the wolf vest she made for me?"

"I did, son. She's making me one, too. Get your slicker and let's head to the barn. You can work with Mama later."

5

"I KILLED Sheriff Mallory fast as you've ever seen." Josh Baker fell from the saddle, blood streaming from his wound. Baker rode all night, the pain of the bullet deep in his left leg throbbed the whole trip. He pulled into the outlaw camp, high in the hills above Cajon Pass after sunrise, barely able to stay in the saddle.

Adrian Nestor ran to his side. "Let's get you inside, boss. What's that you said about Sheriff Mallory."

"Kilt him," Baker said. "But he was with that man they call Dog-man and he was able to shoot me before I got out the door." He groaned as Nestor dragged him into their make-shift cabin. "He killed Victorio, too. Gotta get that damn bullet out."

Baker wasn't a big man, thin and not particularly strong. He had long stringy hair, a gaunt face with a three or four day's growth of whiskers. His gray-blue eyes always looked sad, and his mouth was permanently turned down at the edges.

"You gotta drink the whiskey, boss. You ain't strong enough to take the pain." Adrian Nestor wasn't a doctor, he's the one who changed the brands on stolen cattle, but on this ugly and rainy morning, he was a surgeon.

"You ever call me weak again and I'll kill you," Baker growled through the pain. He was trying to haul his revolver out, cocked, and ready. "I ain't no weakling." Baker's gun arm was weaving around aimlessly and he reached out for the bottle of bad whiskey with his other hand and drank two full gulps. That was followed by a coughing fit, and he laid his head back. Nestor pushed the gun aside and saw the man's eyes swimming about, unable to focus.

"You pull that gun on any of these other yahoos and you'd be dead, Baker. I'm of a mind to shoot you myself. That's how lucky you are." Baker took another long pull on the whiskey and groaned.

"A couple more like that and I'll get the bullet out," Nestor said, easing the gun from Baker's hand. The man was so weak from loss of blood and the all-night ride, he couldn't lift it to shoot anyway. "Take another couple of swallows and I'll get that bullet."

Nestor was short and heavy, strong as a bull, and kindly to most people. That he was an outlaw seemed out of place for the man. He was educated in the northeast, moved to Texas as a bored young man and worked several cattle outfits before heading ever more west. His move into the ranks of outlaws came in Arizona Territory when he became drinking friends with bank and stage robbers.

Nestor killed his first man on his first job, robbing a stagecoach as it was leaving Gila Bend. Banks in and around San Diego and Los Angeles were hit before he joined up with Josh Baker rustling fat cattle. He planned to stay with Baker through one or two more jobs and then find some good men to once again hit the banks. The money was better, and it was easier.

I ain't fit for this kind of life, just sitting around waiting to grab a few head of cattle. Runnin' 'em down to Mexico ain't much fun nether. Bank robbin's the way for men like me. Plan it, do it, and spend the money on women and liquor.

Nestor looked at Baker and picked up one of his razor-sharp knives. *Cut for his bullet or just cut his neck.* The chuckles that were heard in the room were soft and gentle but the eyes told a different story. Nestor had to make a decision. *Killin' a man ain't particularly hard, even if you've known him for a spell. Workin' with this fool has been good as far as the money part is concerned, but bank robbin's better me. Hold still little man and I'll get the bullet out.*

Baker was drunk, humming some tune off-key as Nestor made the first probe for the chunk of lead buried in Baker's flesh. A sharp skinning knife opened the wound enough for him to grasp the bullet with some small tongs and pull it free. He washed away the blood with splashes of whiskey, pulled a wad of tobacco from his mouth and put it in the wound, spread some bear grease over the wound, and bandaged it.

"He gonna live?" Juan Vasquez asked, picking up the jug of whiskey for a quick snort.

"We'll see," Nestor said. "You gonna stick around?"

"Take what we can from that herd that Snake and Dog-man will be moving and drive them to Mexico. Might not come back."

Nestor looked at the man, knew he was able to think, not just react, and wondered if he would be good at robbing banks. "What would you do in Mexico that you can't do here?"

"You ever robbed a train, Nestor? They move a lot of

gold from the mines. Bars of gold, heading to where they make coins."

"Hundreds of guards on them trains?"

"Not too many. I will use my money from this next rustling job to put together a good bunch of men. Most of the guards die or are injured during the train wreck that I won't need too many in the gang."

"Something to think about, Vasquez. Something to think about."

———

SNAKE, Louise, and Dog-man were on the porch at Dog-man's cabin drinking coffee. "I forgot to tell you about the letter from George Dawson," Dog-man said. "He's coming our way, be here in the next day or two." He pulled the letter from his shirt pocket and read it out loud.

"Dear boys, I'm once again expanding my business and this time into the hopefully lucrative Southern California regions. I'll be at Lane's Crossing late summer. Want to talk to you. Important. George".

"You suppose it has anything to do with the railroad they're talking about? Lots of folks are looking forward to that bein' put through." Snake looked out across the wide pastures at the cattle grazing. "Sure will make our life easier."

"Easier?" Louise laughed. "Look at you two, rocking away in your big old chairs drinking hot coffee, watching your steers get fat. How much easier could it get?"

Snake tried to cough, Dog-man just looked off into the distance, and nobody said a word for some time. All three had smiles, however, thinking about what Louise said.

Life is just a little bit different than this time a year ago, Snake thought to himself, taking a long drink of hot coffee. *Me and old Dog have had some excitements these last few years. Makes a man feel good to have his own ranch, to have a woman like Lion Killer. She's just about right as rain.*

"Dawson's got a good thing going with his express and warehouse business," Snake said. "This wouldn't be the time to open a route. Not with the railroad coming through. He must have something else in mind."

It was dust off to the left, on the main trail into the ranch headquarters, that caught their attention.

"Would you look at him?" Snake stood up and walked to the edge of the porch, putting his coffee cup on the rail. The man's buckskins were covered in amazing bead patterns, sprinkled with shells, feathers, quills, and other things, such as rabbit feet and bird legs. He wore an outlandish hat made from a buffalo head, and his horse was walking with a limp.

"That, my fellow ranch hands, is Slim Ferguson," Louise said. She wore buckskins regularly and they were fringed but purely utilitarian. "Man looks like one of the clowns at the traveling circuses."

Ferguson didn't wait to be invited and stepped down from the horse. "Morning. My name is Slim Ferguson and I'm the range rider for this district." He tied his horse off and walked toward the porch.

"Might want to wait 'till you're invited before comin' onto the porch, Ferguson," Snake said.

"I'm here on official business. Here to put a stop to whoever it is been killing wolves and lions. That's my responsibility."

"Not on our ranch, it ain't," Dog-man said. "You

might want to work on your manners, sir. Ain't nobody on this ranch called for the so-called services of a range rider. We take care of our own problems."

Louise stood up and walked to the edge of the porch and looked down on the man. He straightened up just a little bit and took in a quick breath. "Lion Killer? You the one been doing all the hunting? You ain't got the rights to this area. They're mine."

"Haven't seen you for some time, Slim. Don't look like you've changed much. Attitude and otherwise. You ain't got no official responsibilities here or anywhere. Your services are for hire and you know it."

She looked him right in the eye, took another step forward and backed him up a step. "This is my place, Ferguson. You are a hired hunter and we ain't hiring. My man will see to that."

She took a deep breath before continuing. "Your type ain't good for the ranchers, neither. Most won't allow poisons to be spread. Kill as much stock as you do wolves. You ain't a hunter, Ferguson."

Ferguson glared at each of the three in order before saying anything. Snake got a crooked grin on his face, winked at Louise, and took a step toward the edge of the porch. "Why don't you take your range riding official duties off to some other range, Mr. Ferguson. Your services aren't needed and for that matter you aren't welcome here. Gotcher self a bad attitude and it ain't welcome either."

"I'll leave," Ferguson said, "but before I do, a little warning. I'm the official range rider for this area and if I find someone else taking wolves and lions, I'll be forced to file a complaint with the county sheriff."

"You've got no official standing on this ranch," Dog-man said again. He rested his hand near his big sidearm. "Best light out, Mr. Ferguson and don't come back."

Ferguson kicked some mud, whipped his tie loose and climbed into the saddle. "You ain't heard the last from me," he said, turned his horse and rode off at a limping trot.

"Like to shoot that sumbitch," Dog-man said. "Got some nerve, he does."

"He's got no more standing with the law than I do," Louise said. "He's hired out to keep wolves and lions at bay, same as me and Pa were, same as I'm doing for us right now, except he kills 'em with poisons. He don't take care of the skins or even tries to sell 'em."

"Suffering from gas, I expect," Snake said, and that broke up the coffee session.

6

"SEE what you can do about that limp," Ferguson said. "I've got business at the courthouse."

"I'm a blacksmith, Ferguson, not a horse doctor. It's a dollar a week or twenty-five cents a day, in advance." Ray Lassiter gave a disgusting look at Slim Ferguson and spat some tobacco juice into the dirt. "Shouldn't have been riding that horse when the limp started. Ankle's all swole up."

Lassiter was not a large man, but swinging heavy hammers on hot steel every day has made him into one of the strongest in Lane's Crossing. His attitude was as hard as the steel he pounded on. He wasn't exactly telling a lie when he said he wasn't a horse doc, but for most in the community he was as close as they'd ever find. "Go on about your courthouse business but if I find you've abused this animal, be prepared for a bruising when you get back."

"You ain't got no call to talk to me like that. Do your job and I'll do mine. Do your preachin' somewhere else."

Lassiter jerked the lead rope from Ferguson's hand

and led the limping horse into the barn. "Remember my words, Ferguson and you better have some coins in your hand when I tie this boy off." *Man's got a bluster just waiting for a hard fist. Come in my stables with a limping horse and just swagger off to the courthouse? He'll be lucky to crawl off if he gives me much more of his crap.*

Lassiter tied the sorrel off and stepped back to the range rider. "Twenty-five cents or a dollar, Ferguson," the blacksmith said, holding his gnarled hand out. "Extra two-bits if you want that critter to have some oats."

"You'll have to wait until I go to the bank. Been on the trail for weeks."

"You walk away from the stables without paying, that horse and everything on it is mine," Lassiter said. "You ain't goring me, Ferguson. You've gored about every business in this camp but you ain't goring me." Ferguson made some noises that might have been cursing as he walked to the horse, got into a saddlebag, and came back with fifty cents.

The two men stood just short feet apart, glaring at each other. Both were strong but Lassiter had the advantage. Pounding a four-pound hammer hours at a time, day after day, gave him more than just advantage. Slim Ferguson backed down and walked out the doors of the barn, doing his best to swagger.

Lassiter stood at the big doors, jingled the coins about in his hand, and watched the man walk off toward the courthouse. He tucked the coins in his apron pocket and snickered just a bit. Lassiter walked back inside and removed tack from the horse, brushing him down good and offering him, first some water, then a couple of hands full of oats. He pulled the leg up for a look. He picked the hoof clean and found the problem immediately.

"All the man had to do was clean the damn hoof once in a while." The rock was eased away from the frog, there was no blood, no broken pieces, and he put the foot down. "You need a better man, horse." He dropped a fork full of hay for him and walked back to his forge, cussing softly to himself. It didn't matter what the hot piece of metal was going to be, for the moment it was simply a means of beating out frustrations, and they were beat out.

FERGUSON WAS in the south county courthouse to offer his services to the sheriff. San Bernardino County was large and there were offices in the north and the south. They were supposed to work as a team, at least in theory, but the North county felt it was senior. South county bowed to the system. As an example, the South County Sheriff was actually a San Bernardino Deputy Sheriff.

After finding the office empty Ferguson slipped into the county clerk's office. "Where's the sheriff? Got business with the man," he snapped.

"Sheriff's dead," the clerk said. "Somebody else be able to help?"

"Dead? How's that? Why ain't somebody been appointed? This is out of line."

"Ease off, Ferguson," County Clerk Tom Sanderson said. Ferguson was a blowhard, was as arrogant a man as lived in the county, and public officials barely gave him the time of day. "Mallory was killed last night. Commissioner Whiteman is in his office, just next door." Sanderson scowled at the range rider and went back to the paperwork on his desk.

Ferguson muttered something and slipped out the

door and into the office next door. "Whiteman in?" he barked at the man behind the counter.

"Yes, he is. May I tell him who's asking?"

"I'm Range Rider Slim Ferguson. Had business with the sheriff but will have to do with Whiteman."

"I'll tell Commissioner Whiteman you would like some of his time," the man said with emphasis on the word commissioner. The office clerk stepped to the inner office door, knocked lightly and went in.

"A gentleman calling himself a range rider and named Ferguson is here to see you, sir."

"Range Rider? Are we hiring wolfers now?" The clerk smiled and shook his head. "Well, all right, send him in."

Gordy Whiteman was an old timer in the great Mojave Desert, had been a prospector, sheepman, and hunter himself in his earlier years. He was in his sixties, walked with a distinct limp from being mauled by an angry mule he was trying to break, had scars from knives, and one from an arrow wound to his right arm. In his day, he might have been considered a bit of a rounder, and was still in more than fair condition.

He was a gruff man when it was needed, had a wonderful sense of humor, and like many of the old time desert rats loved to sit with a glass of whiskey and tell wild and often ribald stories of their past activities. He settled into his comfortable armchair and waited for the range rider. *County has never bought their services before. It's always up to the ranchers. Sounds like a man with a scheme coming to see me.* There was just the slightest smile on his tanned face.

The clerk knocked softly and ushered Ferguson in. Before he could offer introductions, Ferguson started talking.

"I was here to offer my services to the sheriff, Whiteman. Didn't know the man was dead. Understand there's a wolf problem in the area."

Whiteman stood at his desk to welcome the man but was fully taken aback by his approach. Men were supposed to have manners, were supposed to be proud to introduce themselves, should at the very least offer a handshake. In the most primitive tribes, the meeting up of two men required certain niceties. *This man is a lout. How dare he burst in like this.*

Whiteman looked at his office clerk. "Please, Mr. Kendricks, be kind enough to introduce the gentleman."

"Yes, sir. Commissioner Whiteman, say hello to Mr. Slim Ferguson, who claims to be a range rider."

"How do you do," Whiteman said. His voice was cold, his eyes penetrating, and he did not offer a hand, waited instead for Ferguson to do so. Ferguson did not. Was there a code of the desert? Were these old desert rats like Whiteman anachronistic? Has the time of gentlemen and manners passed?

"Please, sit down. Just what is your business with the county? Range rider, is it? Certainly nothing in our budget for such a position."

"There have been reports of problems with wolves and lions. That's what I do. I hunt wolves and lions."

Whiteman thought that the way the man looked, he might kill a wolf through laughter but held his tongue. "If predators are causing problems on some of the ranches I'm sure the ranchers might think about hiring you. For certain the county wouldn't." Often, when Whiteman had visitors, he would ask his clerk to bring in a pot of coffee. He might even open that special desk drawer and bring out the bottle.

"If there's nothing else, then, good day to you. Mr. Hendricks, be kind enough to usher Mr. Ferguson out."

He smiled at his clerk and turned back to the papers on his desk. One was a seed catalog, the other an invitation to supper with the Bannister family.

"As a public servant, I believe I should at least be heard," Ferguson snapped.

"I'm the public servant," Whiteman said. "I believe you're a hired hunter. We're not hiring. Good day."

Ferguson started to say something else, saw Whiteman open a desk drawer, and thinking he might very well be looking down the barrel of a pocket pistol soon, he stormed out of the office, not bothering to close the door behind him.

Kendricks saw the smile on Whiteman's face before he saw the bottle emerge. "Bring us some coffee, will you, Mr. Kendricks?" He sat back in his chair and let his mind wander off to better subjects. *Jose Diaz said he found some color out on Full Moon Mesa last week. Maybe I'll just take a ride out there. There's a ledge of quartz that's just begging to be blasted out. Range Rider indeed.*

Kendricks came back in with the coffee and two cups. "A dollar to a dime that man leaves town with a bloody nose and black eye." The commissioner laughed. "I'll be gone the rest of the week. Only in an emergency should you attempt to find me."

"And where would I look, sir?"

"Full Moon Mesa or thereabouts."

7

THERE WERE two freight wagons and three outriders slowly making their way through Lane's Crossing on a hot late summer afternoon. The wagons were covered in desert dust, the animals haggard, and the outriders were in no condition to stop a runaway. The lead wagon, its contents covered in canvas and tied down was pulled by a six-up rig and the smaller trailing wagon by four-up mules.

One of the wagons, the one with a six-up hitch, came to a stop about halfway through the little village, across the street from Peterson's large emporium. "Ain't gonna take these critters another ten feet today," the teamster said to one of the outriders. "Tell Osborne." He looked around and had a hard time holding in his smile. *I wonder if those people who said I was biting off too large a chaw were right? Well, we're here.*

George Peterson stepped out of his general mercantile store, saw the wagons and walked up to the driver of the first wagon. "This the Dawson Express?"

"It is. You must be Peterson. I'm George Dawson. Where do you want us?" George Dawson had been a teamster most of his adult life, owned one of the more successful haulage and express companies in New Mexico and Arizona Territory and was making his first foray across the great Mojave Desert. Was his timing off? Why would he want to expand his business to offer shipping services across that killer country when two railroad companies were in the process of doing the same thing?

There was product being shipped west from Prescott and Tucson and from farther north, and there was product being shipped east as well. George Dawson wanted some of that business but so did dedicated railroad people. Was Dawson late in this venture, or did he have something else in mind?

Peterson looked at the grizzled and dusty gentleman and pointed to a side street. "Right around the corner, Dawson. You'll see the loading docks. It'll be tight with a six-horse rig. The four-up will fit in nicely. You made good time."

"No Indian trouble, no water problems, and no storms. Just once in a while a man gets lucky." The two men chuckled at the thought and Dawson picked up the reins and snapped them, getting the leaders to start off. They made that wide turn into the side street, and another equally wide turn to run up to the loading dock behind Peterson's Mercantile Warehouse. Making ninety degrees with six horses and a wagon takes up a lot of countryside, making two of them took an artist, but Dawson had confidence in his horses and himself. Didn't even have a smile on his face as he called the rig to a stop.

Like I said, sometimes a man just gets lucky.

Dawson left the unloading to his and Peterson's crews and stepped up to a large water barrel in the warehouse. Peterson was already there. "I need to find a couple of fellers," Dawson said. "You familiar with a man called Snake and his partner Dog-man? Best two young men I've ever met."

"You bet I know Snake and Dog-man. Their ranch is about five miles west of here. Prettiest piece of land you've ever laid eyes on. How is it you know 'em?"

"They was almost trail tramps when I met 'em. Busted up a couple of attempted robberies, protected some of my men and merchandise, and did some grand favors for me just a few years ago. Got wagons through Apache country, for one thing. I could go on and on about those boys. Almost like sons is the way I feel about them."

"They're damn well liked around these parts," Peterson said. "They should be starting to bring their herds into the home range. Getting ready for fall drive and sale. You'll find 'em at the ranch, I'm sure."

Dawson walked back out and had Osborn get him a saddle horse for the short ride to the ranch. "Thanks," he said to Osborn. "I'll probably not be back until tomorrow. See to it these horses and mules are taken care of, pay the men and make sure they understand they're still employed." He had a little grin on his weathered face. "Don't want 'em running off somewheres."

"We going on to San Bernardino? It's about forty miles and we'd be running empty."

"While I'm gon' see if there might be a load for us. This entire trip is to find out if it's even possible. We ain't looking to make money this time. They've proved up north that even when there's a railroad, there's business for the haulage boys. Costs a lot of money to run a railroad, Mr. Osborn. They charge more than I do." Dawson laughed.

Osborn got the two big wagons unloaded and called the crew together. Smiley, O'Brian, and Shorty had been with the Dawson company for a long time. "Ain't the end of the line, boys. We'll rest up a day or two then head to San Bernardino before making the long haul back to Las Cruces. Got your pay envelopes here." He handed the payout and with each man, said, "Don't get throwed in jail."

THE FIVE MILES to the Rocking Snake ranch would have been quick if it hadn't been such a pretty little ride. *I'm still covered in desert dust and look at what I'm riding through.* Dawson simply wouldn't let the horse ride out at a trot, not with rolling hills covered in emerald green grass and live oak trees so old they seemed to have whiskers. Billowing white clouds stood out in a sky the deep blue of cool mountains, not the high, thin blue of desert heat.

Dawson walked the horse the entire five miles, letting his mind rest after the arduous journey across that hell called Mojave. When he crested the ridge that led him down to the big ranch he had to take a deep breath. "I'll bet those boys are playing in the grass when I get there. Ain't seen nothing like this in a long time." He talked to his teams driving large freight wagons and talked to saddle horses on every ride. He liked to tell youngsters learning the trade that it was the code of the teamster to talk to their animals.

The main road branched off and Dawson rode into the ranch headquarters and up to a substantial building. Two men and a woman were sitting at a table on a broad veranda-type porch. "By god, Snake, you're right," Dogman said. "Sure as I'm right here, that's George Dawson. Well, I'll just be damned," he said.

The three got to their feet and stepped down from the porch as Dawson rode up. "Morning, boys. Who's the fetching young girl in buckskins?" His smile was as bright as the boys could remember.

"Mighty glad to see you, Mr. Dawson," Snake said. "This charming lady is Louise and I'm just proud to say she's my wife."

"Wife? Snake, you old devil, good for you." He jerked his hat off, ran fingers through his thin and graying hair, and bowed slightly. "I'm proud to know you, ma'am. I'm George Dawson. These boys have helped me and my business so many times you'd think they owned it."

She reached out to shake his hand, and he surprised her half to death by taking it and giving it a gentle kiss. "Oh, my." Snake watched the blush start at her neck and crawl to the top of her forehead. "Ain't never," she started to say and just giggled like a little girl.

"Her nickname is Lion Killer, Mr. Dawson. You might want to remember that," Snake laughed. "How about we step into the house and find some refreshments. Want to hear all about your trip across the desert."

"Got plenty to tell you, and some good news about your money, not that in the bank, but what you left with me. I used some of it to buy an interest in a stables and carriage making business." He held the door for Louise and the boys and followed them in. The ranch headquarters building doubled as Dog-man's home and he led them into a large kitchen.

"What is this all about?" Snake asked. "You mean we own part of a business in Las Cruces?" He looked at Dog-man, then to Dawson, and finally to Louise.

"We do," Dawson said. "It's a busy little place and making money. Quite a bit of traffic up from El Paso and down from Socorro. I've got all the papers with me."

"Are you looking to open a haulage business in this area?" Dog-man asked. "Are you aware of railroads looking to do the same?"

They were settled in at the dining table, a hot pot of coffee along with an earthen jug making their way around. George Dawson had been asking himself those same questions for a long time and hoped he was right in his answer.

"I was in Denver a short time ago, boys, and learned something about railroads. They go from here to there." He chuckled seeing their faces. "What they can't do is bring the product that needs shipping to the rails. Somebody has to do that. And they can't service all the little communities that are off the main line by a few to several miles."

Snake looked at Louise and smiled. "See? Just what I said. Those that have something to ship needs to get it to the rails. Them that'er receiving needs to get it to the store." He looked at Dawson. "You old dog. You're talking short hauling, aren't you?"

"That's it," Dawson said. "If that rail line goes in, it can't have lines into all the little communities in this area. There will be a main rail yard and surrounding warehouses with companies like mine distributing to the towns off the rail line. I'm here to plot out distribution routes from what I know of the railroad's plans."

"Peterson, in Lane's Crossing, is already planning a stock yard there. Would you have a warehouse in Lane's?" Dog-man refilled the coffee pot and brought it back to the table and went to a cupboard to get the honey pot as well.

"I think I'd have my main business somewhere around San Bernardino, maybe Riverside. That's why I'm here. Getting the logistics figured out. Lane's Crossing is way out on the edge of civilization, so to speak. Need to be centralized with distribution routes leading out as spokes from the axel. We'll be serving the communities that aren't served by the railroad."

The conversation went well into the evening and by suppertime, half the crew was involved. Jeannie Nichols, Wayne's wife, Louise, and young Pedro spent a few hours in the kitchen preparing a feast and it was served on the patio of the home with everyone sitting at picnic tables scattered about. It didn't take long for the Mexican charros to get their guitars out, and the festivities went well into late night.

"Isn't that something, Louise?" Snake said as they eased themselves under the sheets. "We own a stables and a company that builds wagons, buggies, and carriages. I never would have thought of something like that."

"I like Mr. Dawson. He's a real gentleman. He said that you and Dog-man were accused of being outlaws when you all got together. You ain't never been an outlaw, have you?" Her little tinkle of a giggle softened the question.

"Never," Snake said, then coughed. "Well, when me and Dog-man first got together, there was a question of selling maps to gold mines. Sheriff in Deadwood thought we was wrong in doing it. That ain't really being an outlaw, though."

She snuggled in close to the long skinny Texan, said something soft, kissed his ear, and the evening had a pleasant ending.

8

PETERSON AND OSBORN made sure all was accounted for and George Peterson left the store for a well deserved cold beer at the Desert Rat Saloon. "You boys really know how to pack a wagon," he said to Osborn and nodded to the barman, Claudio Valenzuela.

"Been doing it a long time," Osborn said. "Your store's pretty well packed, too, I'd say."

"You boys filled it up." Peterson laughed. Valenzuela brought the beers and a bottle for them and the two clicked glasses. Valenzuela moved back a step or two, seemingly to wait for someone else to call for service.

"This whole area, from here all the way down to Los Angeles, is growing daily," Peterson said. "I got stuff in that store that five years ago I would never have thought to carry. Civilization is coming to the Mojave, I'm afraid."

Peterson was almost sad as he said that and looked around the saloon. "Just look at that feller there." He nodded toward Slim Ferguson who was standing at the end of the bar. "He's called a range rider. Hired out by the ranchers to kill off the wolves, coyotes, and lions that kill stock. Another year or two and his work won't be needed. More likely, won't be tolerated."

"If I dressed like that I'd scare off the horses and mules," Osborn said. "Seems more like a dandy than a hunter. No Indian I know would ever be caught out looking like that."

Ferguson's buckskins were covered in wild bead-work, in pelts and feathers, in bones and quills. He was wearing a muskrat skin headpiece and Osborn wondered why. "That hat is as wrong as anything I've ever seen. In this heat?"

Peterson's laugh, his nod, and Osborn's pointing drew Ferguson's attention, and he moved down the bar toward the two men. "You guffawin' about somethin'? Sumpin' funny is it?"

Osborne stiffened up and slowly turned to the man. As a teamster, his weapon of choice was a Bowie knife, not a handgun. He always had a rifle and scattergun nearby, while driving, but didn't carry one. He saw anger on Ferguson's face, he saw the man's hands near his knife, and wanted to laugh at the cartoon he was facing.

"Something funny?" Osborne repeated. "I think, by golly, I do see something funny. In the high mountains called Rocky, I might wear a hat like that. In the blistering heat of the desert called Mojave, I'd call it silly, maybe funny, absolutely stupid." He looked Ferguson right in the eye. "Anything else on your mind? If not, I'll go back to my beer, thank you."

"You got a mean mouth, mister. Do you know who you're talking to?"

"No, I don't. Goodbye." Osborne didn't really turn aside but gave the impression he was about to and Ferguson fell for the ruse, went for his knife and found himself flat on his back, staring at a large, angry teamster holding a knife of his own. "You might be able to poison a wolf or two, maybe even scare a coyote, but you're about to learn a great truth, mister Range Rider."

Osborne jerked him to his feet, ripping doo-dads and goo-gaws from the man's buckskins, and drove a fist into his face without letting go of his buckskins. Ferguson's eyes were swimming about, fully unfocused when a second fist was driven into his groin. It was at that point that Osborne let go of the man and simply let him fall to the filthy floor, wrapped tightly in a fetal position.

"Let's move down a spot or two, eh Mr. Peterson. Got some business to talk about," the powerful teamster said. Osborne motioned for Valenzuela to bring a couple more cold beers. "We're going to make a trial run to San Bernardino, and places in between," he said. "Mr. Dawson would rather not run with empty wagons. Would there be merchandise from Lane's Crossing needing to go? He'll offer a great rate, I know."

Peterson smiled at the comment. "As a matter of fact there are several hundred pounds of high-grade ore that needs to go to the refinery, and there are hundreds of pounds of cow and sheep hides that need to be moved from the Smither's tannery. Won't fill the two wagons but it will come close."

"That will make Dawson a happy man," Osborne said. "Can you arrange it all? You'd get a broker fee."

"Consider it done," Peterson said. "I think I see Dawson's plan now. I wondered why he'd want to buck the railroad. He ain't bucking it, he's using it to his advantage. Good thinking."

"THERE IT IS, amigos. Far easier than trying to rustle cattle and far easier to get rid of, too." Claudio Valenzuela was sitting at a table in Rosita's Cantina with two other men, sharing a platter of tacos and a bottle of tequila. "Two fully loaded wagons pulled by well-trained horses and mules. All we gotta do is shoot the men driving the wagons and drive them ourselves."

Jose Garcia, known as Scarface, and Tony Worthington smiled at the words. "Sounds almost too easy, Claudio," Tony said. "Selling the already tanned leather won't be hard. Run it down to Los Angeles or across the border and it would sell immediately."

"I agree," Scarface said. "Ore, high grade or not, ain't something you can just sell somewhere. What the hell would we do with it?"

"Take it into Mexico. The refineries will buy it. Boys, those two wagons will set us up, and the man wants to make regular runs. Merchandise that will have value. Easier than stagecoaches, easier than rustling cattle." Valenzuela looked at Scarface and got a nod, and Tony smiled his acceptance as well.

"Good. Scarface, make a quick ride to the border and find a good refinery and Tony, ride west and find an outlet for tanned hides. They'll be making that run soon, I think." He smiled and clapped the two on the shoulders. "We're in business."

⸻

"IT'LL BE a real pleasure taking out that herd," Joshua Baker said. "Gonna kill that Dog-man sumbitch, steal his cattle, and burn him out, too." He ran his hand gently over the still angry wound in his leg. "Mr. Nestor, you keep a close eye on that ranch. I want to know when they get ready to move them critters. We'll have several hundred steers to drive to Mexico, boys, and many hundreds of pesos when we get there."

"I don't like hitting the herd on the trail," Juan Vasquez said. "We've always driven off fifty or sixty head, held them while altering the brands and adding to the bunch, and then driven them to Mexico. It's always worked for us."

Baker jumped to his feet. "Ain't no time to be challenging me, Vasquez. We do things my way around here."

"He's right, Baker," Nestor said. "We ain't set up to take a whole herd all at once, take the time to alter brands, and make a large drive like that to Mexico. Half the US Army would be on our ass." Nestor was on his feet, as well, and Baker noticed that both Nestor and Vasquez had their hands near their weapons.

"I think you boys weren't listening right," Baker said with about half a smile. "I did say we'd have a few hundred head to move, but, like we've always done, we'll bring 'em here first, fifty or so at a time, for the branding. Don't get yourselves all in a twit. You gotta listen better."

Nestor nodded to Vasquez and eased himself back into his chair. "That's good, Baker. Pick out a couple hundred from Snake and Dog-man." He sat back and smiled at Baker, knowing he made the man back down. *He ain't the man I thought he was when I joined up. I like the idea of busting trains, though. Vasquez is a good man.*

"We gonna hit the YL again? They're moving cattle down for winter range now. We could pick up fifty at a time over the next weeks. Good money, boss." Nestor poured a round of whiskey and reached for a cigar. "Them cattle been in the mountains around Cajon Pass all summer. Fat and ready to be taken."

"The YL hands are handy with their guns, Nestor, but I like the idea. Grab fifty or more, move 'em to Mexico for a nice profit. You and Vasquez put that together. Want to be careful of the YL hands, though. It was the Mexican banditos that made them tough and they've never let up. See if just the three of us can pull this off."

Baker sat back and thought about Nestor's idea. He figured they could take, move and sell two, maybe three groups of steers before Snake and Dog-man started moving their herd. His wound, still tender was healed enough that it might give him some pain, it wouldn't break open or anything. He smiled as he sipped his whiskey, thinking about what they would earn from the YL cattle and then what they would glean from Snake's and Dog-man's herd.

"I like your idea, Nestor. It's even better when you remember that there ain't no sheriff in this part of the county. Ain't no law at all." He laughed long and loud over the thought. "I'll bet we can sell those steers right at the border. Won't have to go deep into Mexico." He took another sip of whiskey and looked up at the ceiling.

"Nestor, get your eyes on the YL people and Vasquez, ride south and find us a buyer or two. Damn, boys, this is gonna be fun. We'll hurt the YL and then hurt the Rocking Snake. I want that Dog-man bastard in my rifle sights."

9

"DON'T KNOW if it mean anything, Mr. Lovelock, but we've seen a man watching us move cattle down into the valley the last couple of days." Andy Lovelock was the L in the YL brand, the Y belonging to Pete Youngblood, his late partner.

Lovelock looked at his foreman, Frankie O'Neil, and smiled. "There's always someone wanting our beeves, eh, Frankie? Scare 'em off. If they don't scare, kill 'em. Tired of these damned outlaws thinking they can just ride in and take my cattle. Make sure every hand is carrying a sidearm and a rifle. Don't hesitate."

He sat back and remembered how it was that his partner, Pete Youngblood lost his life. *Rode all friendly like up to a stranger on his range, found the man with running irons to change brands, and died looking down the wrong end of a heavy caliber rifle.* Lovelock made it a rule of his range that he would not tolerate strangers on the range and felt no compassion for those who died not obeying his rules.

A lot of rustling many years before was done by young men looking to start a herd of their own. Snitching a fresh heifer or two as often as possible. Often done on the open range where they might find unbranded cattle. Lovelock was facing a different breed, outlaws looking to take fifty or more prime steers, move 'em to Mexico and sell them at a good price.

"Listen to me, O'Neil. It used to be, back in Texas, in New Mexico, a man could pick some critters off the range, brand 'em, and start a herd. That was wide open country back in them days, but it ain't that way here. These bastards ain't looking to take a free-range heifer or two to build a herd. They's looking to take branded steers and sellin' 'em. My steers! Ain't the time to be nice, O'Neil. Kill 'em."

"You bet, boss," O'Neil said. Frank O'Neil had come west from Missouri and felt no compassion for trespassers, rustlers, or any other type of outlaw, either. "Boys are bringing the cattle down regularly. It's the right time for the damn rustlers to get active. We herd 'em up and they drive 'em off."

"Ain't nobody but YL riders driving YL cattle, Mr. O'Neil. See to it."

"The word came down from Lane's Crossing that Sheriff Mallory was killed. They ain't got a sheriff for this end of the county. That might make some of these men get a little brave with other people's cattle."

"It makes me want to get even more strict with my land and my cattle, Mr. O'Neil. Double the night guards until we start the drive, eh? And keep a good count."

O'Neil walked out of the headquarters ranch house with a big smile, stepped into the saddle and rode off toward one of the holding pastures. Business with his hands first, then with the unwelcome visitor.

He motioned for a couple of the hands to come to the fence as he rode up. "We'll be taking the herd down to the stockyards in San Bernardino in ten days. We've already got eyes on the herd so be sharp out there. Get them steers out of the mountains and ready to drive."

"Should have close to seven hundred, Frank. We'll bring a hundred culls along, too." Sam Bidwell was hired as the ramrod to get the cattle down off summer range and ready for the fall drive.

"That's short," O'Neil said. "We had a good calf crop, we branded far more than that. Get your boys into those rocks and trees, Sam. We should be driving a thousand head. Chouse those calves out of those rocks, Sam. Your boys are sloughing and they'll be looking for work soon. Tell 'em that. Tell 'em Andy Lovelock said it."

Frank O'Neil was more than upset at the fact that Sam Bidwell didn't drive his hands, let them ride easy. "We got us a fifty-mile drive through that long canyon and I want no less than a thousand head being moved. Now, get off your ass and bring those calves down."

He turned his horse and trotted off toward some rimrock a couple of miles away to be able to look out across the large plain of the YL and maybe even run into the hombre who has been keeping his eyes on the place.

"You heard him, boys. Our sunny days of calm are over. Let's ride." Bidwell wasn't pleased at getting talked to that way in front of the men but also knew that Lovelock was behind it and the old man was a terror when he went on a rant. Bidwell's job was on the line and he knew it.

NESTOR RODE out from the Baker camp shortly after sunrise to watch the YL hands bring fat steers down into holding pastures filled with good grass, getting ready for the fall drive to the stockyards. It was an easy ride across open meadows, through rocky ledges and ridges, and into a nest of live oaks along a sidehill some miles from the pens.

Looking out across the lazy rolling hills, one could see a few rocky outcrops, many stands of ancient oaks and other dark green trees, which set off the pure emerald of deep grass. One could feel a warm and friendly solitude; the feeling of being alone was not frightening in any sense.

"If they make the drive to the stockyards with the same ambition I'm seeing out here, we would have had an easy time knocking 'em off and stealing the herd," Nestor murmured watching a couple of buckaroos moving some steers out of the rocks. "That is if that had been the plan. Can't take a whole herd these days. Not enough men, too far to drive 'em to Mexico.

"These hands, though, they don't give a damn. Lovelock won't hire a Texas cowboy and won't hire Mexican charros either. Shortsighted," Nestor said. "We'll take 'em, small bunches at a time." He watched for half an hour and rode across the top of the ridge for a meeting with one of the men who would be helping on the job.

"Looks like Lovelock'll have about a thousand head moving out in ten days or so," the man said. "What kind of a plan does Baker have? He'd be wrong to hit the herd on the drive."

"Won't be doing that," Nestor said. "Stay out of it, and you'll live," he said, turned his horse, and rode off back to Baker's camp.

"LEARN ANYTHING?" Josh Baker yelled out as Nestor rode in. "You ain't been gone very long."

"We got about ten days to take what we want, Josh. They got 'em spread out in the low pastures. Bidwell ain't any kind of ramrod and the men working the cattle don't give a damn if school keeps or not. We can ride in at night, cut out what we want and be gone. The nighthawks sit around drinking coffee." He was laughing as he stepped down from his horse.

"What about O'Neil? He's a real tiger watching a herd." Baker was standing near the door of their cabin, as Nestor walked up. "He gonna give us any trouble?"

"He'll be with Mr. Lovelock most of the time. He's a good foreman but he's got a loser in Bidwell and that's to our advantage. We can cut out fifty or so, drive them out and Vasquez can change the brands to bar XL. Ain't no reason we can't start tonight. I'll show you the layout."

Inside, he used the table top as a map and drew where the holding pastures were and the trail they should use bringing the cattle to camp. Vasquez and Josh Baker were as intent watching as Nestor was describing. "Taking a few at a time and those boys are so lazy they won't even know they're gone," Baker chuckled.

"We kill the Nighthawks if they show up, drive the group across Live Oak Ridge, down along Fiddle Creek and right to here. Be running through enough rocky ground they'd have a hard time following if they tried. We'll be here hours before they even know cattle are missing." Nestor stood back from the table and nodded to Baker. "They ain't ready for us, Josh."

"You said there are several hundred head in each of

those pastures?" Baker looked at the crude map drawn in dust and then at Nestor. "Seems likely that if we don't have any contact with the Nighthawks, it might be days before they detect their shortage. Let's stay as far from contact with the Nighthawks as possible."

"How they got 'em holding?" Vasquez asked.

"Just let'n 'em mill about. Didn't put up no brush fences or nothing. Good grass, good water, and one Nighthawk keeping 'em nice and quiet. Most of the time he ain't even in the saddle. Sitting calm and quiet by a nice fire drinking coffee." He laughed and reached for a bottle.

"We'll ride out at sunset, boys," Josh Baker said. "Pour me some of that."

"I got a question," Vasquez said, handing the bottle to Baker. "We bring the cattle here, change the brands, and then what? Can't keep 'em here. Our buyers are in Mexico."

"We'll drive 'em south to Devil's Canyon, Vasquez, not here," Baker said. Devil's Canyon is close to thirty miles south, along the western edge of the range. It opens to a broad plain and would be a relatively easy drive south to the border. "My plan is to grab, let's say, fifty at a time until we have a couple of hundred and then drive them to Mexico. It would be a five to seven-day drive at best."

Baker had a smug look on his face, Nestor didn't. "We gonna need some hands, boss. Gonna take more than the three of us. We can handle fifty, not a couple of hundred."

"You're right. When we get these fifty to Devil's Canyon, Vasquez, you stay with the herd and Nestor, you ride to Lane's Crossing and find us however many hands you think we'll need. Don't be promising them much, either."

Nestor chuckled, thinking they wouldn't live long enough after the drive to get anything at all, if he had his way. "I'll bring 'em here and we can then bring another fifty or so steers south to the canyon," he said.

10

"Looks like we're going to have a bunch for the drive," Dog-man said. He and Snake were sitting on a sidehill looking down on the milling cattle spread out across the bottom land below.

"We need to increase our Nighthawks, Dog. Sheriff's dead, every outlaw within a hunnert miles knows it and we got fat cattle. They ain't many of us to keep these kids safe."

"I been worrying myself on that question, too. Along with some mighty fine-looking beef, we got us a whole herd of fine horse flesh to protect. All of this won't be a worry when that railroad get put in. Peterson will have his stockyards right there at the crossing." Dog-man pulled his hat off and wiped the sweat away. "That's down the road, eh? This is now. They come in at night and run off some of our fine stock."

"They do," Snake said. "Back in Texas the rustlers picked what they wanted from the open range to build a herd of their own. Ain't so here. Take fifty or so and run 'em south to the border. We need a few more men, I think." Snake got up and busied himself with coffee cups before continuing.

"I'm gonna take a quick ride into town and see if I might find an out of work charro or two. Maybe hear something from the outlaw quarter too." Snake stretched and yawned. "The easy life just ended for this year." He chuckled.

"This ain't the best time for Dawson to make that run, either. He'll be alone. We can't keep our stock safe and ride shotgun for him too. Don't make him no promises we can't keep."

Louise was off in the hills tracking a mountain lion that had killed a calf so Snake yelled at young Pedro to saddle up. The boy squealed his delight and ran for the barn. It didn't take long for the two to be mounted and riding off the ranch. "Got a couple of people to see, son, and after we'll have us a fine meal. Stick close to me."

They reached Lane's Crossing well before the noon hour and Snake slipped into Peterson's large market. "Morning, George. Looks like Dawson filled in all the empty spaces around here. You got your ear to the ground, anybody able to work cattle looking? We need a couple or three hands for the drive."

"You'll have to stand in line for that. All the ranches are in the same boat. Even old man Lovelock is looking for hands. Those trails from here to San Berdoo are gonna be filled with beef this year. Railroad can't get here fast enough in my opinion."

"Can you keep Pedro busy for half an hour? I'll take a quick look in the Desert Rat Saloon just in case." Peterson smiled and nodded, Snake brushed Pedro's hair and walked out onto the street.

He stood in the shade of the store's overhanging balcony and watched Adrian Nestor ride by. *He's got himself a set of nerves,* Snake laughed. *Sheriff's dead and the man rides right through town. I wonder what Josh Baker's number one man is doing here?* He crossed the street and watched Nestor reign in his horse in front of the Desert Rat Saloon. *This just might get interesting.*

Snake was about a minute behind Nestor as he slipped through the bat-wing doors. The humid and foul-smelling saloon air was thick with smoke, stale beer and spilled whiskey and it took Snake a moment to find where Nestor went. Snake walked to the bar, spotted Nestor at the end, and stayed back many feet from him. Snake motioned for a cold beer and did what he could to watch Nestor without actually looking right at him.

Nestor's eyes moved up and down the long bar as if looking for someone in particular, and when he spotted Snake he froze. It was Snake's partner who killed Sanchez and put a slug in Baker. *What's he doing here? Did he follow me? Don't want to mess with him.*

Snake watched as Nestor tried to get the barman's attention, smiled knowing he had been spotted, and waited to see just what the outlaw might do. *Baker must be planning something and Nestor's here to find men or information.* Snake's mind was working fast when he saw the barman point to a feller sitting at one of the gambling tables.

The gambling man wasn't dressed as a gambler, more as a cowhand, was young, wiry, and had a mop of tangled hair showing out from under a well-worn hat. *That ain't no outlaw Nestor's about to talk to.* Snake knew he would enjoy what ever it was he was about to see.

The cowboy had strong, wide shoulders, a deep chest, thick neck, and narrow waist, and spotted Nestor coming toward him. Snake thought it odd that this man would want to talk with Nestor. *Don't seem like the outlaw type.*

Nestor picked up his beer, gave a quick glance Snake's way, and moved to the table. He bent over and said something, then moved to a table at the front of the saloon. In moments the man at the gambling table picked up his money and drink and moved to join the outlaw.

Sure would like to hear what they're saying about now. Snake used the big mirror behind the bar to keep track of the activity and saw the gambling man almost get angry, slap the table, get up and walk back to his card game. Nestor stood up, grabbed his beer and quickly strode back to the end of the bar.

Before the outlaw reached the end of the bar, the gambling man yelled out something that angered Nestor and the two found themselves glaring at each other from less than ten feet apart. *This is getting most interesting,* Snake thought with just the hint of smile on his rugged face. He knew Nestor was tough but didn't recognize the other man.

"I ain't no kind of dog what would work for Josh Baker. Ain't no kind of outlaw, neither. You got yourself some kind of nerve wanting me to help you steal another man's beef."

Nestor was standing with his feet slightly spread, facing the gambling cowboy, and Snake was sure that cowboy was about to die. *Ain't my fight but that old boy ain't up to facing Nestor and I have a hunch he might be the kind of man we could use at our place.*

"You looking to pick a fight, Nestor? How about picking one with me," Snake said, turning around to face the outlaw. Snake's hand was hanging loose, his fingers ready to grab hold of the weapon at his side and Nestor spun to face him. Men on both sides of Snake moved away as quickly as they could. Lead would be coming that fast.

"Ain't got a fight with you, Snake. Ain't got a fight with nobody. Just came in for a beer." There was some general laughter along the bar, even at the gambling tables, and Nestor tightened up. The laughter was aimed straight at him and he wasn't going to let that sit for long. "Don't make me do something I don't want to do," he said.

"What would that be that you don't want to do, cattle rustler. You trying to hire someone to help you and Josh Baker steal cattle? That why you're here?" Snake was good at prodding, knowing a man who got riled is sometimes also sloppy as a fighter. "You and Josh Baker aren't much good at rustling, Nestor. How are you at fightin'?"

The gambling cowboy spoke up. "That's exactly what he wanted me to do. Help him drive stolen cattle to Mexico. I ain't no outlaw and I told him so."

"Maybe it's time for you to ride right out of town, Nestor. Your kind ain't fit to be in this town." Snake stood away from the bar by a foot or two, his legs slightly spread, and Nestor could almost feel the coiled strength of the man, the quickness, and ability.

"You think you're gonna ride me out of town? Snake, say your last prayer 'cuz you're a dead man talking." He was fast as his hand whipped a big wheel gun out but never got the shot off. Snake had his piece in hand and got two very fast shots off, both through the middle of Nestor's chest. The force of the shots knocked him back several feet where he fell to the filthy floor, dead.

"Like to talk to you, cowboy," Snake said, pushing spent shells to the floor. "They call me Snake and me and my partner, Dog-man, are short a hand or two. You got a name to go with that fine attitude?"

The lanky, tanned cowboy walked up to the bar and shoved a hand at Snake. "Jeremiah Hillyer, sir. Come in from Waco a few days ago. Looking for a good brand to ride for."

"Ours is the Rocking Snake. Let's walk down to Peterson's and pick up my son, have something good to eat, and talk about moving cattle." The two shook hands. Hillyer grabbed his money from the poker table and walked out the door. "Waco, eh? Got some fine cattle in that country," Snake said.

"All I got is my horse and tack, a bed roll and rope, Mr. Snake. Ran into some bad hombres in Arizona Territory. Stripped me clean."

"We'll fit you out," Snake said.

Walking from Peterson's store to Lucy Gonzalez's cantina, Snake saw two men riding out of town at a fast clip. *Josh Baker ain't gonna like what those boys gonna be tellin' him. Without Nestor and Sanchez, he ain't got a gang.*

Young Hillyer, maybe twenty, maybe younger, made friends with Pedro immediately. "So, Pedrito, are you the ramrod of this outfit?"

"Papa calls me his little gopher. I go for this and then go for that." He laughed. "But I can throw a good riata. I'm learning the vaquero way from our foreman, Francisco Alvarado."

"Vaquero, eh? I've heard about that," Hillyer said. He looked at Snake, almost with a question.

"It's a slightly different way of handling all the animals. A little more gentle than the Texas way, Hillyer. The Spanish school of horsemanship, Hillyer. We're breeding Spanish Andalusian stock horses, and you'll fully realize what the vaquero way means after riding one."

They had enchiladas, tacos, and roasted peppers on their plates hoping that there would be enough for the three. All of them were digging in as if they hadn't eaten in a month. Lucy brought a platter of churros and Pedro's eyes lit up. She ran her hands through his black hair and gave him a big smile.

"Don't mean to change the subject," Jeremiah Hillyer said, "But what's gonna be the outcome of you killing that fool back there? I hope we ain't gonna get a visit from some angry sheriff."

"Ain't no sheriff," Snake said. "If there was one, he'd tell me I did the town a service. Nestor is the brains behind the Josh Baker gang of cattle rustlers and he's the second man in the gang to be killed in that bar in the last few weeks. I'd say that Baker is just about out of business."

11

"YOU TELLIN' me that Nestor's dead? Fast as he was and that bastard Snake did him in?" Joshua Baker was lost, he was just walking around the open fire, his fists opening and closing with each step. He lost a good man when Dog-man killed Sanchez and now, his best man, Adrian Nestor killed by Dog-man's partner, Snake. "Them two gotta die, gotta be burned out."

Baker looked at the two men who rode in from Lane's Crossing with the bad news. Was it rage? Anger? Or maybe just a ripple of fear that Baker was feeling. He'd been screaming about killing Dog-man. Now he needs to kill Snake as well. "I'm gonna burn those two out before I kill 'em," he said, storming around the camp. He gave another long slow at the two men who rode in.

"Ain't done business with you boys," he said. "Why is it you rode out to tell me this?" He had a fear that one or both were about to draw and kill him, or, maybe they were there to take what he had. There wasn't really any reason for these two to bring him the report. That ripple of fear was becoming a wave.

"You boys ain't been in this area but about ten days. Why'd you ride out like this?"

"Knew about you losing Sanchez, and with Nestor down, thought you might be looking for some new hands," the one called Dan Mansfield said. Mansfield, despite being new to the area had the reputation of a small-time crook working on the trails along the western edge of the great Mojave Desert, sneaking around camps late at night, pilfering from the travelers. He rarely had any more than enough cash on hand to pay for a beer or two.

"That so?" Baker snarled. "Lookin' to gain something from a man's death is it?" In the world of outlaws of the north county, Baker was lead man, these two were scum. He shook his head and looked at the second man. "You too?"

"We was supposed to meet with Nestor later," Mansfield said. He looked over at his partner hoping the man would say something before Baker decided to go for his gun. Baker cocked his head in disbelief.

"Nestor was going to meet with you two? What for, to get his boots polished?"

"That's right," the man called Dusty Moran said. "We was gonna have a meeting with Nestor after he had his meeting with the Texas kid. It was that meeting that got him killed dead."

Baker stopped walking, looked at the two and saw what appeared to be second rate thieves at best. He couldn't believe Nestor was actually going to talk with these types of hoodlums. What the gang needed were specialists. Real cowboys. Men who could alter brands. Men who could fight with guns, knives, teeth even.

"Never got to meet with him, then? Well, then, you're meeting with me. What have you got to offer me?"

Mansfield felt the anxiety wash off his shoulders and walked up closer to the fire. "I got some time working runnin' irons, Mr. Baker, and I'm good with a rope. Been working cows ever since I was a boy."

Baker nodded slowly, looking Mansfield up and down. Dirty shirt and pants, no chaps, no spurs, no rope on his horse. "You ain't roped a cow since you were a boy, Mansfield. My man Vasquez is my iron man. Show him you're as good or better, but it's always good to have another man who can do it." He didn't offer a hand, didn't really say Mansfield was in. Baker turned to Moran. "You?"

Moran whipped his revolver out and put two slugs into a tree trunk just feet from Baker's torso. Baker was stunned, just stood there, his face ashen, his eyes bright with the fear of instant death. He couldn't breath, wasn't able to say a word, just stood quiet and still. "Anything else?" Moran said and slipped the heavy iron back into its holster.

A two-bit sneak thief, a man who stole from those making their way through a deadly desert, is the best shootist Baker had ever seen? Moran had looked Baker in the eye and in a split second had pulled down on him and got two shots off. Stunned, Baker stood near the fire, an empty tin cup still in his hand.

Mansfield had a slight smile on his face and stooped down, picked up the coffee pot and refilled Baker's cup. "We been working up north in some of the gold camps, Mr. Baker. A little heat from the law moved us down this way. Been tough getting things put together down here. You gonna say something or just stand there?"

It was an open challenge and Baker knew it. This was supposed to be his gang, these men were supposed to look to join his gang, but that isn't what he saw. *They want to take over. That Moran is faster and more deadly accurate than anyone I've ever seen. Gotta do something special and I mean right now.*

Baker looked at Mansfield and smiled, took the coffee and splashed it in his face, drew his gun and aimed it at Moran, fully cocked. "I need two good men to work for me, got some good plans already underway, but it's my gang, my plans. Got it?"

Mansfield was screaming as he fell backward into the dirt, trying to protect his face from the scalding coffee and Moran stood quiet, looking down the barrel of a forty-five, ready to blow his head off. A slow smile crept across his taut face, but the eyes showed scorn, maybe retribution for that little piece of drama.

"I think that's fair," Moran said, about as calm as a man could be. "Don't you Dan?"

———

SNAKE, Pedro, and Hillier rode up to the ranch headquarters late in the afternoon. "Got one, anyway," Snake said, stepping down from his horse gesturing to the new man as if he was showing off a trout freshly caught. "Good man, too. Texan, you gotta know." He dusted himself off and walked up onto the porch. "This here's Jeremiah Hillyer. Hillyer, meet my partner, Dog-man."

Dog-man watched as the lanky young man stepped down from his horse and took the steps two at a time coming up onto the porch. "Good to meet you, Jeremiah. Texas, eh?"

"Yes sir," Hillyer said. "Come this way from Waco. Heard good things about California cattle country. Shore is pretty country around here. Ain't seen this much green grass in a long time."

"Ran into Nestor in town," Snake said. "Nestor's looking to add to Baker's gang, wanted to hire Hillyer but this old son of Sam Houston turned him down flat. Nestor got all riled and went for me, Dog. Sure as I'm standing here, Nestor pulled down on me."

"I take it that didn't turn out well," Dog-man said. "Means Baker's left with one man that we know of. Vasquez is the only one left."

"Saw two of Lane's Crossing's sneak thieves ride out to tell him about Nestor. He'll bring 'em in." Snake chuckled. "Mansfield's only been in the area a short time and already has a bad reputation for stealing. The other one's call Dusty Moran. Don't know much about him."

"I do," Hillyer said. He took the cup of hot coffee offered by Dog-man and settled in at the porch table. "The man's a killer. He's come out here from Texas and New Mexico where he ran with some nasty people. Robbing banks, killing for hire, too. He's wanted in half of Texas counties. He and Mansfield been robbing banks and businesses up north recently."

"How is it you know that, Hillyer?" Dog-man's attitude changed quickly. "Snake said you were fast to claim not being an outlaw. How is it you know so much about these two?"

Jeremiah Hillyer smiled as he looked Dog-man in the eye. "I've been up near Angel's Camp the last few weeks myself. Tried my hand at diggin' gold and those two were all the talk. Robbed a store owner and killed the man right in the middle of the camp. Sheriff's posse couldn't catch 'em. Those that saw the robbery said that Dusty Moran was the fastest with a gun as they'd ever saw."

"Baker might just still be in business, Snake." Dog-man settled back in his chair and gave Jeremiah a long look. *Young, strong, and seems to know something about a Texas bad man moving into California's San Bernardino cattle country. I wonder if there might be a little bit more to this Jeremiah Hillyer.*

"Been working cattle, Mr. Hillyer?"

"My pa had a spread but drank it away. I've worked cattle since I could walk. Been looking out across your ground out there." He pointed toward the herds off in the distance. "You've got yourself some fine beef, but what I'm seeing is horses the like 's I've not seen."

"Them's Andalusians, Jeremiah," Snake said. "Finest breed of Spanish horse flesh you've ever sat. Fast, strong, and savvy. Quick to learn, easy to work. Spanish and Mexican vaqueros love 'em."

"So do you." Dog-man laughed. Snake stood there with a smile on his face, nodding in full agreement. "Let's get you settled in, Mr. Hillyer, and meet the crew. they'll be coming in shortly. We've got extra Nighthawks out because of rustlers. You can meet them before they leave out," Dog-man said.

"I'm feeling mighty good about this, Dog-man," Hillyer said. "You'll get your money's worth, I promise. I ain't a gunman, though. I can shoot straight but ain't never kilt a man."

"You'll fit right in." Snake laughed. "Dog-man ain't much of one, either. It ain't that he can't draw fast, it's just that he can't hit nothin'."

"Got Sanchez, I did," Dog-man said. He pretended to be hurt by the comments and then laughed right out. "I prefer a rifle, Hillyer. Snake's the shootist. The real protection we have around here is Snake's wife. You'll meet her at supper."

He didn't go into detail and Jeremiah Hillyer had a strange look on his face as they walked toward the barn. He had the good sense not to question what was said. *These two big men, surrounded by cowboys and charros and protected by Snake's wife? And the little Mexican boy, Pedro is his son?* Jeremiah shook his head and got a little smile going. *They do have some fine horses.*

12

THE BUNKHOUSE WAS large and roomy with cots down the length of both walls offering a narrow pathway through the middle. Most of the cots had clothing or tack on top and extra pairs of boots underneath. The walls had hooks where clothing and hats could be hung, as well. "Ain't the same as bein' ta home," Dog-man said, "But it's warm and dry."

There were two tables with chairs at one end and a cast iron wood stove at each end. The one near the tables was a cookstove although it was used mostly for making coffee. The hands all ate in the big house with meals cooked by Wayne Nichols Paiute wife Jeannie.

Hillier found an empty bunk and tossed his gear down, giving the bunkhouse a good look. "You've got quite a crew, Dog-man. Why so many?"

"Run two separate operations," Dog-man said. "We've got a nice herd of cattle on the one hand, and we breed, raise, and train Andalusian horses. We'll have a big sale come spring. Let's walk out to the corrals and meet some of the boys."

"This is built up country I'm seeing. Why is there such a worry about rustlers? Ain't a lot of open range for someone to build a herd."

"These rustlin' bastards ain't looking to build herds, Hillyer. They sneak off fifty or so head of beef during the night and hustle 'em south to Mexico or run 'em through outlaw feedlots. The most important man in the gang is the one who can alter brands. They ain't afraid to kill anyone who gets in their way." It was Snake's turn to shake his head in disgust. "Nighthawk is one important job in these parts."

Wayne Nichols led Jose, 'Tonio, and Juanito up to the corral fence and brought his horse to a dusty stop. "Hey, boss. Somebody up on the hill earlier today looking us over. Ran off before I could get to him."

"They'll be watching regular, I'm afraid," Dog-man said. "Say hello to our new hand, Jeremiah Hillyer." Dog-man looked around the open area near the barn where several corrals were laid out, where tack rooms were built, and where winter feed was stored. *Me and Snake been talking about a place like this for some time now. We are gonna have to be more than just vigilant now that we ain't got a sheriff. Every drifter and no-account's gonna have visions of gold seeing herds like ours.*

The group formed around Hillyer, each one introducing himself when ranch foreman Francisco Alvarado rode in. "Party time, is it?" he said, stepping down. "Found some track on the east sidehill, Snake. Followed 'em for a bit. Angling around so to get a good look at our entire place. We're gonna get hit and soon."

Snake nodded and kicked at a little rock. "Got that fool Josh Baker puttin' a gang together, Valenzuela gettin' his bad boys all riled up, and the sheriff gets himself killed. Gonna have to keep our eyes open wide.

73

"Say hello to our new hand, Cisco. This here's Jeremiah Hillyer coming all the way from Waco to care for our beef."

"Right nice of you, Hillyer. Ride with me tomorrow and I'll give you the complete tour." He looked around at the crew. "Wayne, you and Jose take first watch tonight, and Tonio, you and Juan take second. Everybody rides day shift tomorrow."

"If they're out looking us over today, you can bet they'll be back. It's one thing to run 'em off," Snake said, "But it would be better to catch one so's we can have a nice little conversation. Ain't got no law to help us out, boys, so it's up to us."

The group headed to the stock tanks to wash the dirt off and heard the call of the iron triangle as they were doing so. "I do believe that Mrs. Nichols is calling us in, boys," Snake said. "Wayne, I think I'll ride with you and Jose tonight."

Faces scrubbed clean, the crew made their way to the big house and a welcome supper. Long days in the saddle, hard work moving cattle down out of the high mountains, some of the men were nursing bruises, some rope-burned hands, some just tired bones and muscles. "Never will understand why a fat steer wants to spend his time in the rocks and not in a field of green grass," Wayne Nichols said.

He was answered in chortles and chuckles, but not in understood logic, since they were, after all, talking cattle. One can't talk cattle and logic in the same conversation. Jeannie Nichols had two platters of grill fried steaks, a bowl of boiled potatoes, a bowl of bacon grease gravy, and a large basket of biscuits spread out on the long table. "You fellas eat good," she said in her limited knowledge of English. "Apple pie comin' up."

Wayne Nichols learned more of the Paiute language than Jeannie did of the English language and Snake always enjoyed being around the two. Trying to make sense of what they were trying to say to each other was more than interesting.

It was about halfway through supper that Louise came through the door, dragging a man covered in blood, mud, and debris. "Found me one, Snake. Broad daylight and trying to run off with a calf."

Her buckskins were almost as muddy as the man's she was dragging, and there was considerable blood, probably his, on her as well. She flopped the almost unconscious rustler on the floor and grabbed Snake for a hug and kiss. "Sorry I'm late for supper. Got us a wolf today, too. Good hunting."

Snake reluctantly let her go and reached down to lift the outlaw to his feet. "Who we got here?" he said. "Anybody recognize this rat?"

"I think that's the fella they call Scarface," Dog-man said. "Runs with Valenzuela's gang." Dog-man looked at Louise. "He was trying to move one steer? Just one?"

"Actually had a rope on him," she said. "Broad daylight, too. Ain't like they usually do."

Snake had the man standing, weaving some, but standing, and slapped him across the face. "We hang rustlers, Scarface, so you ain't got nothing to lose to tell us what you were trying to do. Puttin' a rope on another man's beef, well, it's goodnight to you. Why just one?"

Scarface Garcia knew he was a dead man and cringed, his eyes wildly taking in the crew at the supper table, giving hateful looks at Louise, and kept his mouth shut. Snake drove his fist into Garcia's belly, folding the man over but wouldn't let him fall to the floor.

"I asked a question," Snake said. "I want an answer. Why just one calf?"

"Leader," Scarface said through a hard-fought breath.

"Seen that done in Texas," Hillyer said. "Take one of the strong animals and use it to lead part of the herd away. Cows follow each other, hell right over a cliff if the leader goes first."

Those at the table chuckled and nodded knowing it was a good story but awfully near the truth. "Seen it myself," Wayne Nichols said.

Snake moved Garcia to a chair and slammed him into it. "Tie his feet together and his hands behind his back boys. We're gonna learn a few things about a man named Valenzuela before this night is over."

Dog-man noticed that Jeremiah Hillyer couldn't keep his eyes off Louise. "Ain't never seen a real Lion Killer, eh, Mr. Hillyer? Meet Snake's most lovely wife, Louise. This is our new hand," he said to Louise. "Meet Jeremiah Hillyer."

"Ma'am," Hillyer said, jumping to his feet and offering a gnarled hand. "I don't mean nothing, but I guess I was staring. Ain't never seen a pretty lady in bloody buckskins before."

"Better get used to it." Snake laughed. "Better get used to her whippin' on people who don't like us. Best damn varmint killer in a couple hunnert miles. You got a wolf today?"

"Big one, too. Interesting thing, he was alone and well fed. Had his eyes on some steers up high in the rocks. We got to get them out of there 'cuz I know for a fact there a whole pack of wolves in that country."

"Take us to them in the morning," Snake said. "Dog-man, you, me, Pedro, and Lion Killer will bring 'em down. No wolves and no rustlers gonna be gettin' 'em first."

"Me and Hillyer will ride with you," Alvarado said. "I'll get to watch two Texans bring some beef down out of the rocks."

Alvarado and Snake picked up the chair holding Scarface and moved it out onto the porch and came back in. "We'll be back for our little talk, but suppers on the table gettin' cold." Snake laughed as he closed the kitchen door.

"Think we'll learn anything?" Francisco asked.

"I doubt it. Might get a name or two. I think just finding him here means we already have learned something. Valenzuela is plannin' on taking some of our cattle and you can bet will have eyes on those horses, too. The worst of those horses is better than most men have ever seen."

"Maybe we should just hang him and get it over with," Alvarado said.

"Me and Dog-man did something some time ago that brought us some good times. We were dealin' with a particular outlaw who just wouldn't give up and we took all his clothes from him, might have left him his boots, can't remember for sure, and made him walk back into town naked as all get out. I think that man quit bein' an outlaw right that minute." Snake laughed.

"We'll run him into town first thing in the morning, then," Alvarado said. "Beats hangin' a man. Hate doing that."

13

SUNRISE in the mountains on the western edge of the Mojave Desert was spectacular and the six mounted riders enjoyed every second of it. They had Scarface Garcia, naked and shivering, his hands tied behind his back, sitting on a horse. "We get half a mile or so from town, and we'll kick that horse loose," Snake said. "He'll run right through town. Be a hell of a show."

"Wish I was sittin' at the front window of Lucy Gonzalez's cantina to see him come runnin' through." Dog-man laughed.

The deed done, the bunch turned back for the ride into the high rocky peaks to bring down the last of the steers before the wolves and rustlers find them. "Gonna be just a fine day," Snake muttered. Louise rode up alongside him and smiled. "Oh, yes, a fine day."

Louise led the pack into the rocks where she had been the day before, and they made their way through fallen trees, rock slides, and steep terrain to where she had last seen the cattle. "Green grass right down at the bottom of this hill," Wayne Nichols said again. "Why do them critters want to be up here?"

"Makes 'em feel good knowing we have to come up and chouse 'em down." Dog-man laughed. "They ain't as dumb as we think they are. Their way of getting even."

The small bunch, maybe ten head, was spread around a square mile, finding nibbles of grass poking up through cracks in the rock, and the men worked hard bringing them together. The rocks formed a razorback ridge in places, stood in high spires in others, and there were small caves and even what looked like fortresses spread about.

The cattle had their minds made up they were staying put and the men had theirs made up the other way. The men on horses won the contest but it was late in the afternoon before they got the bunch down and into the grass with other cattle. More than one horse was suffering bruised or cut ankles and more than one of the riders had the same problem. Only one horse put on a demonstration of defiance but wasn't seriously injured in the program. "For a while there I thought it might be best to just leave 'em." Snake laughed. "That's a lot of work for ten steers."

"Ten steers at market price is a lot of money," Dog-man said. "Our money."

"Haven't heard any gunfire today," Louise said. "Either the boys didn't find anyone or they were able to capture 'em. Did you see those wolf prints in the dirt way up there?"

"You were right about a pack moving in," Snake said. "You got a plan?"

"Same as always, Take 'em out one at a time until they don't want to be around these parts." She said, her smile lighting up the afternoon. Snake couldn't take his eyes off her, smiled and rode right up alongside.

"Just in case I ain't told you yet today, I sure do like you. You just keep right on being you."

She gave him one of her best smiles and her eyes told him he didn't have to worry about that. "Funny, ain't it, Snake. I like you, too, but I also just love the hell out of you." They rode together for the rest of the afternoon doing more talking than any of the others.

The steers moved in with other groups and began eating right away. "They'll be fine now and safe," Dog-man said. "How's that leg, Mr. Hillyer?"

"Gonna know it's there for several days, I think," he said. He was moving a steer down a steep slope and the horse slipped and leaned into a standing spire of solid rock, bruising Hillyer's leg. "Good thing these chaps are thick or I might have a big problem. Don't think it's bleeding, just sore as hell."

"A pint or two of horse rub and you'll be fine," Louise joked.

Spirits were high when they rode into the ranch yard near the barn and corrals. Jose and Tonio were there to meet them. Their horses were already rubbed down and their tack put away.

———

"FIND ANYTHING ON YOUR ROUNDS, BOYS?" Alvarado asked, stepping down from his tired horse. He wiped his face with his wild rag and reached for his canteen. "One hot day."

"Found prints where someone has been recently but didn't chase anyone out." Jose pulled a thin cheroot and lit it, letting the smoke slowly curl out from his nose. "May have been prints from Scarface."

All the horses and tack were cared for, the hands headed for the bunkhouse and Snake, Louise, and Dog-man walked toward the headquarters house. "Looks like someone's there," Louise said. Two horses stood at the hitch rail and Snake picked up the pace. Jeannie Nichols was alone at the house.

The three were almost sprinting when they leaped onto the porch and forced their way inside. "Wondered when you'd get back," George Dawson said. He and his number one man, Osborn were holding cups of steaming coffee, sitting in large wingback chairs near the unlit fireplace.

"George," Snake said. "I'm glad it's you. How are you?"

"Just fine, Snake. Just fine. Mr. Osborn has rounded up some freight for us and we're going to make the run to San Bernardino day after tomorrow. Got time to go over that route with us? We have a map but it doesn't have notations on where an ambush might happen, or where bandits might have an advantage."

"Shortsighted, I'd say." Dog-man chuckled. "Let's spread that out on the kitchen table and see what we can figure out. You taking both wagons?"

"Yup," Osborn said. "Both filled. I'll drive one and George the other, and we'll have both outriders. Could use an extra hand or two."

"We've got at least two groups of gangsters operating in this wide canyon of ours," Snake said. "They've been concentrating on taking cattle, messing with the stages, but haven't gone after any of the freighters working the area."

"So far," Dog-man said. "The mail express wagon has

been hit several times. What are you going to be hauling? That might be an incentive."

"It will be," Dawson said. "Some high-grade ore for one thing and already tanned hides for another."

"That's incentive," Snake said. He looked at Dog-man, Louise, George, and finally down at the table. *Now what the hell are we gonna do about this? Cain't none of us ride out with him. Do that and leave our cows and horses? Cain't not ride out with him, neither.* Snake looked up and just shook his head. "George, I don't know what to say."

"I know," Dawson said. "This is very awkward. We both need every man available but one or the other of us is left defenseless."

"Don't have to be," Louise said. "We're gonna be driving about a thousand head down that long road and if there was two wagons right in the middle of the herd, ain't no outlaw dumb enough to make a move. Your two outriders know how to work cattle?"

George Dawson sat very still, as did everyone else in the room, all eyes on the Lion Killer. It was Osborn who broke the idyl. "Our people ain't as cow savvy as your people, I'm sure, but I think this might just be the best idea I've heard in a long time. They couldn't hit the freighters without coming through the herd and all the guns associated with the freighters would hold off rustlers for sure."

"Damn me," Dawson said. He stood and grabbed Louise and held her tight. "You're even smarter than Snake said you were. Wonderful idea. Let's look at that map with new eyes."

"I AIN'T NEVER SEEN nothing like it, Mr. Baker. Me and Dusty were puttin' our stuff together when this fool come riding into town wearing nothing but his boots." Dan Mansfield was laughing loud and long, trying to tell the tale. "Even had his hands tied off behind his back."

"I swear, Baker, it were a sight." Dusty Moran chuckled and took a long drink from the jug on the table. "Not as funny as Dan seems to think, though. The thing is, somebody caught that fool doing something he wasn't supposed to be doing, stripped him naked, and sent him to town with a message."

"Message?" Joshua Baker growled it out, more as a statement than a question. "Damn right, it was a message."

"Don't do it again is the message, Baker. Got a funny sense of humor," Moran said.

"Ain't no kind of funny," Baker said. "That naked man was Scarface Garcia, one of the men who rides with Valenzuela. Word I got, Snake and Dog-man caught him on their range trying to move some of their cattle and did this instead of hanging the fool."

Moran glared at Mansfield and Baker. "Seems as though a threat has been laid down, to me. You still looking to take some of their cattle?"

"Even more so, now," Baker said. His eyes had narrowed, his face was full of fury and passion. "Even more so, Moran." He poured himself another goodly amount of whiskey and looked at the two outlaws sitting across from him. "Starting tonight, gentlemen."

The three talked about the terrain around the holding pastures at the ranch, and how best to run off some fifty head and get them to the corrals at Devil's Canyon. "Snake and Dog-man are putting their herd together fast meaning they might pull out soon." Baker's angry face was black with hatred as he said that. "I want to run at least a couple hundred of their cattle south to Mexico and I mean as soon as possible. It'll just be the four of us, you two and me and Vasquez, so we take at least a hundred tonight, get those brands altered, and then take another hundred. I want to hurt those two."

The pastures were actually large meadows measuring in the hundreds of acres and Snake and Dog-man had about one thousand head of cattle milling in good grass. More than one stream ran through the grassland and cattle tended to gather along the banks. During the daylight hours, one or two men could oversee the herd with no problem, but come night, Snake saw to it that there always several Nighthawks roaming through the herd.

Baker knew he could never take the entire herd but hurting Snake and Dog-man was more important than stealing the cattle. The pain of his gunshot wound was there every day, and the loss of two men was evident in now having to work with Mansfield and Moran. The thought that Moran could take him any time he wanted seethed in the back of his mind, wanting to boil to the surface.

Would Baker shoot a man in the back? A look at his early outlaw history would tell you, yes, he would. Robbing storekeepers in his hometown as a boy of twelve grew quickly to strong armed robbery of fellow citizens of his small town, which blossomed to robbing banks around the territory. When he was ten, Baker squealed on his neighbor after the two robbed old Mister Smith of some hard candy. And at a bank job near Missoula, he shot his partner in the back and took all the loot while running from the law.

Moran was more than equal to Baker in background

and was well aware that he far better with a weapon than Baker ever was. *The man's an ape, unable to think past this very minute. I'll be running this little gang after we diminish Snake and Dog-man's herd.*

Moran knew that Baker's hatred of those two ranchers would override common sense. Four men can move a hundred head of cattle, but fight off Nighthawks, too? And move through unknown terrain at night? Moran would much rather move fifty at a time over several nights. *Baker ain't thinking straight. We should be gathering up a small herd and head out for Mexico, not try to hurt a couple of dumb cowboys.*

14

"We have close to one thousand head of cattle ready to move out and the eyes of at least two gangs of outlaws watching, ready to run off what they can," Snake said to the crew at supper. "Me, Francisco, and Jose will ride Nighthawk tonight, and everybody will be in their saddle at daybreak to keep watch over the herd during the day."

"We don't want the herd riled up, either," Dog-man said. "George Dawson will have his wagons here sometime the day after tomorrow and we'll move out for San Berdoo. Between now and then we can look for at least one, probably more, attempts on our beef."

The usual din of a loud and boisterous crew was missing as everyone accepted the fact they were going to be attacked and probably much sooner than later. Dog-man was more subdued than Snake could recall and realized that he too was.

"I think we have to make a little change in our plans," Snake said. He looked at Alvarado in particular. "We were going to keep the horse herd here and have a big spring horse sale, but I'm of a different thought right now." "I've had that same thought," Alvarado said. "Too many banditos. We need to bring them in with us for a fall sale at the sale yard itself."

Dog-man started to say something but the sound of horses coming up to the front of the house caught everyone's attention. Snake was on his feet and at the door, weapon in hand as the sound of boots pounded up the stairs to the porch. He flung the door open and stood spread legged, the big revolver cocked and aimed at the intruder.

"Damn, Frank, I almost shot you." Frank O'Neil, YL Ranch foreman, covered in trail dust stood at the top of the stairs, breathing hard.

"Sorry about that, Snake. Mr. Lovelock wanted you to know that we caught two men trying to run off some cattle last night. They said they were working for Valenzuela and that you would be next."

"Come in," Snake said. "We were just talking about that. Did you get names of the two?"

"Got what they said about your herd before we hung 'em and that's all. I recognized one of 'em. It was Scarface Garcia. Valenzuela picks up men from wherever he finds 'em, don't matter to him."

Snake, Dog-man, and Louise traded glances and tried to hide their grins. "We had a little run-in with Garcia yesterday, O'Neil. Instead of hanging him, we sent him back to town naked. Guess he didn't get the message."

O'Neil laughed. "Heard about that, too. Didn't know it was Scarface. Be ready, Snake, they're coming for your cattle."

Talk of rustling, of moving the herds, and of the two known gangs went into the evening hours and Snake begged his way out. "Gotta get out on watch, Frank.

Thank you for telling us about what happened. Come on, Jose, we got work to do."

"I'll join you," Dog-man said, "just as soon as I can." He wanted to wait until O'Neil was gone and the rest of the crew was taken care of. Louise walked out to the barn with Snake.

"I'm going to do a little sniffing around, Snake. Valenzuela doesn't have that many men left, but Josh Baker sure does. I'd be far more worried about those men who ride for Baker than I would Valenzuela."

"You're right about that," Snake said. "At night, your scattergun would be better than your rifle. Carry that ten-gauge monster."

She smiled and split off for their home while Snake and Jose saddled up. "She don't ride?" Jose asked.

"No, she'll be on foot on the hill sides and in the trees, watching. If she can spot lions and wolves, she can surely spot a man trying to be hidden." Snake was in the saddle. "You take the north end of that big meadow and I'll take the south. Keep your eyes open, keep the herd nice and quiet, and yell out if you see anything. Remember that Francisco will be joining us shortly as well as Louise. Make sure of your target before you shoot."

BAKER LED the others off the main road well west of Snake and Dog-man's canyon meadows. "We'll make the run to their place cross-country, boys. Remember this pass we're going over. We'll bring the steers back this same way."

Juan Vasquez had serious doubts about working with Mansfield and Moran and spoke to Baker about them before they left. "Mansfield is not good with running

"Better'm gettin' kilt by some screaming woman," Mansfield yelled back.

"Don't think they ever saw me," she whispered. She saw that three men had grabbed leather and were riding toward where she was tucked in. She shoved the pistol back in her belt and brought the ten-gauge up to her shoulder. The first blast blew Juan Vasquez back off his horse, screaming in pain, holding his hands to his bloody face.

Joshua Baker didn't hesitate. He jerked his horse around and set the spurs hard in the animal's side, making for that ridge they had just cleared. Dan Mansfield started to do the same but saw Moran, his leg a bloody mess, trying to get mounted and rode toward him.

Louise dropped the shotgun and grabbed the revolver from her belt, took another long aim, and put a bullet in the middle of Mansfield's back. He fell face first at Moran's feet and a second shot echoed across the San Bernardino Mountains and lodged in Dusty Moran's shoulder, knocking his arm away, forcing him to let go of the horse's reins. He hobbled a few feet in an attempt to catch the horse and fell to the ground. He no longer had a weapon or a horse.

Louise heard the sound of several horses racing toward her and stood up, using the rocks and brush for cover and watched for Snake to lead the Nighthawks in. She also heard loud complaining coming from the cattle closest to where she was. "Damn," she muttered. "Dogman will have my hide if I spooked those steers into a stampede."

"Go for the cattle," Snake called out to Jose and Alvarado, and skidded his horse to a stop where Moran lay bleeding. He saw Louise, shotgun in hand, move toward Vasquez's body and knew she was safe. "How many were there?"

"Four," she hollered. "One crawled into those rocks over there..." She pointed to an outcrop fifteen feet or so from Snake. "The fourth one ran off."

Snake ducked down low and ran toward the rock outcrop, his rifle in hand. He spotted blood immediately and eased himself around the rocks, finding Dan Mansfield face down in the gravel. "You got 'em all, darlin'," Snake called out. He rolled Mansfield over, made sure he was dead, and moved toward where Moran was sprawled out.

"Dusty Moran and Dan Mansfield," Snake said. "Who you got over there?"

"I think it's the one they called Vasquez," Louise said.

Jose came riding up, followed by Alvarado. "Herd is going to be fine. Coulda had a stampede with all that gunfire. What have we got, Snake?"

"The remains of Josh Baker's gang. That man is out of business. Vasquez was one of the better artists with a running iron and he's dead. Mansfield was just a hired killer, but Dusty Moran has wanted posters out all over the California gold camps. Jose, why don't you ride back and hitch up a wagon so we can bring these bodies in. Ain't no sheriff to take 'em to, but we'll bring 'em into town anyway."

Snake took a long breath and grabbed Louise, wrapped both arms around her lithe body and held tight. "You got a way of scaring me half to death woman, and at the same time, I'm so damn proud of you." He stepped into the saddle and offered her a hand and she swung up behind him.

She had a big smile, wrapping her arms around her

man. "Think this might be the end of Baker? Think he'll move out of this country?"

"He's got a hate for me and Dog, and right now he's got one for you. Nope, we ain't seen the last of Joshua Baker. What I'm remembering is what Frank O'Neil said about Valenzuela. We need to stay awake and aware, I'm afraid." He chuckled as he moved the horse closer to the herd.

"With all that gunfire, I doubt any fair-minded cattle rustler would make a move tonight."

"Baker didn't hesitate, Snake. When I shot Moran, he turned his horse and raced away. Ain't no kind of man in my opinion. Even the nastiest of outlaws wouldn't run off and leave his men."

"Outlaws ain't like us, little darlin'," Snake said. "They don't have feelings for their men or their women. Only for themselves. They'll watch their own kid drown if it means they can get away."

15

Claudio Valenzuela was sitting at the kitchen table in a small line camp several miles from the Snake and Dogman ranch and watched Tony Worthington ride up. The man sat tall in the saddle, held his head high as if to look down on those below him. In his opinion most were well below him. He came west following a flawed attempt at robbing a bank in Boston. During the attempt, a woman and child were killed.

Worthington left his partners to fight their way out and ran west, robbing and killing along the way. He dressed as a successful businessman, starched shirts and all. Never as a gambling man, not as a trail bum. He shaved regularly and carried a walking stick that doubled as saber, a Colt Peacemaker, and usually had a small pocket pistol hidden away somewhere close to hand.

The cabin, tucked in a tight little canyon, was fitted out with a couple of rope bunks, a table and two chairs, and a wood cookstove. Valenzuela had taken possession more than a year ago, fitted out some holding corrals, and tried his best to obliterate tracks when he left. Valenzuela smiled as Worthington rode up. He liked the man's attitude and abilities, the fact he was usually rather optimistic, and rarely argued.

"Might have some good news," Worthington said. They walked into the cabin and plopped down in the chairs. "Just watched Snake and Dog-man bring most of Josh Baker's gang into Lane's Crossing. Dead as dead could be."

The smile spread across Valenzuela's dark face, and his eyes rested on the bottle of tequila. "Best news I've heard in some time, Tony. That's what those gunshots were that we heard last night." The two men had been sitting on the crest of a rolling hill north of the large meadow overlooking the Snake and Dog-man herd. After hearing the gunshots they quickly agreed that last night was not the time to run off a few head of fat stock.

He poured a drink and motioned Worthington to join him. "Going over the maps. Dawson's getting ready to leave out but I don't understand why he's going to spend the first night at the Snake ranch. Did you hear anything in town?"

"Sure didn't hear anything about what you just said," Worthington said. He sat across from Valenzuela and poured some agave juice for himself. "Why would he spend a night at the ranch?"

George Dawson hadn't tried to keep it a secret that he would spend his first night on the trail with Snake and Dog-man. What he did keep as a secret was that his wagons would move out in the middle of a herd of cattle. Other than his own crew, he never mentioned a word of making the long ride with the herd.

Valenzuela had his finger on the map, following the main road that Dawson would have to drive his wagons to get to San Bernardino. "Somewhere along this trail is where we have to hit 'em, Tony. We want those wagons and stock in good condition and we want those men with them dead. How many times have you ridden that road?"

"Enough to know every bend and turn, every steep climb, every damn rock to jar one's teeth," the outlaw snickered. "It's a long, rough road." He bent over the crude map and saw immediately that it wasn't accurate. "Ain't a good map."

He put his finger on a switchback. "That's a double switchback, Claudio, and steep. That's where the mail express has to slow way down coming down and is even slower going up. In the middle, between the two steep turns is a small canyon that opens up to a wide valley. More than one express wagon has burned in that valley." He chuckled.

"It looks like a good place for us to make our hit. There are two wagons, loaded and heavy, two drivers, and two outriders. We gotta keep those horses and mules alive and well and see to it that all the men are dead. How many people are we going to need?"

"Be best to have us two and four more," Worthington said. "Ain't got much time, not sure where to look for 'em either."

GEORGE DAWSON, Snake, and Dog-man had held that very same conversation the day before. "We'll be following that main roadway, George," Snake said, "but the cattle will be spread wide and the herd will be spread in a long line. Can your wagon stand up to that kind of cross-country ride? We'll be well off the actual road almost the whole way."

"Absolutely," Dawson said. "We'll spend most of our time off the main road is what you're saying. Five hundred head of cattle in front of the wagons and another five hundred or so behind, and not on the road itself. If there are outlaws thinking about taking what we'll be carrying, that'll change their minds."

"Let's hope so," Snake said. "When you put your plan into operation, George, we can't be runnin' a herd of beeves for you."

Dawson laughed. "Well, just damn," he said. "I was so hoping for that. This will just give me an idea of what's to come as far as the road goes. We'll see enough of it, I'm sure."

"Get back to town and find two, Tony. If you can find more, good, but bring me two men who know how to kill a man. Promise 'em anything, it don't matter, they'll never get any anyway." He laughed too loud, too long. Worthington didn't cringe, but there was the slightest smile as he mounted up and rode back toward Lane's Crossing.

I was kind of thinkin' that same way, he thought, holding back a slight snicker. The two men, it seems, may have been planning things that they didn't want their partner to know about. Worthington was not above running off and leaving his partners to fight the fight, and Valenzuela had proved more than once that his life was worth far more than his partner's. There was considerable money involved in this project and both men knew it.

Tony Worthington made the quick ride back to Lane's Crossing trying to think where he would find two men. It wasn't the right time of the year for this. Every ranch had hired every out-of-work joker within fifty miles to make their fall drive and the men working the mines in the area weren't about to give up their well paying positions, either.

"I'll just start at the Desert Rat Saloon," he muttered. "Sure won't be too picky about this. All they need to be able to do is shoot somebody." He tried to chuckle, but it didn't work.

16

Joshua Baker sat alone at his cabin, a bottle of whiskey in front of him, a filthy glass with the dregs of the last bottle grasped tightly. He made the ride back at a full gallop and his worn out horse was standing just outside the door still fully dressed. Baker didn't know or care that the sun had been up for two hours or more, the only thing he knew was that he was safe. He never once gave a thought whether or not Moran or Mansfield escaped.

"I ain't got one thing to show for everything I've done and it's not my fault. Those men let me down and they deserved to be dead. I told 'em. I told 'em more than once." His head was bent down and the babbling continued on, not making any sense.

The words were slurred, he couldn't tell you right that instant what it was he thought he might have told those dead men. All Baker knew was, they let him down. They were the cause of the problem. They failed him. "Snake and Dog-man are going to pay for this. I don't have cattle to sell in Mexico and it's their fault. All of them, but Snake and Dog-man are going to pay. They'll pay," He screamed and threw the glass across the room to break against a rock wall.

"Don't need no damn glass. I don't need no glass," he yelled out, picked up the bottle and took two long drinks of warm whiskey. He laid his head down on the table, whimpering like a little boy.

It was late in the afternoon when Baker woke up and stumbled out of the cabin. His horse was still standing at the hitch rack, spent the day without food or water, still saddled and bridled. Baker didn't even look at the bedraggled animal, walked straight to the well, and poured a bucket of water over his head. He dipped a second bucket and used it to more closely wash his face. It was the third bucket that he offered to his horse, which had whinnied during all the splashing. Baker stumbled his way back into the cabin and all but fell into his chair.

"Gotta think now," he muttered. "Gotta think straight. Need a plan." He reached for the half-empty bottle, shook his head and let it fall back to the table. "No, gotta think straight, gotta kill Snake and Dog-man. Gotta burn them out." He remembered that they were making ready for their fall drive to San Bernardino and knew that he had just a day or two at best to kill the two. "I gotta be at their ranch tomorrow morning before sunrise."

Despite the long drunken sleep, Baker was not in control of his thoughts, didn't take the time to care for his horse, and made plans to ride out within the hour for the Snake and Dog-man ranch. "Gotta eat first," he muttered, and began his search of the cabin. There was a can of peaches, some coffee beans, a sack of beans, and some rancid side meat sitting in a cupboard, which turned his stomach and sent him outside to puke up what whiskey was left inside.

Baker was on his knees in the dirt, retching, when he heard hoofbeats coming toward the camp. He stumbled, trying to make a run for the cabin and his rifle. He fell, got up, and was almost to the door when Slim Ferguson yelled out his hello.

"Hello, Baker." He stepped down from his horse and looked at the man. "My god, man, you look like hell." He tied his horse off next to Baker's and helped the drunk to his feet. "Let's get you inside, eh?"

Baker wasn't much help and Ferguson didn't seem to understand what was happening. Ferguson almost dropped him twice getting up to the table. "Thought you might like to know that Snake and Dog-man will be moving their herd out sometime tomorrow or the next morning."

"They need to die," Baker slurred. "Why do you think I care? What do you want here?" Baker's true personality came to the surface immediately despite his drunken condition. Baker's thoughts were in a jumbled mess and he looked a long time at the so-called range rider. "You here to create trouble, Ferguson?" he challenged. "Because if you are, you come to the right place."

Baker saw his gun belt hanging from a peg across the small room, saw his rifle standing near the open cabin door. Both were far out of reach and Baker grabbed the empty bottle on the table. He gave it a solid whack, breaking it and stood with the broken shard, shaking it at Ferguson. "You here to give me trouble, wolfer? Get out!"

He menaced the man, took a stumbling step toward Ferguson who simply stepped aside as Baker viciously swung the ragged edged glass. "Take it easy, Baker, take it easy. I'm here to help you. I heard in town what happened. how your men were killed and you got away. I hate Snake and Dog-man as much as you do. I'm here to help."

Ferguson's hatred wasn't aimed at Snake and Dog-man, but rather at Snake's wife, Louise. "That woman embarrassed me in front of the men, tried to make me feel small in their eyes. You want to kill Snake and Dog-man? I'll help, because I plan to kill that woman."

"Why would you hate 'em?" Baker slurred. He held the broken bottle tight, continued to threaten Ferguson with it. "Why would you help me? I don't need no help." He tried to lunge at the man, tripped on something, and fell to the floor, cutting himself on broken glass. "Damn," he cried out, dropped the broken piece he was carrying, and tried to stop the bleeding in his other arm.

Ferguson picked up a dirty rag near the stove and kneeled down next to the outlaw. "Let's get the bleeding stopped, eh, Baker. Then we can talk some." He had a fight getting Baker off the floor and back in his chair, cleaned the gash in his arm and got it wrapped. *Drunk or not, I need him if I'm going to kill that woman.*

Baker was drunk, fought Ferguson off, flailed his arms around, fending the man off, sputtering foul language and threats. It took all the range rider's energy to finally get the bleeding stopped, get the wound covered, and step back from the filthy man.

Ferguson's mind was as twisted as Baker's and he continued talking while getting Baker cleaned up some. "Woman said some nasty things about me, Baker. Nasty. She thinks she's the only one who hunts around these parts. I've throwed away more pelts than she's kilt."

Ferguson let Baker spout off for a while and when he calmed down the two sat at the table with a fresh pot of coffee and tried to plan their attack. "We gotta go in at night," Ferguson said. "They got too many people around all the time. Snake and that woman live in a house out behind the barn and Dog-man lives in the main house. We gotta burn both of them and kill whoever comes runnin' to help."

"You burn Snake out and I'll kill Dog-man," Baker said. The coffee started to have its desired effect on the man. "If we leave out now, it'll be dark by the time we get there." Ferguson had doubts about Baker's condition, about Baker's horse, but the outlaw seemed to be ready to ride. Was he ready to fight?

———

THE AFTERNOON WAS SPENT GETTING the various herds brought down and gathered all together in one meadow and every man had plenty to do. "Just like back in Texas," Snake said, a smile half a mile wide plastered across his bronzed face. "I'll lead us out with the chuck wagon following. Francisco, you, Jose, and Louise lead the herd. Jeannie, you and Pedro ride in the chuck, and Pedro, you fill that wagon with wood all along the way."

Snake looked over to Dog-man. "You and the rest of the crew work the herd. A couple out on the sides, and at least one riding drag."

"Looking forward to this, Snake," Jeremiah Hillyer said. "Heard all those stories growing up, but the railroads and all the homesteaders ended those long trail drives. That and Texas fever." He shook out a loop and started doing some fancy rope work and little Pedro stood with his mouth open.

Snake saw that and decided it was time that boy learned just what an artist his new papa was. Snake shook out a loop and started twirling it, letting that loop get bigger and bigger, then brought it back and forth, dancing in and out of the loop, and finally letting a figure eight show as it dropped around Pedro.

"Wow," is all the boy said, trying to step out of the double loop. Hillyer laughed and helped him out, and nodded at Snake, giving him that round. It was obvious to everyone standing around that there would be more displays of rope work in the coming drive days. Both men had variation of their own with handcrafted riatas, some as much as fifty feet in length.

The Mexican charros took up the challenge and were throwing loops that a rope couldn't. The braided leather riatas were singing, Pedro was sitting with his mouth open watching the demonstration, clapping and yelling along with everyone else.

"Looks like you've got it covered, Snake," Dog-man said. "It'll take most of tomorrow for the herd to find itself, but you've got a good bell steer and we've got some fine men who know cattle. Gonna be a long but good drive."

Dog-man was just as excited as Snake was and found himself riding around the group of cowboys and charros until Alvarado finally told him to settle down. "You're going to be one tired man if you keep this up," he laughed. Dog-man harrumphed a time or two, then smiled slightly, nodded at his foreman, and rode off toward the big house.

Snake and Louise followed him and the three settled in at the kitchen table. "We'll have the whole crew with the cattle tonight, just as if we were already on the trail. Nighthawks will pull two-hour shifts and that way everyone gets a decent night's sleep and the herd will be protected."

"I'm keyed up like we were gonna fight the whole Apache nation, Snake." Dog-man reached for the coffee pot and refilled his cup. "Our first drive, our first chance to sell some of what we raised. Can't help it, I'm as excited as when we found that gold mine."

"That were one fine day, Dog." Snake sat back in his chair, looking at Louise. "We climbed up onto a flat area above the trail we was followin'," he said, a big smile on his face, "and stumbled into a mine that hadn't been worked in some time. The skeleton of the miner was still in his lean-to."

"All the tools were still there," Dog-man said. "It was a working mine and hadn't been touched in years. We just laid our claim down right there."

"Didn't know it," Snake cut in, "but we were probably somewhere well south of the border."

"That's right," Dog-man said. "We were in Mexico. Didn't matter to us, we worked that hard rock every day and come out of there with a bunch of money." He looked at Snake, smiled, shook his head, and took a long drink of coffee. "I miss those days," Dog-man said.

"Yeah," Snake said. "Me too, but I don't miss how hard it was getting out of there. Don't miss that at all. Hope moving this herd of ours is easier than that ride was."

Louise was taking it all in. She had heard the story more than once and it still thrilled her to hear it again. "Wish I'd been around in those days," she said. "But I'm sure glad I'm around right now." She heard something and stepped up to the door. "Looks like George and the wagons are coming in. That's a real sight," she said.

The two men joined her at the open door. "You would have enjoyed the time we brought some of Dawson's wagons from New Mexico to Arizona," Snake said. "We escorted three wagons through Apache country for Dawson's company. It were a ride." Snake laughed. "Some strange people along with us, eh Dog-man?"

"Ain't the right word for it," Dog-man snorted. "Well, break time is over. Let's help George and his boys and get this operation underway."

Louise smiled as they walked toward the large open area near the barns, where Dawson and company's wagons would spend the night. *Me and my daddy done a lot of things in my short life, but I ain't done nothing like what we're about to do. Ain't no man in the world like my Snake. I just hope I don't embarrass him with not knowing what it is I'm supposed to do.*

17

GEORGE DROVE the four-up rig and Osborn drove the six-up and made a grand circle leaving the two rigs ready to pull out at first light. Dawson's three men, Smiley, O'Brian, and

Shorty had the teams undressed and in corrals in no time, spread food for the mules and horses, and joined with the Snake and Dog-man crew for introductions.

Conversations among the group were in English and Spanish, flavored with a few invectives, but generally pleasant. George, Snake, and Dog-man moved up to the main house. Louise and Jeannie had the first night's supper well planned and decided to put it together from the chuck wagon rather than the house kitchen. It was going to be a party on the one hand and an opportunity for everyone to make sure what was planned would actually work.

Pedro's wood supply, gathered as the afternoon wore on, was more than enough for the cookfires, and Jeannie had steaks, roasted potatoes, and hot biscuits ready for the crew. Pots of coffee made their way around and

Louise surprised everyone with a display of apple pies for dessert.

"Ain't gonna be this way every night," She laughed. "My pa used to love my pies, and I had to fight Snake off from eatin' ever one of them."

Early riders from the herd rode in and the Nighthawks rode out as the day's light slowly turned to dusk. George Dawson sat with Snake and Dog-man. "Heard anything at all? No kind of tall tales making the rounds at Lane's Crossing?"

"Being off the road, being a large herd with your wagons, I don't think any of the gangs operating around here would be foolish enough to try," Dog-man said.

"We've got more guns than any of the gangs," Snake said. He looked around at the ranch crew and Dawson's crew, and shook his head. "I think this is gonna be a nice peaceful drive." It was the thought that Dawson wanted to hear.

"My freighting business in Colorado, New Mexico, and Arizona has been a good one, Snake, as you know, and this expansion has been in the back of my mind for a long time. When I saw how those freighters in Colorado responded to the railroad coming in, I knew I had a chance with this project. You boys have always been there for me, and I want you to know how much I appreciate it."

"Well, now, Mr. Dawson," Snake drawled out in his best Texan, "I do believe you have pulled us from the tar pit more than once. We've grown into a pretty good family."

FROM BAKER'S filthy camp to the Rocking Snake ranch was a five-mile ride on the main road, and about seven miles cross-country, which is how Baker and Ferguson were riding in. The dusk turned to night and a few scattered clouds dulled the stars some.

The two were on the crest of a rolling hillside looking down and across the wide valley, home to the big ranch. Fires could be seen among a gathering of men a hundred yards or more away from the main ranch house, barns, and corrals.

"They'll be pulling out at sunrise," Ferguson said. "Looks like everyone is gathered around a campfire, like they were already on the trail."

"That's good," Baker said. He had sobered up but suffered from a massive headache. It had been more than a day since he had anything to eat, many hours since he puked up his bottle of whiskey, and he hadn't bothered to drink any water either. What was it that drove these men, created such hatred over what might be considered simple problems? Baker was in far more physical trouble than Ferguson, who only had a lack of intelligence on his side.

"We'll ride up to the main house, you move over to Snake's, that's the one that looks like a log cabin off behind the barn there." Baker couldn't help thinking he still was the boss.

The men had tins of kerosene tied off on their saddles and had put together torches made from the clothing left behind by Moran and Mansfield. "Anybody come runnin' kill 'em," Baker said. "I'm gonna throw my torches on the roof and duck into the trees back there. I'm good with my rifle and ain't nobody gonna put that fire out."

Ferguson looked at the still filthy rustler and almost

laughed. *He's so damn sure of himself yet he ran off and left his gang, was so drunk I had to get him in the cabin. They'll find him and pick him off and that will give me a chance to kill that woman.*

"I think you've got a good plan, there, Baker," Ferguson said. "It's plenty dark, let's ride on down."

They walked their horses off down the hillside and veered off to the south to make their way well out and around the cookfires and all the men there. The dark was intense but they were in open country and let their horses pick their way through the meadow toward the trees behind the big ranch house.

Ferguson saw riders coming in from the herd off to the north and other riders heading out. "Looks like their main concern is watching over the herd, Baker," he said. "They ain't worried about their buildings." *That woman said I ain't got no right to be on this property. I'm showin' her, eh? I'm huntin' on her property and it's her I'm huntin'."*

He held in his chuckle as the two eased their way into the trees. "Time to split up, Ferguson. You're on your own from this point. Good luck." Baker rode into a copse of trees, deep in the dark of night and tied his horse off in a patch of grass.

Ferguson wanted to shoot the outlaw but continued riding toward Snake's house. *On my own, am I? You bet I am, you little coward. I've been on my own since before I met you.* He dismounted as he neared the barn and corrals, stayed deep in the trees and worked his way slowly toward the log cabin. He had three torches in one hand and a tin of kerosene in the other.

There were no lamps lit that he could tell. Noise from the camp, maybe a hundred yards off, rumbled across the open space, bringing the melodies of Mexican guitars, some singing and laughter, and the general noise of men in camp. Ferguson had three torches with shirts wrapped and tied and doused them with kerosine from the tin.

Gotta get close enough for me to throw these onto the roof. He kept a close eye on the campsite watching for anyone venturing up out of the meadow. It was a good hundred yards from the cabin and he was deep in night shadows.

——————

SNAKE AND DOG-MAN, Louise and Pedro, along with George Dawson were sitting on their bedrolls back away from the general din of the campfires. It was nearing the end of a lovely evening, the first of many they would share on the trail to San Bernardino. Stars were slightly misted by high, thin clouds, there was no wind to speak of, and the night air was cool. It carried the aroma of a large herd of cattle and horses, grasses, and trees, along with the smoke of several fires.

"I think it was in Las Cruces, Snake," George Dawson said. There was a slight grin on his face, like he was going to tell a secret. "When that sheriff from El Paso was going to throw you boys in jail that you said something about never ever getting tied up with a woman, wasn't it?" Dawson chuckled and watched Snake reach out and take Louise by the hand.

"Might have been, George, but you know what a damned old liar I am. Took a special kind of woman to change this old boy's mind. The kind that saved my life more'n once. Yup, I can't say that I miss Las Cruces or El Paso. We did have some good times, though."

"I don't have my blankets, Mama," Pedro said, getting to his feet.

"Wait," Louise said. "I'll walk with you." She grabbed

her shotgun and she and Pedro started the long walk to their home. "I thought you brought them down earlier."

"I put them on the bench on the porch and forgot them." He was on her left side holding her hand as they walked through deep grass and skirted around bushes. "You'll need them on this trek of ours. We'll be sleeping outside every night."

"I like sleeping outside, trying to watch the stars move around. Then I go to sleep and the stars are gone when I wake up." He was laughing as he talked.

Her mind strayed back to when she and her father were on the trail constantly, hunting for good skins to sell. "Me and Pa were on the trail for weeks at a time, Pedro. You would have loved him. Big and strong, and the most loving man I've ever known, except for Snake."

"I've got the best mama and papa in the whole world," he said and squeezed her hand. "Sleep under the stars, ride my horse all day long, and eat as much as I want." He was laughing when Louise shushed him.

She stopped quickly when she saw what looked like a man hunkered down behind a tree, not ten yards from the side of their cabin. "Run back and get Snake," she said to Pedro. "Hurry. Don't ask, run." Pedro turned and ran as fast as he could back to the campfire and Louise moved slowly toward the figure. She was sure he hadn't seen the two of them walking up.

What's he doing there? He ain't one of our men.

He had something in his hands but she couldn't tell what it was, didn't recognize the silhouette either. She moved slowly through the darkness, placing each foot carefully, not making a sound. Louise could stalk lions, she surely could stalk whoever this was violating her home. She wasn't twenty yards from the man when she saw sparks being struck and a torch coming to life.

"Stop!" she cried out, raising the shotgun and firing just as the man reared back to throw the torch. It was a long distance for the ten-gauge but several of the double-ought buckshot struck the man, at least two in his face.

Ferguson dropped the torch, screaming in pain and went immediately for his sidearm. Louise didn't hesitate after firing and ran toward the man, saw the revolver coming up and let fly with the second barrel. She was much closer and this round did its business. Ferguson was down, writhing in pain, surrounded by burning brush and grass. The torch was close enough to where he fell that the feathers and doo-dads on his buckskins caught on fire, and then the skins too were hot enough to flame up. The man was engulfed in flames.

It was a horrible sight and Louise knew she couldn't get close enough to help. She tried to stomp out the fire, but it was getting away from her, burning right up to the side of their home. Ferguson's screams came to a sudden end and Louise knew he was gone, but the fire wasn't.

Soon men were all around her, stomping out the flames. Buckets of water from a nearby trough were dumped and the fire was doused. Louise stood close to what was left of Ferguson, tears running down her cheeks. "Why would he want to burn us out?" Snake put his arms around her and squeezed tight. Pedro, almost out of breath from the long run, wrapped his arms around the two of them.

"Some men just ain't right, Louise. I'm afraid he was one of them." He held her tight, lifted her face to his and kissed her. "Ain't a man in the world got a wife like mine. You're gonna have to put up with me for a long time, lady." Tears were streaming down her face, mixed with the dirt and dust of the long day, Snake had to chuckle at the sight. "All mine," he murmured.

A great cry rang out and several men started running hell-bent-for-leather toward the big house. A torch had arced through the night, landing on the roof, spreading quickly into the dried wooden shingles. Snake let go of Louise, pushed Pedro's arms aside, and was at a full run in half a second.

Two people wanting to burn us out? Louise gathered Pedro in close and held him tight. "Remember everything you're seeing," she said softly. "We'll be talking about this for a long time." She watched men climb onto the roof of the big house and literally stomp out the fire, other men were putting out a small fire in the brush and grass.

Gunshots echoed across the meadow and men's voices were heard cursing. "He's going south," someone yelled out amid more gunfire, and then it was quiet. "Let's go," Louise said, getting to her feet, grabbing her shotgun in one hand and Pedro in the other. She was stuffing shells as they hurried along.

She had loaded the two barrels as they walked and found most of the men standing around the back of the house. There was a man spread out in the dirt and Louise's heart almost stopped. *No, no, no,* echoed softly through her mind and it took several seconds for her to realize the body was not Snake's.

Snake grabbed her and held her tight. "Ferguson had help. Never did get a good look at the man. He shot one of Dawson's men, O'Brian, but he's going to live. Got him in the leg and then ran off. You and Pedro stay with the crew at camp. Me and Dog-man are gonna follow that fool's trail." He took a quick look at the shotgun. "Keep that shotgun loaded."

She didn't want him to go, needed him right close, and knew, too, that he had to go. This was their ranch that had been attacked, their homes. Snake and Dog-man had to go, had to catch and kill the intruder. After all, she thought, she killed Ferguson. Just who was the man who tried to burn down the ranch's headquarters building? "Go get him, Snake. We'll be right here waiting for you."

She and Pedro stood quiet watching the long tall Texan walk toward the corrals. *Why would Ferguson want to burn us out? He's always been strange but I don't recall the fool being dangerous. Who was with him and why? Ain't gonna get those answers standing around in the dark.*

"Come on, little man, let's get that blanket and walk back to camp. Ain't the right way to start off a cattle drive, I don't believe."

There was a line of men making their way back to the welcoming campfires, some from the Snake and Dog-man crew, some from Dawson's wagons. Louise looked up into the sky, saw long thin threads of clouds, stars brightly shining, and even this late in the fall, it was still fairly comfortable outside.

18

JOSH BAKER SAW what was going on at Snake's big cabin and shook in fear. Men with guns running toward the fire, more gunfire, and the fire being put down. He quickly doused a torch in kerosene, lit it, and threw it high up onto the roof. The coward that he was, he didn't hesitate and ran back for his horse. Men came running, yelling, shouting curses, and he pulled his handgun and shot the first man who showed up. There were answering shots but none came close.

Baker jumped on his horse and sunk his heels deep, leaning out across the horse's neck as it sped through the trees and out into the open meadow. He never let up, drove the horse, whipping it with the ends of the reins, kicking its sides, and never looked back. It was two hours, because he didn't know where he was for some time, that he got back to his filthy hideout.

Baker was exhausted, his horse could barely walk the last half mile in, and the man didn't even bother tying it off, just dropped the reins and made for the front door. He fell across his bunk and coiled into a fetal position.

"They'll come for me in the morning," he muttered. "Hungry." No water, no food, too much strenuous activity, and Joshua Baker passed out.

Outlaws have never been known for their intelligence and Baker never considered that someone might be following not too far behind. He never gave a thought to anything other than himself and that's why he didn't care if his horse lived or died. He would have been highly insulted if the horse simply rolled over and died instead of waiting for him to feed and water him.

Baker hadn't had anything to eat because he depended on his gang members to keep the cabin supplied. When they died off, supplies ran out. Once one is dehydrated, his energy is gone, and when coupled with a lack of food, the man becomes helpless. Baker considered himself the boss of his gang and yet had no idea how to take care of himself.

He never heard the soft whinnies from his horse, nor the thump as it crumpled to the dirt. There was an even softer last breath as the life of the driven beast ended.

"CAIN'T MISS THESE PRINTS, Snake. The man was at a full gallop and he's thrown dirt and grass everywhere." The two men found Baker's trail out from behind the big house and followed it south and then west across the great meadow. Baker wasn't on a trail or road, but was running cross-country, giving the boys everything they wanted to see.

"Ain't got no thoughts for his horse, this fool we're chasing," Snake said. They were riding at a quiet trot, easily following the trail left for them. "Soft ground like this could hurt a horse if he steps in a hole. We got badgers and ground squirrels enough to kill a company of cavalry."

The trail worked its way up and through great stands of timber and into the rocks. They slowly made their way over craggy ridge tops and into better ground to follow. They had to slow down once they hit the rocks and use all their knowledge of following a trail to stay on this man's tail feathers. A print in loose dirt here and there, rocks kicked aside from time to time, and broken and bent brush and ground cover led them over the top and into the long canyon that eventually leads one into the Los Angeles basin.

Whoever it was they were following found a roadway but didn't slow down. His prints still stood out, even in the subdued light of late night. "Where is this fool going, Snake? '

"He's working his way toward the YL. This road cuts right through their range. For some time, I think he was just running and didn't care where he went, but now, he's staying on this road. He'll lead us to wherever he's going."

Dog-man had to chuckle at the way Snake explained all that but also saw the truth in it. Instead of just crossing the road in his mad dash to get away, the man stayed on the road and didn't seem to have any idea of getting off.

"That old horse is gonna give out on him," Snake said. "He's been pushing him hard for this entire time. I'm gonna kill him just for the way he treats his horse. Then I'll work him over for attacking us."

Baker had followed the main road that would have taken him almost to the front door of the YL ranch, but where a creek came down out of the hillside, he turned onto a narrow trail up into the trees, following the creek.

"Good thing you spotted that, Snake. I would have ridden right on by," Dog-man said. "Best start thinking about ambush. Thick timber along this little canyon."

"And rocks and caves, and hairpin turns, and everything else one could hide behind or in," Snake chuckled. "Ever wondered how many times we've found ourselves chasing somebody? Seems like we're always chasing somebody."

"'Cuz they're outlaws and we're not, Snake."

Following the trail Baker left was the easy part. Trying to let their eyes see everything that might be in front or off to the side as they rode along, was difficult and tiring. "Canyon is about to widen out some," Snake said. The trail up and through the trees also involved crossing the little creek often and Dog-man welcomed the broader scene in front of him.

They worked slowly over a flat ridge and looked down on a cabin tucked into a little bend of the creek. "I'm gonna whip that man until my arm falls off," Snake said, looking down onto a terrible scene. Baker's horse was on its side and even from this distance Snake knew he was looking at death. "Still saddled. Just laid down and died. Best thing that could happen to him, though. Ain't the way a good horse should die."

Snake's anger had been building almost from the time they took to the chase. There were only a few things that got Snake fully riled, Dog-man thought, looking at the long man. Cruelty to a horse would ignite the flames faster than anything.

"Let's tie off and work our way down," Dog-man said. He looked up the hillside to the east and saw the first tinges of dawn in the high clouds. "It's gonna be light enough to make us targets before too long. Hope whoever's in that cabin is alone."

"Ain't no other animals in that wreck of a corral behind the cabin. Ain't no smoke from the chimney either." Snake moved through the trees, angling into the front corner of the dilapidated cabin. It's always the coldest at sunrise and Snake was glad the men had worn their heavy coats before leaving out. "I'd have a fire going if I was in there."

"If you was conscious." Dog-man chuckled.

"You've got a point, there, partner. Let's see how close we can get." The ground was rocky in places but soft in others. Dead leaves and twigs were scattered everywhere and being quiet was difficult. Snake led the way through the trees, not on the well-worn footpath, to within just a few yards of the cabin.

"Ain't but one window that I can see. Damn door's closed. Got a plan?" Dog-man asked.

"Always," Snake murmured. His smile was bright and he quietly, almost sauntered across the small open space and right up to the cabin's door. Dog-man watched him pull his sidearm and kick the door open. He stepped inside and Dog-man was at a run across the open yard.

"Ain't seen nothing like that in a long time," Snake said. He reached out and lifted the revolver from Baker's holster, Put his own away, reached down and jerked the cot up, dumping the outlaw onto the dirt floor.

Baker came up cussing, screaming, swinging fists, reaching for his weapon. Snake laughed and looked over at Dog-man. "Quite a show, eh?" Snake grabbed the man and pulled him close, drove a fist into his midsection, then swung straight up into the man's jaw, and before Baker could fall to the floor, slammed him across the side of the head with his own pistol.

"That's better," Snake said. "I like the quiet."

"Should have shot the fool, Snake. What are we gonna do with him? His horse is dead."

"Well, now, ain't that a pickle," Snake said. The realization hit both men at about the same time. What would they do with the man?

Dog-man went up the side of the hill to retrieve their horses while Snake tied Josh Baker up tight. He slapped him a couple of times to see if he could bring him to, but gave it up and sat down at the table. "Now just what do we do with you, Mister Baker? You ain't riding behind me and I'm sure Dog feels the same. You ain't in no condition to walk back, and it would be cruel and inhumane to just put a rope around you and ride off."

Dog-man walked in, chuckling. "I could hear you halfway up the hill. I do got an idea, though. Take a couple of those tree limbs he used for that corral and make a travois."

"Well, now, will you listen to that?" Snake said, right to Baker's face. "By golly, you're gonna get the ride of your life." He turned to Dog-man, a grand smile across his face. "I'll romp my horse through the longest, biggest, nastiest field of rocks I can find on the way home."

The two were laughing and joshing each other for the hour or so it took to fashion a travois and get it attached to Snake's horse. "Now, this fine old horse of mine ain't never pulled nothing, Dog-man. No carts, no buggies, no wagons, and surely no travoises. If he starts kicking and carrying on some, Mr. Baker there just might find he has a mouth full of horse hoof. Well, don't matter none, the man ain't got a pretty face like mine to start with."

19

IT WAS a long ride back to the ranch and Josh Baker spent most of the time crying out that he was dying, that he would kill the two hauling him through the rocks and streams, and generally making a fool of himself. Both Snake and Dog-man were disgusted with the man well before they reached the ranch.

Baker saw fault and failure in everyone around him but never saw it in himself. It was Ferguson's fault that he was forced to flee before burning out the Snake and Dog-man ranch. It was his horse's fault that these two malicious cowboys were able to track him back to his cabin. It wasn't his fault that the plan to burn out and kill Snake and Dog-man failed.

"We were supposed to be moving the herd, Dog-man. Ain't even got started and we're already a day behind our own schedule."

The camp was alive with activity from both the herd hands and the wagon hands. Cook fires were burning brightly, men were eating while working, and Snake rode up to where Louise and Pedro were settled in. "Got him," he said, stepping down from his stock horse. With a flourish, he introduced his captive. "Joshua Baker, no longer a member of the Baker gang."

"What are we going to do with him?" George Dawson said, walking up. "We should have been on the trail hours ago."

"I know, George, but this is the man that shot your man. We ain't just turning him loose. Ain't gonna hang him neither. Not our way." Snake was just a bit grumpy having been up all night on the chase, having to put up with Baker's bad mouth for the hours-long ride back to camp, and wasn't in the mood to be questioned.

"Got to get him locked up in Lane's Crossing," Dog-man said. "We got enough people to get this drive started. I'll take Baker in, which makes our ranch crew one man shy, and you've got a wounded one, George making you one man shy. We still got more than enough people to get started and I'll catch up."

Snake nodded his head, looked at Dawson who did the same, and everyone standing around seemed to agree as well. "Yup, rule of the majority." Snake laughed. "All right, this fool is all yours, Dog-man. I'm gonna get a belly full of something and we'll get this drive on the trail. Boys, start moving the beef, George, get your wagons ready, and Louise, please feed me and bring coffee too."

Snake was in command and there was no doubt in anyone's mind. Even George Dawson started moving a little faster than what would be considered the norm. Dawson looked at the man and smiled remembering the first time that lanky Texan walked into his office bringing news of an attempted stage robbery.

That man looks at the world through a completely different

125

set of eyes than most of us use. He sees beauty, danger, and warmth in hues far superior to what we see.

It must have looked like an ant hill come alive as men found their horses and moved out toward the bunched herd, others found horses and mules and got harness straightened out and in place, and fires not being used were stomped out.

Dog-man attached the travois to his horse, made sure Baker was tied down tight, and lit out for Lane's Crossing. He had a tin cup full of coffee in hand and a pocket full of biscuits waiting their turn. "Five miles in and five miles back," he muttered, touching his spurs lightly to his big Andalusian. "Piece of cake. There won't be any catching up, they'll just be getting underway."

He took a look over his shoulder and smiled down on Baker. "All comfy are we? Hang on tight and I'll find as many rocks as I can." Dog-man was laughing loudly, Baker was screaming obscenities, and the dust rose in waves as he rode away.

Pedro took Snake by the hand and pulled him toward one of few fires still burning. "Mama has food, papa." Snake yelped a cry of joy, threw Pedro over his shoulder and did the Texas two-step across some open grass to where Louise had his platter waiting.

"This is the way to start a cattle drive, eh, my lady? A pound of beef, half a dozen eggs, and biscuits to sop up the leavings. It's gonna be a fine day."

DOG-MAN DRAGGED HIS QUARRY, still screaming his head off through the small community and up to the courthouse just as County Commissioner Gordy Whitman was coming down the stone steps. Dog-man still had a grim look on his face despite the fun he had waving to all the folks lining the street and making fun of Josh Baker. Baker of course responded with howls of displeasure filled with vile language, which of course brought on even more loud cat-calls and comments.

"What have we got here, Dog-man? Haven't seen a rig like that in a long time." He couldn't hold in the chuckles but also glared at the prisoner.

"This is Joshua Baker, commissioner. He and Slim Ferguson tried to burn us out last night. Ferguson is dead, we're starting our fall drive today, and the county will want this man under wraps."

"Ferguson, eh?" Gordy Whitman remembered the strange meeting he had with Slim Ferguson just a week or so ago. "This is the exact problem I presented to the commission yesterday," Whitman said. "We have a sheriff's office, we have a jail, but we still don't have a sheriff. Well, you say Baker and Ferguson tried to burn you out?"

"That's right, and Baker shot a man, besides. This man needs to be locked up tight. His men attacked our herd two nights ago, also. He's got a lot of paper hanging around the county."

"Bring him in, then, and we'll get him under lock and key. I'll take charge of the situation. I wish either you or Snake would take the job."

"You want to run our trail drive?"

"No, Dog-man. that's all yours." He laughed. "All yours." He thought about what the rancher said. *I'm swamped with south county business, desperate to find someone to be acting sheriff until the next election. Driving a thousand head of cattle to San Bernardino? I wouldn't know where to begin.* His deeply tanned face told another story, though. Gordy Whitman had spent the last several days in the mountains, busting rock, dry panning the busted pieces, and had filed his claim earlier that morning.

This will be my last year as county commissioner because of those rocks. I'll live on the claim, eat off the land, and store away some fine-looking specimens of gold. Sell just enough to keep me in food and beer.

Whitman was the kind of man who should have been sheriff, not a county commissioner. When his new claim pans out, he'll give up that position. It doesn't take a lot of gold dust for a man and wife to live well, and with his wife helping, they would do fine. "No, Dog-man, I may have plans of my own and they don't include cattle."

Dog-man got Baker untied from the travois and on his feet. Baker had a hard time standing up, keeping his balance. He'd been lashed to the rough pine poles for hours, was suffering a ghastly hangover, was as stiff as the pine boughs that framed the travois, and was still cursing a blue streak. Loud enough that George Peterson came out from his store to see what was going on.

"Well, well," Peterson said. "Joshua Baker, in custody. Best thing I've seen in months. What happened?"

"Tried to burn Snake and Dog-man out," Commissioner Whitman said. "Shot a man, too." Whitman shook his head as Dog-man shoved Baker toward the courthouse steps. "Seems he and Slim Ferguson were working together. Dog-man said Ferguson is dead."

"That don't surprise me none at all," Peterson said. He followed everyone into the courthouse and the sheriff's office. "Need to have a word with you, Dog-man when you get Baker settled in."

Dog-man nodded and pushed Baker into one of the empty cells. He pushed the man onto a bunk, face down, and untied his hands that Snake had tied many hours before. "You're gonna be here a while, Baker, so make yourself comfortable."

He backed out of the small cell and slammed the iron door shut, made sure it was locked tight, and turned for the door. He hadn't taken half a step and Baker started in with his screaming, about where he had left off.

"He's all yours, commissioner," Dog-man laughed. He turned to Peterson. "Something else going on?"

"Afraid so," the storekeeper said. "One of my boys heard some men talking about robbing Dawson's wagons on the road to San Berdoo. Anyway you and Snake can get word to him? It sounded like it might be Claudio Valenzuela and company."

Dog-man didn't say anything about Dawson's wagons moving in the middle of their herd, just looked at Peterson. "Thank you. We'll get the word to Dawson right away. He's got men riding with him and they've protected his wagons before."

Dog-man made the quick ride back to the ranch and saw that the herd was moving out across the rolling ridge to the west and would drop down to flank the main road to San Bernardino. "What a sight," he murmured, pulling his horse up. "Most beautiful sight I've ever seen. Our herd, moving out to market. My god, Snake, what have we done?"

20

THE CATTLE, a long line as broad as fifty yards of almost a thousand head, snaked up the hillside and over the grassy ridge, a dust cloud hovered in the clear fall air. Dawson's wagons were tucked in, surrounded by slowly walking steers that would bring top dollar at the sale yard. "Walk 'em easy, boys. That weight is gold and we don't want to lose any." Alvarado's last words before leaving out was still strong in the men's ears as they pushed the cattle.

Texas and California cowboys, Mexican charros, and a sprinkling of Dawson's teamsters, all calling out in loud voices and several languages, urging the animals along. The sounds of the voices and the rumble of thousands of hooves could be heard in the still air, and the smile on Dog-man's face would have lit up the sky if the sun hadn't already been up.

He rode up on the herd, waved to Hillyer riding drag, already covered in dust, moved along the flank, said howdy to a couple of Mexican charros, and rode up on the two Dawson wagons. "Everything looks good from my angle," he called out.

"Couldn't be better, Dog-man. Terrain pretty much like this all the way?"

"It'll be good all day today, but we'll be in rocky country tomorrow and the next day. Figure this to be a five-day drive at best," Dog-man called out. He waved and moved back out on the flank and rode toward the head of the herd. It was miles long, snaking along following the lay of the land. Looking back, all he could see was the backs of steers and dust, and his smile never wavered.

He found Snake riding alongside the chuck wagon, which was being driven by Louise instead of Jeannie Nichols and Pedro was in the seat next to her. "Something wrong?" he asked.

"Not a thing. Jeannie is our wood gatherer for an hour or so, Pedro is learning the fine art of driving a team, and Louise is telling him stories of how to hunt lions and wolves. I'm just along for the ride." Snake had a unique way of riding when there wasn't an issue of some kind. He leaned as far back in the saddle as he could, stretched one leg up and around the saddle horn, and Dog-man was sure that the man actually napped from time to time.

Snake chuckled. sat up straight in the saddle and motioned for Dog-man to ride alongside. The two rode off in front of the wagon. "I've got a fine trail laid out for us," he said. They were in a trot moving through grass, a few rocks that could be avoided, and low brush. "Both Louise and Jeannie are good with the wagon and Pedro's learning. This is the way to drive cattle."

"We may have company, Snake." Dog-man broke the reverie and Snake sat bolt upright. "Peterson said there was talk of Valenzuela looking to hit Dawson's wagons. Neither Peterson nor whoever was talking knew about Dawson being in the middle of our drive."

Snake draped a yellow ribbon on a piece of brush and made a slight turn to the left, following a draw through some tangled live oak. Dog-man saw how quickly Snake could read the terrain, how he knew the wagons, all of them would be able to keep right on without even slowing down.

"If they're gonna hit us, Dog, it will be when we're at camp. Ain't no way they're gonna bust their way through the herd. We'll spread the word when we make camp tonight. Night guards out on two-hour shifts and ready to fight."

Dog-man smiled and nodded in agreement. "They'd have to work their way through grazing cattle to get at the wagons, Snake. I don't think we'll see 'em."

"They wouldn't have to, Dog-man. They might try to stampede the herd. Either way, we'd do 'em in. I'd bet when they see the wagons inside the herd, they'll back off," Snake said.

"I know I would." Dog-man and Snake were well in front of the chuck and the herd, continuing to lay out the trail and continued their conversation on how they would probably not get hit by outlaws anyway.

"THAT AIN'T what you was telling us, Claudio," Wally Lippincott said. He and Claudio Valenzuela were sitting on their horses under an umbrella of live oak watching the large herd across a wide expanse of meadow. "Them's Dawson's wagons tucked in the middle of all them beeves."

Lippincott was a small-time confidence man working the stage stops in the great desert. He was good with a knife, good with hidden cards in table games, and good at fleecing unsuspecting travelers at the Mojave River water holes. He joined up with Valenzuela when the word gold became part of the conversation.

"You said that we was raking the two wagons, Claudio. I brung Pepe and Silas along 'cuz you said all we needed to do was knock off a couple of drivers. What are you trying to get us into? Ain't rustlin' no cows. No sir, ain't."

"You're right, Wally, we aren't rustling no cows. I think Mr. Dawson is trying to pull a fast one on us. There's water about six or seven miles in front of that herd. Bring your boys and let's get there first." Wally Lippincott had two sons, Pepe from a joining of the flesh with a Mexican girl eighteen years ago and Silas from a blessed night in El Paso sixteen years ago. Both boys were handy with guns and knives and both had wanted posters plastered along the trail defined by the Mojave River.

The four men rode quickly to a small stream running down out of the high country and through a large open pass on the trail to San Bernardino. The main road was a mile or so to their west. "That herd will have to stop here tonight," Valenzuela said. "There's water and grass. The one thing drovers watch for is a stampede. It draws everyone out to stop the herd. You savvy?"

"I think you got a corn cob stuck somewhere, Valenzuela," Wally said. Pepe and Silas laughed and passed a bottle back and forth. "You saying that tonight we start a stampede?" He looked at the two boys and then at Valenzuela who nodded his head in affirmation.

"That's exactly what I'm saying. they'll be so busy

chasing them damned cows they won't even know we've run off with Dawson's wagons. Probably won't even have to draw our weapons." The lean Mexican outlaw sat with his back resting on a log and tossed a small twig into the fire. "Couldn't be easier the way I see it."

Wally looked at his two sons. Pepe was the oldest and also the brightest of the two. Silas was the meanest. Only sixteen, he was known to have killed two men and there was talk of others. "What do you see in all this, Pepe?"

"Might be just as easy as Valenzuela says if that old teamster leaves the horses and mules harnessed and hitched. That ain't the way teamsters do things, though. Ain't the way I'd do it, Pa."

"What do you think, Silas?" Wally was shaking his head, looking at Valenzuela, then each of the boys. "Pepe has a damn good point."

"Ain't never seen a teamster leave his animals harnessed and hitched overnight, Pa. We been at every water hole from here to Arizona Territory, and I ain't never seen it done."

"You got us all the way out here on a fool's errand, Valenzuela. Them wagons ain't gonna be driven out from that herd if they ain't got animals attached."

Claudio Valenzuela knew he was in trouble, saw in Wally Lippincott's eyes that murder might be next on the agenda. "I didn't know that Dawson was going to be coming along with a herd of cattle, Wally. It was never mentioned but I do have an idea."

"You'd best have the brightest idea of your life," Wally said.

Lippincott was not a large man, stood in the neighborhood of five feet and seven inches, weighed one thirty at best, but was wiry strong, quick as the fastest titmouse, and mean as cat shit. His eyes at the moment told Valenzuela he was moments from death.

"When they drive those cattle into that glen down below there," and his arms spread to show what he was talking about, "everyone will be dog tired," Valenzuela said. "That's when we spook the cows. Create a wild stampede, and grab the wagons. There's gold ore in one that a mill in Mexico will take care of for us, and the other wagon is loaded with fine tanned skins ready for sale."

He said gold with heavy emphasis knowing Wally's love of the stuff. Both Pepe and Silas smiled at the word as well. "I weren't messing with you, Wally. I didn't know Dawson would be with the herd. Ain't nothing was said about that. But starting a stampede will draw every man away from those wagons."

"We got time to think about it, Pa," Silas said. "Herd won't be here for several hours. Maybe we can come up with a good plan."

"We're coming out of these hills with a wagon full of gold or you, Claudio ain't coming out. You lied to us and me and the boys ain't likin' it. This works, or you die." Wally took the bottle away from young Silas and drank deep before continuing. "Pepe, you know a little about cattle, Claudio, you say you do, so the two of you put together a plan on how to start that stampede. Silas, you and me will work on how to get that wagon with the gold. To hell with the skins."

"Remember when we snatched that wagon out near Bendix, Pa? We rode up, each of us on a side, shot the teamster, which spooked the team into a good run, but we was able to keep them on the trail. It worked good." Pepe had just enough liquor in him that he wasn't thinking straight.

"Put the bottle away, son, and start thinking. You don't see no trail, do you? You see rocks, do you? Ain't busting axles or wheels and losing the gold." He spat tobacco juice into the fire and motioned for Silas to follow him. "You worry about cattle. Me and Silas will worry about gold."

"You might want to give those hides another thought, Pa," Silas said. "Hides is a big commodity still. If we can get both wagons, I think we should."

"All I wants is that gold, son. If you want them hides, go ahead and get 'em but don't get in my way gettin' that gold."

21

"IF YOU WAS Claudio Valenzuela and you was looking to hijack Dawson's wagons, how would you do it?" Dog-man and Snake were a mile or so in front of the herd and nearing the first night's stop. Snake had found a decent meadow earlier. It featured a creek running through so the herd would have good grass and water for their first night on the trail and he and Dog-man were leading the circus in.

Considering the size of the herd, the inexperience of some of the men, and it being the first day, Snake was in a good mood. There hadn't been any major problems and the day was slowly coming to an end. The idea of some damn fool outlaw wanting to hijack George Dawson's wagons just didn't seem to be the right way to end the day.

"There's good water and grass not far in front of us," Snake said. "If he's after Dawson's wagons, he has to hit us as soon as we arrive or just as we are leaving in the morning. If he's after cattle, then late tonight." Snake's eyes told a grim story. "Any fool tries it ain't gonna live no matter which it is."

"How would you do it?" Dog-man asked. "The only thing that would defeat his chances would be waiting until Dawson unhitches the teams."

"You're right," Snake said. "That fool wants Dawson's wagons and not our herd? He can't wait until we get settled. George takes care of his animals before anything and Valenzuela sure as I'm breathing ain't gonna steal no wagon that ain't hooked up to horses or mules." He had to laugh at the picture in his mind of a skinny little Mexican bartender trying to pull a wagon. "Gettin' serious, though, If Valenzuela is going to hit us for Dawson's wagons it has to be within the first half hour of our arrival in that little valley. He'd have to scatter the herd, fight off all our people, and keep Dawson from his teams. Once those wagons are unhitched he ain't gettin' 'em."

"You're thinking he'll ride out and try to scatter or spook the herd? With all the guns we have driving them critters?" Dog-man shook his head.

"Well," Snake drawled out. "All them guns would respond by chasing the herd, gotta say that for sure. But Dawson's men ain't drovers, are they. That's not how they would respond." Snake chuckled at the thought. "Let's ride back, have us a pow-wow with George Dawson and Francisco Alvarado. We'll have our own plan, Dog-man."

Snake felt sure that even though some of George Dawson's men were working cattle during the drive, if a gang attempted to grab one of Dawson's wagons, they would do what they could to defend those wagons. "We got us a large herd, Dog, and we got us plenty of guns. I don't think this Valenzuela feller is very bright."

Their first stop was at the chuck wagon. "When we get to the camping area, stay as close to the wagon as you can. Don't do anything except you and Pedro stay undercover," Snake told Louise. "Keep your rifle and shotgun close to hand. Dog-man thinks we're gonna face an attack."

Louise didn't question at all and turned to tell Jeannie and Pedro what to do. "I'm not always good at just watching, Snake. I think you're right that Jeannie and Pedro should hide in the wagon but you might need my guns." She was dressed as the hunter she was, buckskins, men's pants, and high-top mocs. Her gun belt was tight around her waist and that wicked shotgun was always close by.

"It ain't right for me to be telling you what to do, sweetie, but I sure ain't in the best mood about you gettin' in the line of fire again. You scare me half to death sometimes." He rode close enough to the chuck that she could reach out and touch his hand and gave him a big smile.

"That goes both ways, big boy. I'll help if I can. I've got my rifle, shotgun, and pistol, can hit a running wolf at a hundred yards, and I want to help."

Snake gave her a big smile and nodded his head. "I ain't never knowed anyone like you, girl. Sure glad you're on my side. Just do everything you can to stay safe." He smiled again and joined Dog-man on their ride to find George Dawson.

"That woman's about the finest in the world," he said. "There's Dawson's wagons. I'll ride to him, you find Alvarado and bring him to the wagon."

In less than fifteen minutes, the four men were together, Snake, Dog-man, and Francisco Alvarado on horseback, Dawson in the high seat of the lead wagon.

"Can't picture it myself," Dog-man," George Dawson said. "Start a stampede and hijack my wagons? Hell's bells, boys, these cattle stampede what do you think these horses and mules are gonna do? They'll join the party sure as I'm sittin' here." Dawson had a way of creating a picture with his words and Snake laughed right out, seeing the mules dancing with the cattle.

"Ain't something I'd call a party, George, but you're probably right. The thing is, Claudio Valenzuela ain't a cattleman, don't know nothin' about the critters other than he can sell what he steals. He knows they will stampede, sometimes for the least cause, and he don't care who might get caught in the middle. In this case, he wants your wagons, but they might be part of the stampede."

Dog-man had to laugh remembering when a gang tried to run down one of Dawson's wagons and gunfire spooked the six-up rig into a full run, creating more problems than the outlaws could handle. "He's right, Snake. We've seen it."

Snake laughed and turned to Alvarado. "Make sure all our people understand what might happen. Dawson's men will protect the wagons, it's up to us to protect the herd, get the beeves settled, then we can run the outlaws down and kill 'em dead."

"I'll spread the word," Francisco said. "Hillyer will be among those leading the herd and he's more than capable of helping turn the leaders if they do spook. How much further, boss? We're running out of daylight."

"When we drop over the ridge we're climbing, the meadow is on the other side." Snake looked at Dog-man. "Grab a couple of men and let's get up there quick." He waved, turned his horse, and rode toward the front of the herd at a strong trot. He saw Alvarado motion Hillyer to join them.

Dog-man waved Wayne Nichols and Jose de la Cruz to join and followed Snake. "We're sure there's gonna be an attempt to stampede the herd when we get over this ridge," he told them. "Be ready as soon as we join Snake."

It was an easy ride up the hillside and the herd was moving along at a steady pace. It took less than an hour early that morning for the herd to fall into a pecking order of sorts, with those riding on flanks having little difficulty keeping order. Looking back from high on the hill, Dog-man again enjoyed seeing the long and wide herd moving snake like through rocks, trees, and good grass. *If I keep looking back at them cows, I'm gonna have a permanent smile on my face.*

WALLY AND SILAS were sitting their horses in a stand of live oak watching as two cowboys crested the ridge followed by the herd leaders. "That herd is a quarter mile across, Pa," Silas said. "How the hell are we gonna stampede them?" He sat in the saddle with his mouth open trying to count as the herd and its great cloud of dust came across the top of the ridge.

The two lead riders were joined by two more and Wally was well into having second thoughts about the whole idea. Along with the well-armed cowboys Wally saw the chuck wagon come across and the driver had someone sitting next to him with a rifle across her legs. He'd heard stories about the woman called Lion Killer at just about every water hole across the great desert. When the herd's flank riders rode across the ridge Wally called it off.

"Let's go, Silas, this ain't a good day to die. We'll shoot Valenzuela and get the hell out of this country. There's more guns riding with that herd than we've ever faced."

Wally Lippincott made the right decision just not soon enough. Claudio Valenzuela and Pepe were moving as silently and as hidden as they could get along the herd's route and when the leaders made their way down off the ridge and into the grassy meadow, they rode out, howling at the top of their lungs and firing their pistols into the air.

Snake saw them first and put the spurs to his quick Andalusian stud. They moved from trot to full-out gallop in two strides. He had his pistol out and rode stretched out across the horse's neck right at Valenzuela. When the two were within twenty yards or so of each other, Snake fired off two quick rounds, and Valenzuela was thrown back off his horse, dead by the time he hit the ground.

Snake brought the horse into a tight turn and was about to make a run at Pepe Lippincott when he saw Dog-man race through the grass, firing his pistol and killing the boy with his first shot. Francisco, Jeremiah Hillyer, and the two Mexican charros were already moving to head off any stampede that might erupt. With all the gunfire, screaming voices, and excitement, Alvarado was sure it would start.

Several of the men who were riding on the flanks of the drive came at a gallop, joined Alvarado at the head of the herd, got the leaders turned, and brought them to a stop before anything could start. The herd itself continued streaming across the top of the ridge and slowly filled the large basin. With plenty of fresh water and green grass, they settled down for a long night of grazing.

Cowhands were busy getting the herd settled, Dawson's men swarmed the wagons and then got busy getting the teams unhitched, out of their harness, and into good grass near fresh water. The action turned quickly from possible chaos to normal late in the day cattle drive. "Got lucky on this one, Dog-man," Snake said as they rode up to where one of the bodies had fallen. "It could have gone nasty fast."

"We got us a good crew, Snake. We have to be the two luckiest men around. Always have good people working with us." Dog-man rode off to see if Dawson needed help and

Snake rode toward the chuck.

Louise and Jeannie Nichols had Pedro bring the chuck wagon to a stand of live oak on the far side of the meadow and began making up the camp. It wasn't long that George Dawson brought his wagons in, got the animals unharnessed and staked out near the stream and in good grass.

"Heard the gunfire," George said to Louise, "but don't think there was a stampede."

"Looking at all those cows just standing there eating, I don't think there was one, George. All your men accounted for?"

Dawson smiled and nodded and helped Pedro get what wood he had collected during the day piled up for the night's fires. "Get some of this good oak that's on the ground, too, son. Makes for a nice long fire at night. After a day sitting on that hard wagon seat, a good hot fire burning through the night makes things a little easier."

Pedro laughed watching Dawson rub his backside. Louise, in turn, laughed watching Pedro walk out for wood rubbing his backside. "It really is going to be a nice drive," she murmured, rubbing her backside.

"No!" Wally cried it out, watching Pepe fall from his horse and roll in the grass. He stared long at the boy but Pepe was not getting back up. "Those dirty bastards just killed your brother," he screamed. "No, Pepe, no."

Silas stood next to his father, anger boiling through every vein. "Pepe," he cried out and silently vowed to kill the man responsible for his brother's death. The half brothers were close in age, in background, and in what they wanted from life. Money, mostly, and power. They believed they would get that by riding the outlaw trail with their father. A lack of education helped in that respect.

Of the two, Pepe was the leader and even Wally Lippincott tended to pay attention when Pepe was discussing a possible job. Silas followed his brother without question. If Pepe wanted it, Silas wanted it even more. If Pepe said something was no good, Silas would fight anyone who disagreed.

"It was the one called Dog-man, Papa. He was the one, and I am going to kill him, slowly, with my knife."

Wally looked at his son and did not see a young boy standing there. He saw an avenging angel with a Bowie knife in his hand and knew it would happen. "You and I, Silas, will sneak into their camp tonight and we'll kill everyone we see. They are all responsible for Pepe's death."

22

A COUPLE of the hands brought the two bodies in for burial. "That's Claudio Valenzuela all right, but I don't recognize the young one," Snake said. The two were laid out in the grass while graves were dug in the soft earth. "You seen this boy before, Dog-man?"

"I have." George Dawson spoke up before Dog-man could answer. "We were at a water hole and they hung a poster with his face plastered on it. Seems he, his brother, and their father prey on travelers coming across that wild desert." He tilted his head in thought before continuing. "Name's Lippincott."

"Wally Lippincott and his boys," Snake said. "Yup, we've sure heard about them. Valenzuela must have brought them in because of the gold ore you're carrying, George. Those rocks would mill out to a pretty sum. Me and Dog-man know all about that, eh?"

Dog-man chuckled remembering their mining days in Mexico. "That means that somewhere out there is Wally and his one remaining son," Dog-man said. "We better make sure our Nighthawks are aware of that.

They won't be going after the herd. They'll be coming after us. Outlaw or not, losing a son will rile a man, and Wally Lippincott riles easily."

"I see what their plan was now," Snake said. "Valenzuela and this boy would ride out and stampede the herd and Lippincott and his other son would hijack your wagons, George." Snake shook his head and snickered. "They would have needed another four or five men to pull something like that off. Damn stupid if you ask me."

"That's why they're outlaws, Snake." George Dawson laughed. "Smart people aren't outlaws. I've heard you say that more than once."

Snake chuckled and wagged his finger at the long-time teamster. "Yup," he said. They walked back toward camp smelling some meat cooking over an open fire and knowing coffee would be brewing as well. "Can't imagine what it would be like watching my own boy get shot out of the saddle," Snake said. His eyes said far more than his words. "Don't matter none that the boy was a killer or outlaw, it would be the fact that it was his boy he saw bein' killed. Gonna be a lot of anger and loss coming at us later tonight, boys..." His voice trailed off, and he looked out toward where Pedro was bringing firewood to Louise.

Ain't known that boy but for a short time, but he's ours. Ain't the same color, ain't the same background, sure as hell ain't as handsome as I am, but god almighty do I love him. He stood quiet, watching Pedro tease Louise about something, and saw his Lion Killer pretend to chase off the little imp. *I can't imagine seeing what Lippincott might have seen. Can't imagine his rage.*

The thrill of how well the first day of the long drive went was dulled with the thoughts of two men with guns and knives coming down on them later that night.

"Let's not spread this camp out too wide, boys. Gather in nice and close. We'll keep the fires burning and at least two guards in camp. Three Nighthawks on the herd in two-hour shifts, and two guards in camp on two-hour shifts. Everybody's gonna get their chance tonight, I'm afraid."

Dog-man looked at Snake, knew that meant just about every person on the drive would find himself pulling guard duty at some point that night. "Might make for a long day tomorrow, boys, but it's better than the alternative."

That brought some subdued chuckles from around the fire and plates full of broiled beef and beans were eaten quietly, as everyone thought about that alternative. A long, cold knife blade between the ribs would not make for a pleasant night.

Jeannie Nichols in her broken English changed the mood quickly. "Found me some wild apples and whupped up pies while you guys bury 'em bad guys. You like?"

She could have been elected president at that moment, and she and Louise brought the pies out of the chuck. "This is gonna be a nice drive," Louise murmured for about the tenth time that day.

SNAKE ARRANGED for two fires to be burning with half the crew around each one. Guards were picked for the camp and for the herd, and those not on guard grabbed bedrolls to catch as much sleep as they could. Everyone, except for Jeannie Nichols and young Pedro would be pulling at least one shift of guard duty that night.

"I really wish you wouldn't," Snake said as he and

Louise sat near the fire with their coffee. "We got enough people to cover everything."

"It wouldn't be right, Snake. You know it wouldn't. You know I have to pull my share. I have to." Her mouth and eyes told Snake that all the words in the world weren't going to change her mind. "You and Dog-man will be out with the herd, I'll be here in camp. Just like it was when we were roaming the desert, Snake. You protecting me and me protecting you."

He wrapped his arms around her and held her tight. "We're a pretty good team, old girl. I got my lion killer, and you got a beat-up old wreck of a Texas cowboy. Ain't no gang of outlaws mean enough to take us on."

She giggled some, nuzzled his neck, and let him hold her as tight as he wanted. "I'm worried about Pedro being alone when I'm on guard," she said.

"I've thought about that," Snake said. "We won't be on guard at the same time. One of us will always be with him all night. Wayne Nichols will also be close with Jeannie. That little Paiute lady insists she's going to pull guard with Wayne. They're really a close couple."

"She's a lot of fun to be around. Wonderful sense of humor. She's teaching Pedro her language and he's teaching her Spanish. This is gonna be a fine drive, Snake."

THE TWO MEN ate cold meat and drank cold water for their supper. No fires to give themselves away. The night came quickly in the mountains, and the fires from the cow camp could be seen about a mile off and down below them. "Ain't gonna be easy boy, not the way they got that camp laid out." Wally Lippincott had gotten as close as he dared once it got dark and hurried back to report.

"They got trees on one side, men stretched out in bedrolls between two campfires, and then the wagons stretched out. Ain't gonna be easy to pick out Snake and Dog-man, but them two have to die."

"It's quiet down there. Let's go," Silas said. He'd been testing the keen blade for half an hour, shaved most of the hair from his left arm, and felt the rage continue to grow. "I ain't never really enjoyed killing any of those men we've done in, Pa, but I'm gonna enjoy tonight's. I'm gonna look right into Dog-man's eyes when I slice his heart into pieces."

Wally Lippincott could feel the hate radiating from his son, could feel the rage boiling in his bile, and slowly got to his feet. "Best if we come in from either side, Silas. Don't know which of those bedrolls holds Dog-man, which might hold Snake, or even if either man is there. They have riders out on the herd, too."

"Don't matter none. We'll kill 'em off until there ain't none left." Silas made a crazy sound that was supposed to be a laugh.

The night was dark, only the stars shedding some light. A most gentle breeze wafted through the trees, spread soft waves through the grass, but didn't carry the sound of boots for any great distance. The wide and long meadow had some low rolling hills to the south and more rocky ridges to the north and Wally elected to cross over to the north and descend on the camp.

The two did not make plans to meet in the middle but rather, when their work was done to return to their camp and flee back to the great Mojave Desert. "Good luck, boy," Wally said, moving off into the dark. Silas just nodded as he, too, slipped into the darkness.

Silas grunted, stumbling over rocks as he moved down off the hillside, staying as much as possible in the trees and rocks, using the natural terrain to stay out of sight of the fires. Silas made his way well to the west, around the herd and back toward the cow camp. He would be a long time getting there. The fires were burning bright, which kept him on a good line, but he knew they would hamper his ability to get close.

He spotted a Nighthawk riding slowly around the herd and stopped, crouching behind a rocky outcrop. It was one of the Mexican charros, singing softly to the herd, watching the cattle, glancing about from time to time. It was several minutes before Silas felt comfortable moving out and made for the trees on the opposite side of the meadow, away from cattle and Nighthawks.

He was surprised at how long it took him to begin his stalk on the camp. That meadow was broad, the herd was large, and he encountered two Nighthawks before he reached the trees. *I wonder if they're expecting us?* He was good at being quiet, stealthy, but started worrying the closer he got to one of the fires. *There are too many people up and moving about for this late at night.*

It took but a second contemplation for the rage to come back, for the scene to play out in front of him. He again saw his brother thrown back off his horse knowing he was dead. *I don't care how many people are waiting for me. It just means that many more will die.*

He saw a man carrying a rifle get up from the fire, put his tin cup down, and walk slowly out and then around the fire, always looking out from the fire, never right at it. He moved cautiously through all those sleeping, quietly. *Don't know who that is but I gotta get rid of him before I can even get close to those sleeping. Don't matter none who he is. He's with Dog-man and that means he's my enemy.*

Silas didn't even attempt to calm the rage, instead, he let it boil, let it loose to kill and maim those who killed his brother. Kill the man with the rifle and then those sleeping near the fire. Scream out Pepe's name with every slash of the knife, with every drop of blood.

The camp guard's movement was haphazard as Silas watched. He never took the same path on each round of the sleeping men, never ventured too far out from the fire. Silas moved in as close as he dared, staying in the shadows, behind trees and rocks, and expected the guard to come close enough for him to attack on his next turn around the fire.

Juanito Morales was nineteen and loved working on the Snake and Dog-man ranch. Training horses was what he loved most, and working with Francisco Alvarado was more than exciting. Alvarado had been trained by Spanish Vaqueros straight out of Spain, had the reputation that young Juanito was hoping might be his one day. Tonight was not pleasant, walking around the fire hoping that what Snake feared never came his way.

Morales had never killed a man, had only been in a few fights growing up and wondered if he would even be able to kill. He was raised by devout Catholic parents but wasn't that religious himself. But, to kill another human? Could he? More to the point, would he?

The path he was following would take him within five feet of where Silas Lippincott was hiding, waiting for an opportunity to drive his razor-sharp knife deep into the boy's back.

All at once there was a loud commotion at the other fire, men running around in their underwear, shouting curses, and then a loud, ugly scream.

Silas didn't move, Juanito Morales started to run

toward the ruckus but changed his mind and moved toward the fire, letting his eyes roam all around the no-longer-sleeping cow hands. *My job is to protect these men even though they have awakened.* He spotted Silas moving away, deeper into the night, fading out of sight among trees and brush.

"There," Juanito cried. "A man running," and he moved quickly around the fire and into the shadows. He couldn't see anything, had his rifle at the ready with every step, but turned back to the fire in moments, unable to see anything. "I couldn't see," he said to no one in particular.

The camp was in chaos with everyone now up and armed, moving about trying to find out what had taken place. Who let out that horrible scream? Is someone hurt? What's going on?

Snake had been out with the herd, but Dog-man had been one of the camp guards and saw Wally Lippincott slowly make his way toward one of the sleeping crew members. He attacked at once, slamming his rifle butt into Lippincott's head, driving the man to the ground, but Wally wasn't out of the fight. He scrambled to his feet, had his knife in hand and leaped toward Dog-man.

Lippincott was too slow. but it wasn't Dog-man who drove a knife deep into the outlaw's back, it was Lion Killer herself. She knew the knife went deep and heard the blood-curdling scream from the man. She pulled back on the knife, ready for a second thrust, which never came. Wally Lippincott took his last breath as he fell to the ground, driving his face into scattered rocks, not feeling anything.

Louise stood silently as the men dragged the body to the fire. Pedro ran out from under the chuck and threw his arms around her legs, holding her tight. She reached down and rustled her hand through his long black hair, and softly sobbed at the death of the man. She had killed before and, just as before, she suffered from the pain of knowing she had killed. "It's all right, Pedro. We're safe now," she murmured.

"That's the old man," George Dawson said. "That's Wally Lippincott."

"And that means his son Silas is still out and around here. Maybe close. Let's get back to paying attention," Dog-man said. Some men were still trying to get their pants and boots on, others moving in small groups through the trees. Juanito showed where he spotted the man running away, but it was too dark to try and find footprints in the grass and rocks.

Louise and Jeannie put pots of coffee on the fires and Dog-man sent someone out to fetch Snake who rode into camp within minutes. "Juanito saw a man run out at about the same time

Wally died," Dog-man said. "Did you see anything out there?"

"Not a thing. Didn't see or hear anyone passing through the herd. That would have got the animals moving about some, too. That boy's loss is gonna be our problem, I'm afraid." Snake stepped down from his horse, accepted a cup of hot coffee from Pedro, and squeezed Louise tight. "You done good, girl. You done good." He looked up through the trees at the stars, then off to the east, where the night sky seemed just a bit lighter at the horizon.

His eyes flicked down and drove deep into Louise's. "You did the right thing, the only thing you could do. You killed the man who was trying to kill Dog-man. You kept the rest of us safe. It ain't easy, but you got to take it for being the right thing to do. Look at that boy of ours and know you did the right thing."

She burst into tears, wrapped her arms tight around Snake, buried her head in his chest and felt his big hand reach down and pat her on the bottom. That was his way of showing his love, and then she felt Pedro wrap his arms around her legs and just let the tears flow. It seemed like minutes before Snake eased her back some.

"Ain't much sense in trying to get back to sleep. Let's get day number two off to an early start, eh?" Snake smiled at Louise, nodded to Dog-man, and waved George Dawson over. "Any reason you can think of to not get started some early, George?"

Dog-man squatted down at the fire, a cup of coffee in hand and watched Snake and Louise. *That's one hell of a woman that man has. Strange, but I can't imagine what that must be like, to have those kinds of feelings for another person. So personal, so close. Me and Snake been partners for a long time but that's a different kind of close, not man-to-woman close. I've watched him with the woman and her kids near Tucson and then that other woman. Maybe someday I'll stumble into one of my own.*

Dog-man sat by the fire through another cup of coffee, saw Nighthawks come in and new ones ride out, saw camp guards check their weapons several times, and tried to get his mind back on driving cattle not thinking about a woman who may or may not exist.

"Cattle, that's my business," he said right out loud, causing one of the hands standing nearby to give him a curious look before wandering off.

23

THE SCENE WASN'T QUITE AS LIVELY as the previous morning, but breakfast was cooked and eaten, horses and mules were harnessed and hitched, saddles were cranked down, and there were a few cuss words heard from time to time.

"You cutting trail again?" Dog-man asked and Snake gave him a big grin, riding off with Alvarado and Jeremiah Hillyer. He saw Louise move the chuck in behind them and smiled watching the rest of the cattle crew move toward the herd. It wasn't long before the cries of cowboys, charros, and teamsters echoed through the mountain air and the cattle were moving through the still very early dawn. It wasn't long and great clouds of dust were rising along with the morning's mist.

"Ain't never gonna forget this sight," Dog-man muttered. "Me and old Snake have moved several herds in the last few years but this time, those animals are ours." He sat in the saddle for some time watching the herd move slowly out of the large depression and across the side of the hill toward what was called Buzzard Peak, about ten miles to the northwest, site of their next camp.

What a world we live in, Dog-man thought. *Our cattle moving through rolling hills covered in the richest grass I've ever seen and not that many miles north, men are still digging fortunes out of solid rock.* He sat silently watching the great herd move out, not even trying to hold back the smile plastered across his face.

Would they be under attack from Silas Lippincott? Would the herd? Were there other fool outlaws out there waiting for them? Dog-man smiled. *Let 'em come. they ain't big enough or strong enough to take us out.*

Silas Lippincott was sitting next to a small fire on the side of the hill watching the excitement going on below. It became more and more obvious that the scream he heard was the death scream of his father. He was alone in the world now. Angry, hurt, and very alone. Silas had never been alone, had always been with his father and brother. The knowledge and fear of what that meant slowly crept through his slow mind.

Silas sat down in the dirt, cradled his head in his rough hands, and the realization hit him straight in the gut. All he had in the world was what was in that camp at that moment. A coffee pot and frying pan, a bedroll, the horses and tack, and his guns and knives. "I ain't even got a dollar," he cried out. "Pa always had the money. Wally kept it in his saddlebags." He jumped to his feet and raced to the horse and found the saddlebags tied to his father's horse.

Still dejected, still angry, Silas brought the saddlebags back to the fire. He poured a cup of coffee and started rummaging through the leather bags. A bottle of wretched, foul whiskey, some shirts, and a leather wallet stuffed with greenbacks.

"I won't starve," Silas said and poured some of the whiskey into his tin cup. "And some of those men out there are gonna die before this day is over."

Reality was slow coming to Silas. First it was knowing he was alone and would be for a long time. Second, not only was he alone, but the only things he had to keep him alive was that wad of greenbacks in his wallet. "Pa knew who to rob, who had to be kilt, even when to do it. Pepe and I did what we were told to do. I ain't got a clue how to plan a robbery."

It was a strange discovery for the boy to understand that he didn't know the first thing about how it was all that money was in that wallet. His murmuring to himself continued for several more minutes. He discovered that Pa knew who had money when they came through the watering holes out there in that terrible desert and he, Silas, didn't. "Even Pepe knew," he muttered, pouring more whiskey into his tin cup.

Moving a thousand head of cattle across rough and open hill country is a long slow process. Distance isn't measured in miles per hour but in miles per day. Snake was hoping they could make ten that day but would settle for eight. Even with all the drama they had moved a solid eight miles the previous day.

The country they were moving through was lush with hardwoods, conifers of many kinds, some pines, lots of brush, and good grass. "Hard not to have fat cattle in this country," he said to Francisco Alvarado who had ridden up to spend some time with the boss. "These rolling hills we're in roll right down to the Pacific Ocean.

157

Every breath of breeze coming up brings some moisture with it."

"I've always found it fascinating that just over the highest ridge behind us is the great Mojave Desert," Francisco said. "All along the coast, first coastal mountains, then broad, rich valleys, and the next step east, high mountains, and finally desert. Where we are right now is as close to heaven as a man can get without dying first."

Snake laughed but also nodded his head in full agreement. "Glad I've got to see it without dying. Have you got more than one person riding drag? That Lippincott boy is sure to be coming at us at some point."

"Jeremiah Hillyer is sure I've got it in for him." Alvarado laughed. "But he's the most likely to see an attack coming. He rode drag yesterday, too. I've got young Morales back there with him."

"Keep a close check on 'em. At our mid-day stop would be the best time to hit us. He's alone as far as I know, but one man out of his mind with rage at losing his father and his brother could do a lot of damage, kill a lot of people and animals."

"I can't imagine what's going through his mind," Francisco said. "How's that horse treating you?"

Snake smiled. He was riding one of the finest animals he'd ever had the pleasure to work with. "Most of my life I've heard stories of these prized Spanish Andalusians, Francisco, and I can tell you right now, there ain't a man alive gonna take this stud away from me. When he gets to feeling his oats and gets to prancing, by god, I sit as tall as a man can."

Alvarado laughed watching Snake get the big stud to prancing and turned his horse back east. "I'll check on

Hillyer and Juanito. Find us some shade for mid-day," he called out, still laughing.

Alvarado moved slowly back through the long line of bawling steers, stopped often to talk with men working the drive. It took him about a half hour to make it to the end of the long line. Jeremiah Hillyer was riding back and forth keeping the herd moving while Juanito Morales was doing the same thing on his side of the end of the herd. Both men were already covered in trail dust and Francisco waved to get their attention.

"What's up, boss?" Hillyer called out riding up alongside. Morales rode up on the other side.

"You're both doing a good job keeping the herd nice and tight, moving along good, but I want to remind you we have an angry man who is probably trailing us, looking to get revenge for the death of his father and brother."

"We've been talking about that," Juanito said. He looked at Jeremiah who nodded.

"Hard to see much with all the dust these critters kick up," Hillyer said. "We're taking turns dropping back and to the side, out of the dust, to see if we can spot anything. So far we ain't seen nothing."

"That's a good idea but I'm gonna send another man back here. If you hang back, make sure there are two of you doing it. You'd be an easy target for a man with a rifle and I'm not sure your partner would hear the shot. Don't do it again until that third man joins you."

The two agreed and Alvarado rode off to find Wayne Nichols to join them. "Those two are leaders in my book. Get them off drag after mid-day."

24

IT WAS easy staying with the herd as it moved at a walk through the valley with the hills on either side, moving slowly toward buzzard hill. Silas Lippincott walked his horse along the sides of the hills, riding through trees and brush, through rock formations, always within sight of the herd. He saw how the men riding drag would drop back to see if he was following and was making plans to take them out, one at a time. That way he would work his way up toward the front of the herd and kill Dogman and Snake.

He was a young man, maybe older boy would fit better, and uneducated. In his mind, racked by the horrible sight of seeing his brother killed and knowing his father was dead as well, all of these men associated with the cattle drive were responsible. The fact his brother was involved in an attempted theft of cattle or that his father was involved in an attempted murder didn't play into his sense of reality.

Silas slowly angled his way down toward the valley floor using the natural terrain to hide his movement. He could see where the valley turned more north and narrowed a bit, which would slow the herd. *That would be a good place to intercept and kill at least one, best if both drag riders.* For the first time in two days, Silas had the slightest smile on his face.

The trees on the hillside were just thick enough that Silas was well hidden but also thick enough to hinder his movements. He remembered his father always saying something funny about that. *You can't ride through 'em and you can't ride over 'em. You gotta ride around 'em and that always slows you down.* He almost nodded as if he heard his father.

He had to quicken his pace if he was going to intercept those riders just before the turn. The herd had slowed as he predicted but he was still too far away to make a clean kill. *That big outcrop is where I need to be. They ain't got nowhere to hide and I can pick 'em off one at a time.*

He nudged his horse just a bit faster, having to work around deadfall, rocks, and standing groves of trees, always making for the outcrop on the one hand, and keeping an eye on the two drag riders. He slipped behind the outcrop, grabbed his rifle, and stepped down from the horse. He moved through broken limbs, around mounds of rock, and settled in behind a saw-tooth ridge.

"Oh, yes," Silas muttered, seeing Juanito Morales just a hundred yards or so from him, casting looks all about, searching for someone possibly trailing the herd. Silas spotted Jeremiah Hillyer closer to the herd, working the cattle, not keeping an eye on Morales. Silas eased down behind the spiny ridge, brought the rifle up, and slowly took a long aim.

He was just beginning to squeeze the trigger when Morales all at once spurred his horse into a run back toward Hillyer. "What the...?" Silas stormed, almost jumping to his feet. He saw a third rider coming toward Morales hard, waving and yelling. The sound didn't carry that far, overwhelmed by the noise the herd made. "No," Silas moaned, watching the two move back to the herd being joined by Hillyer. He saw the new man point up at the ridge Silas was hiding behind, and some kind of discussion kept the three busy. "Oh, no," he said, racing back toward his horse, jumping into the saddle and riding off quickly.

MORALES RODE toward the man waving at him. "There's a man in the rocks up there," Wayne Nichols yelled out, pointing up the hillside behind Morales. Jeremiah Hillyer rode to join the two.

"What is it, Wayne? What did you see?"

"A man with a rifle in the rocks right up there," Nichols said, pointing.

"Let's go," Hillyer said, spinning his horse, and the three moved out at a fast run toward the rocky ridge. "He's running," Hillyer yelled, seeing Lippincott run for his horse.

The hundred yards Silas was thinking about for his shot at Morales, was down the steep hillside, and the boys now chasing, had to climb up through rocks, trees, and downfall to get to the slight, rock-strewn ridge line.

Silas was riding full out, letting his horse pick the trail. He jumped some of the deadfall, made desperate turns around rocks and debris, and managed to get onto a game trail that led back down onto the herd trail. Silas's horse wasn't in that good of condition, was tiring fast, and before moving out of the trees and onto the

good with his men, had respect for the land, and was untiring in his work. "That man has only death on his mind," the ranch foreman said.

Snake looked at Dog-man and George Dawson, then back to Alvarado. "I ain't one to sit around and wait for someone to attack," he said. "Worse, though, I ain't got no kind of plan to go get that boy." He looked around asking without asking if any of them had a plan.

"We been in a fix like this before, Snake." Dog-man swished a biscuit through some stew gravy and took a big bite before continuing. "I'm gonna ride out and follow his track back to where Hillyer lost Lippincott's trail and see if I can pick it up and follow it back. He'll be so interested in you boys he won't think somebody's on his ass."

"Want company?" Snake asked.

"No, you need to be with the herd." Dog-man finished his stew and saddled his horse. Louise stood with Snake and watched him ride off into the trees, trying to stay hidden until he was away from camp.

"Somebody should go with him," Alvarado said.

"No," Snake said. "Dog-man ain't as good at trailin' a man as I am, but he's better than anyone else in the world." He laughed and finished his coffee. "If we hear gunfire, we gotta make a fast run toward it. Let's get these critters re-started."

———

LIPPINCOTT WAS DOWN on the valley floor and moving toward a spot where he thought he could sneak up on the midday cow camp when he saw four riders start moving the herd. He was on his belly almost under a stump of brush when the cattle began moving, and he had to hurry, almost swimming in the grass and dirt to a large stand of rocks.

"I gotta get up that hill. Back into those trees," he said. He was almost breathless, choking on the dust being thrown up by cattle so close he could feel their warmth. Cowboys, charros, and teamsters were yelling out, getting the herd moving and Lippincott, more scared than he'd ever been, made a dash for a stand of trees, hoping that, one, he wouldn't be stomped to death by a thousand-pound steer, or, two, shot to death by an angry cow hand.

No one saw him and he pulled up into the trees, still hundreds of yards from his horse and gear. He'd have to climb that hillside almost in plain sight of the men working the herd. He looked up the hill, tried to plot how to make it from one point to the next place to hide, and moved quickly, just a few steps at a time.

The men working the herd and driving the wagons were far more interested in their jobs than watching for a lone man running up the side of the hill to a stand of rocks and trees. Silas was panting hard when he reached his horse. He almost emptied his canteen before getting in the saddle.

"I'll get them tonight," he muttered, riding a little higher on the hillside, staying as deep in the forest as he could while following along with the herd. Was the death of his father the driving force in his quest to see everyone associated with the cattle drive dead? Or was it the death of his half brother, Pepe? He and his father didn't have that close of a relationship but he and Pepe did.

Wally Lippincott was one of those men who always let you know that he knew far more about any subject that might come up than you. He saw to it that young

Silas was aware that his father was always the boss, was always right, and to never disagree with the man. Wally was not afraid of using switches, latigo leather, or a fist to keep the boys in line.

If I have to, I'm going to spend the rest of my life seeing to it that the men who killed you, Pepe, die a hard and terrible death. He let that thought build in his mind as he slowly followed the herd from his own trail high up the hillside.

IT DIDN'T TAKE Dog-man long to find where Silas had hidden from Hillyer and company, and was able to find where he made the move to return and continue following the herd. He was going slow, making sure that he didn't lose Silas's trail and keeping as quiet as possible. Silas was not a caring man when it came to his horse and Dog-man found he had to go around problems that Silas simply ran through or over.

"He'll have an injured horse before the day is over if he keeps this up," he muttered. The hills that Dog-man and Silas were riding through probably hadn't been ridden through, ever. This wasn't Indian hunting country, it wasn't mining country, and certainly wasn't good grazing country. With every storm that moved across the range, trees were felled, with every winter freeze and thaw, rocks were broken apart, some rolling downhill.

There were few game trails or natural trails to follow and Dog-man found he was following someone who wasn't very good at picking a way through wild forest land. Silas was far more interested in keeping the herd in sight. *He's riding too fast for this country, just not good for that horse.*

Dog-man heard loud voices echoing through the

trees and knew that Snake was getting the herd back on the trail. *Been no gunfire so Lippincott didn't attack during mid-day. He's somewhere in front of me and relatively close if we're that close to the herd.*

Dog-man knew the sounds of the herd would cover any sound he made but also any sound Silas might make, and slowed his pace just a bit. He'd see where the trail went then keep close watch in front of him as he followed instead of just concentrating on the trail. *I'm close enough I could just stumble right up on him.*

He was riding around a tangled deadfall that Silas had simply ridden through when he heard the sound of a horse neighing not too far in front. He stopped, leaned far forward and held his hand over his horse's nose, and listened. A thousand or so beeves down in the valley made it difficult but Dog-man thought he detected movement fifty yards or so in front of where he stood.

"Easy, boy," he muttered, nudging the horse forward. Dog-man reached down and pulled his rifle out of its leather and laid it across the saddle. *There he is.* Dog-man urged the horse on but Silas saw him and sunk the spurs in his horse's ribs.

Silas Lippincott leaned out over the horse's neck, kicking hard, running at a full gallop through tangled downfall, rock outcrops, dodging trees, ducking limbs there to rip his head off, and even made a grab for his sidearm. The horse tried to jump a deadfall, didn't make it, got his front feet tangled in the mess, and went down hard.

Silas was thrown free and rolled up against a dead tree, bleeding from scratches and gashes. His head hurt but he had sense enough to crawl deep into the under-brush. He kept crawling, got moving down the hillside, got to his feet, and scrambled as fast as he could down toward the valley floor. The herd was moving along at a calm walk and Silas spotted a charro working his way toward him.

Antonio Sobrante Rodriquez was twenty years old, they still called him Tonito, making his first cattle drive. He'd been working with Alvarado breeding horses but had never worked cattle. He was watching them, never saw the man, on foot, run up to him and jerk him from the saddle. Never saw the knife flash in the afternoon light, and fell to the ground, dead.

Silas Lippincott jumped in the saddle and made again for the hillside and the safety of rocks, timber, and brush. The herd continued its slow, plodding course down the long valley.

Dog-man rode up to the outlaw's downed horse, writhing and screaming its pain to the world. "Oh, no," he muttered. He could see the front leg flopping as the horse struggled to get up. "Oh, damn."

He couldn't just ride on, couldn't keep up his search for Lippincott. Not with a horse screaming in pain from a fractured leg. He pulled up and dismounted, tying off on a limb. He walked close to the horse, pulled his revolver and shot the horse in the head. The only sound now was that of the herd down the mountainside. "Bastard just ran off and left him. Bastard." Dog-man spat it out.

He left his horse tied and moved in a great circle until finding Silas's boot tracks leading off down the hillside and followed along, slowly. It wasn't but moments he found horse tracks leading up the hill. "What have we got here?" he murmured and almost knew the answer. "One of our men is dead and Silas has his horse."

26

DOG-MAN WAS BACK in the saddle, found the prints again, and began his chase. Down in the valley, Jeremiah Hillyer was riding on the south flank of the herd when he spotted young Tonito's body crumpled in the grass, his neck a ghastly wound from a not-so-sharp knife.

Hillyer spotted another drover and called him over. "Get the word to Snake and Alvarado," he said, and Wayne Nichols raced for the head of the herd. Hillyer moved the body a little up out of the valley floor and began the hard job of digging a grave, all the time watching for someone who might attack.

Snake and Alvarado rode up to help. "Must have needed a horse," Snake muttered. "What would cause him to need a horse?" He was moving rocks and ripping out brush for the grave, and having a good conversation with himself. "Dog-man is following him, he loses his horse, has time to come down to the meadow, kill Tonito and steal his horse?"

Francisco Alvarado couldn't help chuckling listening to the conversation play out. "It don't seem right," Snake said. He looked at the two, Alvarado and Hillyer. "Dog-man is still up there, nobody's heard any gunfire, and Lippincott loses his horse. You boys keep on with that work. If Dog-man's in trouble I gotta be there."

The cattle bawling their frustration at having to give up munching the grass had hidden Dog-man's shot, killing the foundered Lippincott horse. Snake jumped in the saddle and started up the hillside, following the tracks plainly left by Silas. It was just minutes that he found Dog-man's boot prints, and then just another few minutes that he found Dog-man's horse's prints. "Most interesting." He stepped down from the saddle and looked at the prints carefully.

They told a good story. Silas was running his horse, that was obvious, and Dog-man was following at a walk. He knew his partner was not injured, knew he was on Silas's trail, and knew that with he and Dog-man out and Rodriguez dead, they were three men short on the drive. It was a hard decision to make and Snake fought it for several minutes before turning back and down the hill.

"We need to have the herd moving along and that means everyone working it," he muttered, doing his best to justify his change. "Dog-man is all right and he'll stay on Lippincott's trail until he finds the fool and kills him." He rode down to where Alvarado and Hillyer were finishing covering Tonito's grave.

"Dog-man's following him. Don't know what happened. Let's keep this herd moving, boys. Lots of daylight left and buzzard's peak ain't that far away now." It was the right thing to do and Snake knew it, but after riding with the man for several years, it seemed wrong to not go to his aid.

Maybe there wasn't aid needed, Snake thought. Maybe that partner didn't need any help. *That would be just fine.* But he couldn't shake the worries and for the next several hours he spent as much time looking up the steep hillside as he did driving the cattle toward buzzard's peak.

———

DOG-MAN FOUND that Silas was riding just as recklessly on his new horse as he did killing his other one. Following the trail Silas made was the easy part. Broken limbs, kicked-up rocks, obvious signs of a horse jumping a downfall, made following Silas the easy part. There hadn't been anybody roaming these hills for a long time so horse prints stood out like painted signs.

That boy has to know I'm on his trail. He might just pull up and try an ambush. That is if he's smart enough to think of it. Dog-man had to chuckle at his thought. He had thoughts that the boy would soon be walking again if he kept up the fast pace he was setting. *I'm gonna come up on another injured horse and that's gonna get me more riled than I've been in a long time. He's already killed one.*

Dog-man was busy reading the trail left by Silas, moving around some downfall, riding through others. Riding around large rocks, finding where, at a fast pace, Silas had jumped some downed trees and rocks. *It's a shame I'm chasing a killer right now. This is beautiful country with all the hardwood and other trees. Very little grass up this high so probably not much summer grazing, though. Not much game, either.*

Silas also didn't have time to see what he was riding through. Great stands of oak and other hardwood, patches of wild berries, stands of pine, spruce, and fir. The hillside was alive with small creatures and birds, but he hadn't seen a deer or any other large animal. Silas didn't see anything but visions of dead men, particularly Dog-man and Snake.

His was a limited life, running from the law with his father and half brother, having virtually no education, and never a mother's love. His rage at his half brother's death would be from Pepe being Silas's closest friend, relative, being. Wally, despite carrying the name father, was someone who constantly told the boys what to do, when to do it, but never showed the least amount of love.

Is the rage just an excuse to go on a killing rampage? Is this terrible rage something he thinks would be expected of him? The only thing Silas knew as he moved too fast through the forest was that he had to avenge his brother's death.

Dog-man was able to look down on the great herd moving through the valley floor from time to time and could see buzzard hill and the pass just below it. *That ain't three miles away. I wonder if, somehow that fool boy knows that's where we'll camp for the night?* He found where Silas had moved through some damp ground near a spring and stepped down from his horse, dug out a hole and watched it fill. It just took minutes and he was able to give his horse a cool drink.

"Silas didn't even do this simple little thing for his horse. I've never taken killing a man with favor, but he's gonna be a first." The marks in the mud hadn't firmed up much and Dog-man thought the boy might not be too far in front of him. "Better be on my best behavior," he chuckled. "Might be around the next deadfall or outcrop."

SILAS LIPPINCOTT WAS MORE than surprised when he first found Dog-man hot on his trail. Losing his horse, killing the Mexican and getting another was just luck, and now, he was sure he was again being followed, and closely. Had he heard something? Did he see shadowy figures behind every tree? Silas's blood ran cold thinking about someone sneaking up behind him and shooting him in the back.

"I gotta kill that man, and soon. He's gonna catch up when I'm not ready." He started looking for someplace he could hide and wait for whoever was following. Fallen trees littered the ground, rocky outcrops were scattered about, but Silas didn't see them as places from which to ambush the man following him. "Need to be behind some rocks. How would Pepe do this?"

He would have come up with an answer much faster if he had wondered how Wally Lippincott might have done it. The father and brothers had run from posses and others many times, had had to ambush more than one sheriff and his deputies, but Silas was far closer to Pepe than his father. Pepe's death was what needed revenge, not Wally's. It didn't occur to Silas that both he and his brother were followers, not leaders.

As a father, Wally should have been a leader but was a failure at that just as he was in life. He never taught the boys. He simply told them what to do. They did what they were told to do or else, and the or else hurt like hell. Thus Silas had found himself on the side of a mountain, on a stolen horse, being chased by a man who had learned well, the lessons of life.

There was not a trail to follow and the only thing on Silas's slow mind was to keep the herd in sight, to kill whoever was following, and then to kill those driving the herd. Working his way through rough, primeval forest was more than difficult at best and not being able to move fast angered the youngster and he took it out on the horse.

He came to a broad, almost level area that led to a draw he could have followed down to the valley floor. Instead, he worked his way across and into a granite rockfall, stepped down from the horse, rifle in hand, and moved the horse into a nearby copse of cedar. He quickly ran back into the rocks and took up a position where he could see his back trail plainly. "He'll learn not to follow Silas Lippincott," he muttered, making sure his rifle was fully loaded, cocked, and ready for action.

Dog-man was less than seven minutes behind Silas and was working his way through heavy timber when he spotted a horse tied off in some trees. "That's a fine Mexican saddle on that pony," he muttered, stepping down from his horse. Many of the men working the Snake and Dog-man ranch had the Mexican style saddles and Dog-man knew for sure seeing this one that it meant one of his hands had been killed.

He had his rifle in hand, tied his horse off, and visually tried to find Silas's trail through the underbrush. "Looks like he rode right up to that pile of rocks." He could easily visualize the young man checking out the rocks, then moving his horse off into the trees.

He knows he's being followed so why didn't he hide the horse deep in the trees? Dog-man chuckled to himself. *Because he ain't smart enough to know that.* He moved through the stand of trees and was able to get a good look at the rock fall. *He's got himself a good bunch of places to hide in.*

The rocks had tumbled from a ledge onto the flat area, maybe as much as a thousand years ago, but not on down the draw and Dog-man could see that it would be possible to work around the rocks from the south side but not the north. *That boy is gonna be watching his back trail and hopefully not giving a hoot about anything else.* Dog-man began a wide circle around to the south and it took almost half an hour to get on the other side of the rocks.

There you are, watching so intently. Dog-man was looking down on Silas, no more than fifty yards off and started to move toward him, hoping to take him alive. On his second step a rattlesnake whirred its warning and Dog-man jumped back, kicking rocks, kicking at the snake.

Silas heard the rocks rattling, spun and fired his rifle from the hip. He was in a panic and just started running for his horse. He was mounted and racing through the trees and deadfalls at a terrible rate not giving a damn about anything but getting away from the man with a rifle. It was several minutes before he slowed the horse to a walk.

Dog-man felt the bullet tear through his leg, fell to the rocks and saw the snake coiled, ready to strike. He couldn't bring the rifle into play and went for his revolver. The first shot sprayed rocks at the snake and the second shot took its head off. The pain in his leg was severe, blood was flowing, and Dog-man knew he was in trouble. He ripped his pants open with his knife, tore his wild rag free and stuffed it in the wound, stopping the bleeding.

Damn horse is almost half a mile back. He pulled his shirt free and ripped a long strip from it and tied the kerchief tight. "Better not be any more snakes," he murmured, trying to get to his feet. He used the rifle for support and was standing, almost straight, in moments.

"This is gonna hurt," he said right out taking the first step down from the rocks.

He fought his way through the rocks trying to make a quick picture of his situation. *I've got water, have some smoked venison, and a few biscuits that Louise stuffed in my saddlebags. Get to the horse and patch up the wound proper and then ride down that draw. I'll make it.*

27

"HEAR THAT?" Snake turned in the saddle in time to hear two more shots, getting a good idea from where they came. "Dog's in trouble," he said, spurring his horse toward a wide draw coming down the hillside. "I knew I should have followed."

Snake motioned for Juanito, just a few yards off to follow and rode toward the draw. High up on the hill and to the west, he caught the flash of a running horse. It was just a flash but Snake instinctively knew someone was running away and it surely wasn't his partner.

"Dog-man's in trouble, Juanito. Go back and find Alvarado and tell him to keep the herd moving toward Buzzard Peak. Lippincott might be closer than we thought. Got all that?"

The young Mexican charro nodded his yes, spun his horse and rode off at a gallop. Snake smiled and put his big Andalusian stud into a strong hill-climbing walk making his way up the draw. Rocks that have tumbled over eons, downfallen trees, storm-damaged terrain made the trip slow and dangerous. The stud was good at picking his trail and Snake made good, if somewhat slow, progress up the hillside.

It was three distinct shots I heard and from two guns, a pistol and a rifle. Who was firing which? I'll find you, Dog. Just hang on, partner, I'm coming. It was a busy ride up that draw, even if the horse was good at picking trail. Rocks that slipped out from under the hooves, broken timber as overhangs that would smash a head, and no sounds of someone who might be hurt. Snake was listening for the cries of a hurt man. He wanted to hear those cries. Their absence made his blood run cold.

The draw topped out and Snake saw the large rock-fall and knew that was where the gunfire came from. It was a perfect location for a gunman to hide. It took less than five minutes to find the shot-up rattlesnake, which led him to Dog-man's bloody trail. Snake turned east to follow. He found his partner sitting on a log trying to tie a decent bandage on his wounded leg.

"Let yourself get shot, did you? Well, let's see if I can help some. I think I saw Silas running along this hill just after I heard the shots. You hit him?"

"About time you got here. Could have died, you know. No, I shot a rattlesnake. Silas shot me. Damn, that stings some." Snake brushed Dog-man's hands away and poured more whiskey into the wound, getting a good loud yell from the man, along with a fist to the ribs.

"Don't be messing around," Snake said. "I'm trying to help."

"A man could die with your kind of help."

"Be still now," Snake said. He ripped some more shirt from Dog-man's back and wadded it up, placed it on the wound and tied it off. "Let's get you back to the chuck wagon, old man. Jeannie Nichols can dig that bullet out.

Alvarado will have the herd at Buzzard Pass by the time we get there."

Dog-man, using his rifle and Snake for help made the walk to his horse, got on, and the two rode back down the draw and into the meadow. Snake kept a close watch on his partner. Dog-man lost a lot of blood, wasn't sitting that secure in the saddle, and Snake had to keep them at a walk. He wanted to go faster but was sure Dog-man would fall if they did.

Snake had always been the partner who found someone in trouble, was always the first to offer help, was often hurt himself when people didn't respond as he expected. To lose his longtime partner was more than he was willing to even think about. Dog-man had patched him up numerous times, had found Snake in deep trouble more than once, but Snake had not had the same experience.

Ain't never gonna not follow when I know I should. "Can't let you out of my sight, can I?" He growled at Dog-man. "Let you go off chasing a killer and you almost got yourself kilt. Shoulda been with you." If Dog-man heard any of that, he didn't respond at all.

Following the herd was easy enough and getting through slowly moving cattle to the chuck took more time than Snake realized. Camp was being made up as the two rode to the chuck wagon and a scene of activity.

Buzzard Pass was spread out across a break in the mountains with Buzzard Peak standing watch. Hundreds of the birds flocked to the high mountain every year, which gave the area its name. Snake looked across the grassy meadow, across the pass and into the forest on the south side. *He's up there waiting for us to make camp. You've shot your last man, Lippincott. You ain't getting no more.*

"Got a hurt one for you, ladies," Snake said. He eased a slumping Dog-man from the saddle and laid him out near a fire already lit. "He let a bullet hit his leg. He mentioned something about a rattlesnake, too, so you might want to look for a bite. He ain't been talking for half an hour."

Louise gasped seeing Dog-man's bloody leg and got a pot of water on the fire and motioned for Jeannie Nichols to bring out the doctoring kit. "Go on about your chores, Snake. We'll take good care of him. Was it the Lippincott kid?"

Snake nodded, stepped back on his horse and rode out to find Alvarado. Louise watched him until he was lost in the dust. *So casual,* she thought. *His partner's been shot and you'd think something like that happens every day.* She caught herself, smiled at what she was thinking and got to work cleaning up the wound. She was quick to remember that, yes, for the last few days they had been shot at on every one of them. *I have married into a wonderful partnership.*

Jeannie Nichols had a trade knife out and poured whiskey on the keen blade, motioned for Louise to sit on the other side from her. "I slice down, slow, be ready to pick bullet. Wash fingers in whiskey."

Louise did as she was told and watched Jeannie carefully slice open the wound, spreading the skin open and as she got deeper, Louise saw the bullet. She had skinned hundreds of wolves, coyotes, and lions in her short life, so the blood and open wound didn't bother her as she reached her thumb and a finger deep into the wound, felt the bullet, and found she had to exert considerable strength to get it loose and out.

Blood followed the lead and Jeannie quickly poured some whiskey into the wound and pressed a clean cloth over it. She held it firmly in place while Louise worked to get the patch tied up. "He be good boy now," Jeannie said in her way. The lovely Paiute lady's English was improving every day and she and Louise spent hours together talking about their lives and loves.

"You've done this before," Louise said. It wasn't a question.

"Yes," she said quietly, with her eyes cast downward and almost shut. It was just moments and Louise realized she may have accidentally struck a raw nerve, some bad memories. Was her family involved in big fights with other tribes? Or white men?

The two women laid out Dog-man's bedroll near the fire and got him in it, had Pedro get stacks of firewood ready for the long night, and began putting together the meal. Those drovers would be riding in at any minute and they would want coffee and be able to smell the night's supper cooking. Louise chuckled, thinking, *Doctoring took some time but supper had best not be late because of it.*

Snake saw George Dawson coming, saw the scowl on his face, and knew something was wrong. "How much longer are we going to base our operation on a dumb-ass killer?" Dawson started the conversation. "I've contracted to get these wagons to San Berdoo and you contracted to give me safe passage. Why are we letting this fool kid determine when and where we go?"

"Take it easy, Dawson. We haven't made a single change in our operation. This is a scheduled stop. In case you haven't heard, Dog-man was shot trying to stop that fool. We'll be doing tonight what we did last night."

"This drive was scheduled for five days and we haven't made ten miles. We ain't gonna make my deadline, Snake. I'm sorry for Dog-man. Is he going to be all right?"

"He'll be fine, George. Actually," Snake said, "we made eight miles yesterday and I'm estimating a solid nine for today. It's the water, not the mileage that determines where we stop. You know that as well as I."

"I'm just being gnarly, Snake. Those are my wagons and teams, that is my business, and I'm not making any decisions. I don't like it." His tone changed, he tried to get a smile across his big face, and Snake chuckled.

"If it's decisions you want to make, I'll turn the herd over to you, George. You take us to the sale yards in San Bernardino."

"Go to hell, Snake," Dawson laughed and started to walk away. "Where's Dog-man? Maybe I can talk some sense with him."

Snake laughed and pointed toward the nearest of the campfires. "Right over there, George. Be nice, he hurts something awful."

SILAS LIPPINCOTT'S new horse was limping on a sore leg as he rode up behind a large cedar tree to overlook Buzzard Pass and the grazing herd below. A breeze was blowing up the pass but would switch directions when the sun went down, which would allow him to work his way into their camp without disturbing the cattle.

It was the lame horse that bothered him. "Won't be able to depend on him for a clean getaway. That cowboy should have picked a better horse." That was the Lippincott way. Blame the horse for coming up lame, not the rider who drove the animal recklessly. Silas drank some water and ate the rest of the dried meat. Even if he'd been able to have a fire he didn't have coffee or even a pot anymore.

He wasn't able to understand the concept of irony or he might have chuckled knowing he had a wallet filled with cash in his saddlebags but no where to spend it. As the sun slowly made its way into the mountains to the west he began the long walk down from the ridge. "I'll have plenty to eat after I kill those men."

He felt a shudder flow down his back, as a cold wind might bring, and believed it was a call from his brother. "I'm coming for them, Pepe. Know it in your heart, you will be avenged." The words were angry, spat out, not muttered as he worked his way through the trees and into the meadow below. This was the second time he'd had what he believed to be a conversation with the dead Pepe.

It wasn't strange to Silas that he hadn't had this type of conversation with his dead father. Wally Lippincott wasn't in the current picture, but as Silas worked his way down that mountain he could feel Pepe right alongside, urging him on, telling him he was doing the right thing.

He tried to skirt around the cattle, keeping as vigilant an eye as possible out for the Nighthawks. The cattle didn't like something on two legs walking near them and tended to get loud, some tried to move away, and others got a little testy about it. Moving out and away from the herd meant that Silas Lippincott had a long walk in front of him.

There were ragged clouds moving slowly through the night sky, the chill of early evening kept Silas moving at a warming pace. The shadows created seemed to move as some of them came from the herd, some from the forest, and some conjured by a sick mind. Revenge was a driving force but it was slowly being replaced by hunger.

The breeze was such that the aroma of stew boiling in a dutch oven wafted thick in the air. Silas was fully aware that he hadn't had a warm meal in more than two days.

At first the walk made him angry and then he found if he used the time to detail in his mind just how he was going to kill all those men, it made things a bit more pleasant. As he neared the encampment he could smell the great pots of stew boiling over open fires, could smell steaks being grilled, and there was more than vengeance in his mind as he got closer. The driving force was hunger now.

28

"WE NEED to get 'em started as early as possible in the morning," Snake said. He, Louise, Alvarado, and George Dawson were sitting near the fire. Cowboys, charros, and teamsters were at other fires, finishing their meals, mending gear and tack, or just enjoying the twilight. Soon, the Nighthawks would venture out and those with the herd would come in for their supper.

It was a ragged sky they were enjoying, flaming clouds off to the west, but ugly, black clouds promising a turbulent tomorrow were building fast to the north. Tomorrow? How can they worry about tomorrow when they have tonight to face first.

"Tomorrow's journey will start out mostly downhill, following Buzzard Pass for about four miles then turning north toward some good water." Snake pointed out toward the pass.

Looking north, many saw thunderheads building but still miles away. They would be moving down out of the mountains and with wet storms moving in, would this just be a mud bath? "What's the ground like?" Dawson asked. "Seeing those thunderheads makes me think of mud."

"Softer ground for sure, George," Snake said. "Lots of grass, though."

"Dog-man will have to ride in back of the chuck," Louise said. "We've made him a nice little bed back there. Is that Lippincott boy going to attack us again tonight?"

"You can bet on it," Francisco Alvarado said. "His loss has been turned to revenge now, you can be sure. He's a stupid young man and all he can see is revenge right now."

"In a way, we're lucky it's Silas we're facing." George Dawson sat back against a rock, took a sip of coffee and continued. "His father was good at being a sneak thief, at shooting someone in the back. I hope Silas is a slow learner. He'll be here, though. Something you can bet that silver dollar of yours on, Snake." George Dawson remembered how many times Snake had said, 'betcha a dollar I'm right.'

"No bets tonight, George." Snake looked at the group. "If you were a young man with little education and had this rage of revenge pumping through your system, how would you go about extracting its payoff? George? Louise?"

"He and his father were on that trek last night," Louise said. "The old man came close. It was Dog-man who caught him."

"It was you who finished the job," George said. "Silas was about to strike when Wally screamed out his last, otherwise we might have had one of our own die. There are so many of us, so many will be awake at all hours. He might just wait for morning and pick us off one at a time with his rifle."

"That's an ugly thought," Alvarado said. "Damn, but it

would be better than trying to move through our camp on a killing spree."

Snake looked around at the three. It occurred to him that they had the same look on their faces as he probably had. "I think Francisco is right on the money but let's remember that Silas isn't known for his brains. Let's prepare for both, attacks on sleeping men and sitting back picking us off one at a time." He let his eyes roam about the group. "I'm not sure how we protect ourselves from an ambush like that, though."

Dawson said he'd keep his men prepared for both, Alvarado said the same, and Snake moved over next to Louise. "Let's you and me saddle up and take first shift watching those steers of ours out there."

"Do you have something else in mind, big boy?" Snake just chuckled, walking toward where the horses were. The smile would have lit the sky and he gave her thoughts some serious attention. *I think we're on the same page here.*

THE NIGHT WAS MOONLESS, the wind picked up just a bit, and way off in the north, flashes of lightning could be seen in the clouds. "A long way off," Snake said. Louise rode close enough that their knees touched often.

"Might be riding in the rain tomorrow," she said. "Won't affect us, but it sure could have an effect on George Dawson's wagons. I remember how my father used to cuss loud and long when the wagon wheels buried themselves in the mud. Dawson's wagons are a lot heavier than the old one we had."

Snake heard her but his attention was on a small bunch of steers that seemed to be interested in something other than good grass to eat. "Keep riding straight ahead," he said and turned his horse toward the bunch. Louise saw him pull his rifle out as he neared them and reached down and unloosened her massive shotgun.

Snake's eyes were moving fast, trying to see everything within a one-eighty arc. One steer gave a grunt and swung his head back and forth, horns digging down on each sweep. All at once, a coyote howled as a horn gouged a chunk of fur out of a shoulder and fled at a high rate out of range of those deadly horns.

Snake chuckled softly, tucked his rifle back in its scabbard and turned back toward Louise. He watched as she put the double-barreled ten-gauge back as well. "I hope that's our excitement for the night," she said. "I'm afraid I know better."

They made a complete circle of the herd, walking their horses clockwise. Alvarado and Wayne Nichols had passed them working around the herd counterclockwise. No one had seen or heard anything.

Snake had been quiet for a long time and Louise finally had to ask him why. "Thinking what we was talking about at supper. Thinking about Lippincott hiding out somewhere near our camp and picking us off come sunrise. It would be the thing an outlaw would do. Makes more sense than what we've been preparing for."

Louise felt a shudder up and down her spine thinking of someone hiding behind a tree and shooting her in the back. "Don't like that kind of talk, Snake. Don't like it." She'd been shot once and it almost killed her. She lost the baby she was carrying and lost the ability to have future children. It was a dreadful thought.

She looked out across the backs of hundreds of head of cattle, could see the flares and shadows of the various campfires, and wondered if maybe the killer was already setting up his killing place. *How do we defend against that? Can't just hide and hope he goes away.* She looked at Snake, looked at the flashing lightning to the north and felt a cold wave of fear.

"Problem with that is how many people we actually have," Snake said. "Hard to say, but a man could get maybe two before the whole camp would descend on him and the end result wouldn't be what he was after, either."

"You're being a bit careless with people's lives," Louise muttered. "Kill maybe two? No, Snake, we gotta do better than that. We can't let that happen."

"Don't want it to happen, but think about what our camp looks like come sunrise. Fires burning bright, men and women working around them, working out around the animals, working out and around the wagons. Hard to defend against. Damn, if it ain't." He reached out and took her hand as they rode through some tall brush. "With a rifle, Lippincott could be a hundred yards off and we'd not know it until the first shot was fired."

They were relieved by a couple of the Mexican charros and made their way back to camp and warm bedrolls. Snake smiled and reached out and took her reins and carefully led them away from the herd, away from the campfires, away from any eyes or ears. The grass was still warm from the afternoon sun, their bodies thrilled to that, and it was another hour before they returned to their camp

Pedro met them after they put up their horses and tack. "Coffee?" he asked, a grand smile across his young face.

Louise was surprised and had to take a second look. *He's grown into a young man in just two days. A little boy who wanted to be hugged and wanted to play, and now, he gathers firewood, brings us coffee.* There were other thoughts mingled with these. She wondered what the baby they lost would have been like. The thought of never being able to have a child interrupted other thoughts regularly and tonight was one of them.

"Thank you, Pedrito. You should be asleep, you know. These are long hard days for little boys." Louise ruffled his black hair, bent down and kissed his forehead, and watched him scamper back under the chuck wagon.

Louise shuddered again. *What if it was Pedro in those rifle sights? I couldn't bear that. Couldn't.* She took a sip of coffee and motioned for Snake to join her and they slipped into their bedrolls. She knew she wouldn't sleep a minute. *A hundred yards off with a rifle and we make perfect targets.*

It was Snake's strong arms drawing her close that changed the program and she let his hands roam wherever he wanted them to roam. They had no trouble falling to sleep, wrapped in each other's arms. Even the approaching thunder didn't have any effect.

LIGHTNING FLASHED way off in the distance, not so far that Silas couldn't hear the thunderclaps as he moved around the herd and closed on the cow camp. The fires burned bright, he could see men with rifles walking around, could smell fresh coffee being boiled, close enough now that he could even hear snippets of conversation. The night sky was covered in thick clouds as the early fall storm moved in. So dark one couldn't see one's hands, but the campfires gave Silas perspective and he was able to move carefully through the gloom.

It wasn't the people around or near the fires that Silas

worried about, he could see them. It was those who might be coming in from Nighthawk duty, who might have taken a little walk after supper or to relieve themselves, that bothered him. He had to look in every direction at the same time because there was surely someone coming up behind him.

In the intense dark it wasn't hard to remain concealed, but just as the night before, he wasn't able to get close enough to kill anyone. Men, women, even children, were wrapped in their bedrolls just feet from the fires and guards walked in perimeters out and away from the sleepers.

Silas crept around in the brush and grass well out from the fires and thought he might be able to get close to that one wagon that stood so close to the camps. *That has to be the chuck wagon. If I can steal some food I can wait for sunrise and just shoot these people. I want to feel my knife cut deep into their bodies but the important thing, Pepe is to kill them.* The conversations with Pepe were coming more often and it seemed to Silas that his half brother was right there with him.

The chuck was parked in such a manner that the rear was aimed at one of the campfires and the front deep in shadows. Silas worked his way through heavy brush, around some deadfall, and found himself just a few yards or so in front of the wagon, on his belly, under a large sage.

I know there's food just behind that seat up there. He lay in the dirt for a long time and watched the camp guards making their rounds. They did come right up to the back end of the wagon from time to time but didn't linger long. Each man carried a rifle, and Silas knew he would be shot on sight. There would be no warning, no offer to give up.

Two guards walked up and one reached inside the wagon and pulled a couple of biscuits out. He handed one to his partner and they walked off. *Food. Right there.* Silas stood up, pulled his hat down as tight as he could get it, kept his head down hoping if he was seen he would just look like a camp guard.

Two steps, then one more and he was at the tailgate of the wagon. He reached over and his hand felt a cloth over the biscuits. One or two wasn't good enough for Silas Lippincott, he tried to pick up the bowl holding half a dozen large, still-warm biscuits. It slipped and clattered against the wooden shelf it was on, and Silas panicked. He grabbed for the bowl but the alarm was raised by Pedro, sleeping less than two feet from Lippin-cott's boots.

Pedro screamed at the top of his young lungs, loud enough to awaken the herd, and men with guns jumped to their feet. The first one on the scene, rifle in one hand, pistol in the other, was Snake in his underwear. He caught sight of a man running hard through the brush and took the first few steps before having to turn back.

Pedro rushed to his side as did Louise. Snake, bare-foot, pulled some thorns from his foot and pointed into the brush to their north. "That way, men. One man, holding a rifle, on foot. Go get him." He struggled to get free of Pedro and Louise, found his boots and danced around trying to get them on. "Damn it," he said, loud and strong, almost falling down. Louise wrapped her arms around his waist and with some balance he got his boots on.

Five men with rifles and pistols headed off through the brush and Snake grabbed a torch that had been attached to the chuck, lit it at a campfire, and headed out after the bunch. "Stay with Pedro and keep that shotgun handy," he hollered.

That man came right into camp, Louise was shaking thinking how close to Pedro he had been. *More drawn by hunger than vengeance. What a sad thing, his father and brother killed right in front of him, and he's left with nothing. Not even something to eat.*

Those were sad thoughts but Louise shook herself away from them. *No! He's a killer like his father. Distracted maybe by the thought of food, but he was in our camp to kill us. Wake up, girl. He was here to kill us.* She reached out and took Pedro by the hand and walked over to the fire. Together they built it up, got coffee boiling for the men for when they returned. Louise sat down to think about the situation they were in and she didn't like it.

Lightning could be seen coming closer with each bolt that tore through the ragged sky. Thunder, which seemed so far away just half an hour ago, was rolling through the hillsides and into the canyons and meadows. *Ain't been in a situation like this for a long time and I don't like it.* She had to chuckle at her thoughts.

Papa always said not to worry about something you can't do anything about. Well, dear daddy, I'm worrying the hell out of something I can't do anything about. We've got a herd of more than a thousand animals out there about to be spooked by a thunderstorm, I've got a husband out there chasing a crazy man who wants to kill all of us, and we've got a young son who is desperate for love. You got any answers, Daddy? I sure don't.

Louise set her thoughts aside and added some wood to the fire and sat down next to Pedro. Jeannie Nichols sat down beside her. "You brave boy, Pedrito. You scream and bad man run away. Good boy."

Pedro hugged Louise even tighter and smiled at Jeannie. "I was scared. He almost stepped on me." Louise hadn't heard that before and it made her suck in her breath.

"You never said anything," she said.

"I was scared," Pedro said. Louise wrapped her arms around the boy and nodded, fully understanding. *Me too*, she thought.

Other campfires were stoked, men were fully dressed, and horses were being saddled. George Dawson walked up to the fire carrying a short-barreled shotgun. "Looks like we'll have another short night, eh? Anyone hurt?"

"No," Louise said. "Several men are on the chase. We need to get some men out working with the cattle. All this noise and they're gonna start wanting to move out."

"I just left Alvarado," Dawson said. "He and two others are already out there. I'm missing two of my men so I'm hoping they are out there with Snake."

29

WHEN PEDRO SCREAMED, Silas felt his heart almost stop. The boy was right under his feet. He turned and ran as hard as he could run from the cow camp. It was just seconds, he thought, that he could hear men running behind him, yelling, howling obscenities. He was desperate, needing a hole to jump in, a rock to slide behind, anything to keep those men from finding him.

What would Pepe do? Where can I run? Help me, brother. He almost ran full tilt into a tree, and trying to get away from it fell over a deadfall, crashing into leaves, branches, rocks, and dirt. The sound of running feet put the fear of hell's fires into the young man. He started to get back on his feet, knew the men chasing him were too close, and crawled, quickly, under the deadfall. He pulled as much of the scrap in with him and almost held his breath as the men charged past.

It was panic that drove him to run, it was panic that led him to crash into the deadfall, and he knew it would be panic that would kill him. *I have to think. It's always what Pepe said, don't just react, brother. Think and think hard.* Silas had his breathing under control, knew the men chasing him were far away now, and he knew he had to take these few minutes to think his way out of the terrible position he was in.

The night was so black that none of the men noticed the disturbance in the ground cover, as they ran as hard as they could, almost blindly. Silas lay as quietly as he could, not daring to breathe deep, fearful he might cough. He couldn't see anyone but he could hear them and knew when they left to continue their chase. He was amazed to find that he had the remains of a crushed biscuit held tightly in his hand.

He didn't hesitate and shoved the crumbled bread into his mouth. Oh, what he would do with more, what he would do with a drink of water. The sounds of chasing men slowly ebbed and Silas crawled out from under the fallen tree, looked around quickly, and moved off to the left of where the men went.

He didn't know where he was, was trying to figure out which direction to take to find his horse, and it took less than a minute or two for the anger to build. What time was it? Where is that horse? How do I get out of this mess? Help me, Pepe. It was more than his sick mind could handle and calm thinking was replaced by unthinking rage. He didn't care about noise, about being seen, even, as he moved through the trees and brush to be close to the open meadow where the herd was milling.

He took one brief minute to inspect his guns. The rifle took a beating falling over that deadfall and crashing into the ground. Dirt and mud shoved into the end of the barrel, the lever action lock and exposed hammer full of mud. *Damned thing's useless now. Blow up in my face if I fired it.* The revolver, on the other hand, came out of the ordeal in good shape. He cringed, though looking at the holster. A branch of the fallen tree must have been the culprit that tore the leather and gouged the belt. All that leather did protect the revolver, however.

It was the thunder that caught his attention. Lightning had been playing in the clouds all night but now the storms were close enough that he could almost feel the thunder. That meant the rains might be close as well, and Silas was on foot in open country without any way to keep warm and dry. He was out of food, didn't know where his horse was, and not quite bright enough to do anything about his obvious peril.

He walked into a stand of trees on the edge of the meadow and just stood there looking out across the large herd of milling cattle. A great flash of lightning followed almost instantly by massive rolling waves of thunder showed him in bright light where his horse might be. On the other side of the herd.

He saw the hills that led down to open up Buzzard Pass and knew his horse was in the trees right over there. Right over there was at least two miles away, he would have to walk around the herd, and there were men with rifles out there, wanting to kill him. *Those men don't give me any other choice,* he thought, hoping for another flash of lightning to guide him. The first few steps were the hardest, filled with danger. Where were those men? After that, just put one foot in front of the other, use your eyes and ears to stay away from cattle and men with rifles.

He had visions of dead men, could almost smell coffee, beef, bread. He kept a running conversation with

Pepe, and slowly worked his way around the great herd. Lightning crashed into trees, sparking fires, thunder beat down on him like hammers of the ancients, and he was quickly aware that it was raining hard. Worse than that, the storm got the herd anxious and the milling was turning to bunches of cattle running about.

He stayed as close to the edge of meadow as he could, used the lightning to judge how much farther he had to go, and hid behind the trees to fend off roving steers with mean-looking horns.

"We ain't gonna find him in the dark, boys," Snake finally said. "Let's get back, get people out on the herd. They're gonna want to make a run for it soon. That fool boy ain't gonna do well, either, when this storm rolls down on us."

He barely got the words out when the first icy drops of rain beat down on the bunch. Snake could feel the tension in the air, knew those same feelings were spreading fast among the steers and horses spread across that wide meadow. "We got a thousand head of cattle and more than fifty head of horse flesh out there, boys, and that's where we need to be."

Snake and those chasing the killer were on foot and some distance from the cow camp and could hear cattle bawling, knew Snake was right and made their way through the rain back to saddle up and ride the herd.

Francisco Alvarado had those same feelings as he and three of the Mexican charros along with two of Dawson's teamsters rode toward the herd. The rain was bitter cold, the drops were large, and it wasn't but moments that the wind picked up and was screaming its wrath. There was danger in a storm like this. Lightning, falling trees, stampeding cattle to name just a few.

"Gotta keep those leaders as quiet as we can," Alvarado shouted out. He nodded at two of the young Mexicans. "You two, get up near the front of the herd and try to keep them calmed if you can. Be ready to have to turn 'em if a stampede starts."

Alvarado pointed at one of Dawson's men. "Ride with them and do as they ask. They've been moving cattle all their lives and will know what they're talking about." The teamster didn't balk and rode off to join the two charros. They might know horses and mules, those boys knew cattle. Francisco nodded at the men left with him.

"You two work slowly around that side of the herd. Talk to them gently, softly. Sing some fine songs. Ronaldo, you ride with me and we'll do the same on this side. You sing, I just scare 'em when I try." The rain was coming in sheets, lightning was crashing into the forests on both sides of the meadow, and thunder split the air unmercifully, pounding the men and animals.

The cattle had been grazing in thick grass for several hours, were sated, if cattle can be, so despite the intense barrage of weather, most were not inclined to stampede. There were a few, of course, but most of the animals had stood through summer thunderstorms in their own meadows before. Having men on horses riding close and talking or singing made things almost normal for them.

Snake brought his wet and muddy group up to Louise's fire and they got as close, jostling each other to get as close to the hot flames as they could. "Any word from those out with the herd?"

"George Dawson only said that Francisco was able to put together several men and were out there." Louise looked at Snake's well-weathered face and knew they hadn't had any luck in finding the Lippincott man. "You need dry clothes, Snake."

"Later," he said and bent down to kiss her on the top of her head. "Let's saddle up, gentlemen. I do believe I hear some cattle out there calling to us." He looked a long time at Louise before speaking. "It's going to be the worst day of the drive, girl. These men are going to need a big meal before we get started. Nobody's got a good night's rest, and this storm will make handling the cattle difficult. They're gonna need a good hot meal."

She wrapped her arms around the big, wet man and held on tight. "I'll see to it."

There were no arguments from the men about getting underway, no grumbling, just a tired look or two at the almost empty coffee pot and they headed for their horses. "Keep that shotgun close, Lion Killer. That fool is out there somewhere."

Louise and Jeannie refilled the coffee pots with fresh water and ground beans. When the men came back they would need as much as they could drink. Pedro helped with dry wood and they stoked the fire despite the rain that was now falling and tucked themselves under the chuck wagon. "We'll run out as needed to keep that fire hot. Those men will be soaked and half frozen when they get back."

She chuckled softly and scrambled out from under the wagon. "They're gonna want a whole lot more than coffee, Jeannie. They're gonna want as much hot food as we can give them. We've gotta get breakfast going and fast. As soon as they get that herd halfway settled they're gonna want food and fast so they can get the drive underway."

The two women ran a tarp out as a fly under which they could prepare and serve food, Pedro had his stack of dry wood tucked under the front end of the wagon and it was his job to keep the cook fires going strong while the women prepared and cooked. A well-oiled machine went into action. It wasn't long and the aroma of fresh biscuits baking in cast iron skillets filled the air, followed by frying side meat.

30

SILAS LIPPINCOTT KNEW he was still a full mile or more from where his horse should be, was chilled to the bone and moved into the trees at the edge of the meadow to get somewhat out of the rain. Was that a smart move, what with the way lightning was smashing trees all around him? He was only thinking of staying dry. He used a dead oak leaf to funnel rainwater into his mouth. It was sloppy at best, but he kept at it until he couldn't swallow another time.

He knew he could make better time walking out in the grass not stumbling through the forest but when he started to move back out, he spotted three or four men on horses moving through the grass, talking and singing gently to the cattle. Lippincott didn't panic but moved quickly back into the heavy trees and safety.

"Gotta get to that horse," he muttered, stumbling through rotted forest debris now wet and slimy. "Don't panic," he said over and over, the forest forcing him to slow down. "Can't run, don't run," he said. Was he talking to himself or was he hearing Pepe talking back to him? Regardless, Silas did slow down, was able to pick his way, and found that his panic eased as he spent more time worrying about the next step than he did about men on horses, carrying rifles, looking to kill him.

The rain didn't let up and was driven by harsh and cold winds. Lightning slashed the sky and thunder pounded his ears as Silas continued his trek. The forest is usually a calming place to be, giving a person an opportunity to think, create, believe, but not in a raging storm. Incredible thunder, screaming wind, falling trees, driving rain and one's nerves are stretched piano string tight and ready to break.

"Have to be close," he muttered. He stood quiet, catching his breath, hoping for a flash of lightning so he could get his bearings. He was weak from hunger, but the water he drank helped ease the hunger pains.

A bolt of lightning slashed its way into trees just a hundred feet or so in front of him and the intense power of the strike drove him back and dropped him into the mud and detritus. He lay in the mud, feeling the rain pound him and realized he couldn't hear it. That's when the panic set in again. He called out to Pepe and knew he was in even deeper trouble. *I can't hear my own voice.* He reached up and rubbed an ear and when he pulled his hand away, he saw the blood.

The intense force of the clap of thunder, directly over his head, burst blood vessels and he found both ears were bleeding, and he had stains of blood around his eyes as well. Silas sat down in the mud and started crying, sobbing, as if he was three years old. He cried out for Pepe, pounded his fists into the mud and debris, scraping his knuckles bloody.

His was a lost soul, no horse, no food, no brother to help, and not a friend in the world. Silas Lippincott had never been this alone before. He had always had Pepe with him. His father wasn't a positive influence, but he too had always been there. Was it time to die? Is this how he would spend his last day on earth, crawling through the mud, crying like a baby? He was never a leader, always a follower, usually of his brother Pepe. He was supposed to be looking to kill the men who killed Pepe. All he could do was lay in the mud and cry out for his brother.

Panic. The word flooded through his brain and he fought for control. He knew he could hear Pepe telling him to calm down, but, strangely, he couldn't hear the rain pounding his head. His vision was dimmed by rain in his face and the force of the thunder claps, but he slowly got himself put back together. Racing through the forest, falling in the mud had not been good for his clothing. His old, worn shirt was ripped in several places as were his pants.

He managed to get to his feet, found his boots were as wet on the inside as on the outside, wiped what mud and leaves and twigs he could from him, and tried to listen for Pepe. He needed Pepe to keep him from simply wandering off to die somewhere. *I need that horse, Pepe. Where did I leave that horse? I have to be close. Where?* Cold wet air sapped his strength. He shuddered at every blast of wind-driven rain, desperately wanted to build a fire but didn't have the means to do so.

He began walking again, stumbling through the edge of the forest, cattle grazing just yards away. He still carried that rifle, now even more smeared with mud, the detritus of the forest crammed into its barrel. Two men rode by but didn't see Silas crouched behind a pine tree, wishing he dared to shoot both of them. *I should have shot them. There's food in those saddle bags. I know it.* He reached down for his sidearm but found the men gone by then, lost in the rain.

He continued moving toward where the meadow ended and the ground sloped more, and he was close to Buzzard Pass. He stopped, and forced his mind to take a long, slow look all around. *I'm very close to where I left that horse. He's here, I know it.* The more he looked the less he saw, and once again panic began its way in, slowly taking over.

He ran to some trees, but the shadow he saw wasn't a horse, but, over there, there's my horse, and he ran that way. In less than ten minutes, Silas had found five shadow horses, but not one real, alive, horse. He fell to the mud again, crying out for Pepe to help him, and found he could hear his voice.

Was it the return of hearing that calmed him? Or was it fatigue and hunger? The wind and rain were now forces of evil sent to kill him as were those men with rifles. He slowly got back to his feet, covered in forest debris and mud, and leaned against a tree. "What was that?" He said it out loud and looked around. "My horse," he said and walked the twenty yards to where the horse he stole from the Mexican boy stood, tied to a sapling, munching on wet grass.

FRANCISCO ALVARADO and Snake left several men with the herd and brought everyone else into camp. "We're gonna be late getting this circus moving," Snake said, "but we have to get some food in us and some dry clothes."

George Dawson had split his crew as well, some eating and changing while the others got the wagons ready for the day's journey. When the first crews of drovers and teamsters had eaten, they replaced the others so they could eat and change. It was a long process and it was several hours before the trek could begin.

"Think that Lippincott fool will still be with us?" Dog-man asked as Snake stuck his head in the back of the chuck where his partner was stretched out.

"Ain't no doubt, Dog. He'll be a mess, though. This rain is cold and the wind's strong. Sap the strength right out of a man, even one driven by as much hate as that boy has. I see you have your rifle and pistol with you. Keep 'em close."

Snake wagged his head back and forth. "The last time you saw Lippincott he had a horse?" he asked Dog-man. "But the last time I saw him he was on foot. He was on foot when he attacked the chuck. You think he might have had that horse you talked about tied off somewhere?"

"That's my thought," Dog-man said. "He ain't good with animals. I had to put that one of his down. And he was running the one he stole awful hard. If that's what he did then he'll be with us all day and again tonight."

"Pickin' us off," Snake murmured. "This is our first drive, partner, and it's been something from way before we got the herd down from the hills." Snake shook his head and snickered at the thought. "Everybody and their aunts and cousins been after us, I think. Trying to kill us, burn us out, take our animals. Now a killer after us 'cuz we killed his father and brother who were also trying to kill us. Damn me, but I'm gettin' tired of it all."

Dog-man was laughing at the way Snake was trying to tell his story and that just got the long tall Texan even more upset. "Oh, yeah, sure, you're all comfortable in

209

your blankets nursing a little scratch on your leg while I'm fighting to keep our herd from runnin' off, tracking a killer through an early morning tornado and hurricane, covered in mud and grime. I suppose the women brought you hot coffee, did they?"

Dog-man laughed even harder and that brought Louise and George Dawson to the wagon. "What the hell's going on back there?" Dawson asked, poking his head through the canvas. "Sounds like a damn party. We gotta get moving, Snake. Half the day's gone."

"As soon as everybody's fed, George, we're moving. This storm is going to force us to go slow down the pass but when we make the turn north, we'll be on a worn trail and the going will be easier. There's water six miles in front of us and that's where we'll camp tonight. It'll be a push to get there, though."

"Lippincott gonna give us trouble the whole way?" Dawson's face was as stormy as the sky outside the wagon and the cigar he had shoved in his mouth was taking a beating. It hadn't been lit for half an hour but it was well chewed upon.

"Snake and I were just talking about that, George," Dog-man said. He eased his wounded leg into a more comfortable position. "Reminds me," Dog-man said with a smile. "You ruined that new shirt I bought, Snake. We get to San Berdoo, you owe me a shirt. I want a yellow one, too." He laughed and then got all serious again.

"Silas killed one of our men and stole his horse. He was here in camp last night but on foot, so he may or may not have a horse. If he does have a horse, we will come under fire." Dog-man tried to adjust his wounded leg again and Snake could see the pain spread across his partner's face.

"Damn, damn." Dawson stepped back from under the

wagon flap and stormed off toward where his teamsters had the two big wagons ready to move off. "You boys have your rifles near at hand all day today. That fool Lippincott just might be with us all day." Dawson tied his saddle horse to the back of the largest of the wagons and climbed up into the seat, taking the reins from his shotgun rider."

Dawson had been having second thoughts about his decision to start up this new business of his. *These roads and trails aren't in very good shape, there seems to be outlaws behind every rock.* He had to chuckle at his thoughts. *Seems a lot like when we started moving freight from Denver south. Outlaws, Indians, and bad weather every day. Age, that's the difference. These young bucks don't even know they're tired and I'm dying here.* He threw the old cigar into the mud and pulled a fresh one from his coat pocket. "Hiyah, let's get 'em rolling."

Louise led the caravan in the chuck followed by Dawson's wagons, and then the horse remuda, and finally the cattle herd. The line of march would extend over a distance of miles. "Won't be fighting dust today," Francisco Alvarado said, urging the cattle on. The grass was wet, open areas muddy, and horses and cattle found themselves doing little dances from time to time, staying upright.

Dog-man insisted that Louise leave the end tarp rolled up and he was sitting up as straight as the wagon would let him, watching the grand panorama unfold. The grin was wide, the eyes were as bright as day, and he could actually feel his heart responding to the view. Great oaks spread wide, tall pine and fir sparkling in the wet, and a vast meadow covered in an undulating wave of beef and horse blanketing the grass.

"I'll never get tired of something like this. Our cattle,

our horses, and our men driving them. Me and old Snake got run out of Deadwood just a few years ago and look at us now." The only thing missing, and Dog-man refused to let it crowd into his mind, was Dog-man in the saddle helping move that herd. He rubbed the tender spot where the bullet from Silas Lippincott tore a hole in his leg.

There was one other thing missing but Dog-man did what he could to not let the thought come forward. Old Snake, the best partner a man could have found his woman after doing what he could to not become a married man. And Old Dog-man did not have his woman. Except for that little she-wolf in Colorado, Dog-man hadn't even done any flirting more or less chasing a woman and Snake had had affairs with several.

What's that man got that I ain't got? I'm the better looking of the two of us, so why do the women flock to that long tall string bean? I can look at Louise and just feel the warmth she has for that man. I am lonely, Dog-man finally decided. He also decided he didn't have any idea how to change the situation. *Sure as hell ain't gonna tell nobody. I might be looking for more than a new shirt when we get to the livestock pens.*

31

SILAS SAT in the saddle watching the herd move out and when the last of the herd and those riding drag passed by he rode across the meadow to where the cow camp had been set up. He didn't really care what it was that he might find just as long as it was something he could eat. Scraps of anything would be like a banquet on this cold wet morning. His luck held and he found nothing, which made him as angry as he'd been.

The day, though, was glorious. The night's thunder and lightning were gone as was the wind and driving rain, leaving glistening leaves, grass, and pine boughs. Silas saw none of that, never saw the brilliant sunrise nor the white pillows of clouds drifting slowly inland.

It was exactly as he remembered it from the times he spent groveling through people's trash as a youngster. Horrible, knowing people had seen him, understanding, even as a young boy, what they might be saying about him, about his half brother, and about their drunken father. Silas walked through the empty cow camp not wanting those memories but unable to put them aside.

He couldn't remember a time, as a youngster, when he wasn't hungry.

His father, Wally Lippincott, would come to the cabin drunk and the boys wouldn't get supper. Hunger had been a way of life for him and Pepe and it was hunger that led him and Pepe into becoming rather proficient at stealing from various enterprises in whatever town they might have been in. Pepe believed that snatch and run worked, but sneak and hide was better. Bitter memories sat on an ugly and empty stomach this cold late fall morning.

It was when he and Pepe were nearing maturity that their father used their youth and strength and began robbing people on the trail, holding up businesses, even doing a bit of stage robbing. They all had money in their pockets, and they could eat any time they wanted to. Now, just like when he was so young, he was alone, hurt, and hungry.

Silas rode out and got in behind the drag rider and tried to gauge how close other riders might be to him. Could he ride up and not be seen? Could he shoot the bastard and not have the shot be heard? Silas had only the thought of food on his mind. Killing the men moving the cattle as an act of revenge was set aside for the moment. Only food, self-preservation, mattered. There were biscuits in those saddlebags.

It was the constant wind-driven rain and the cold that had made it so difficult. His hands and fingers had no feelings, and his ears and nose, still covered in blood, felt like red-hot pokers were jabbing them. At the moment, killing all the men involved in this cattle drive wasn't nearly as important as finding a pot of boiling coffee and a platter of hot biscuits.

A cattle drive is not something that involves speed.

The drive moves at a walk and this one was stretched out for miles. There were riders out on the flanks separated by considerable distances but in visual contact with each other. The drive filled the wide valley, side to side. The drag rider could see flankers well up ahead of him because of the night's storm. He wasn't eating half a pound of dust every ten minutes.

Silas was frustrated and rode out of the meadow and into the trees to his north. The pass would drop several hundred feet before turning north and Silas knew he would have to hide in the trees and shoot that drag rider from a great distance. "I can't be seen, Pepe," he muttered. "And the sound of the rifle has to sound like a long way off." He had been hearing the sound of a thousand animals plodding through open land for hours. Would that rumble mask the sound of a gunshot?

He didn't spare the horse at all, rode hard through the wet forest, around rocky outcrops, deadfall, and heavy brush. He forgot the horse had been limping the day before and it wasn't long before the horse was limping again. He found he was at least a half mile in front of that drag rider, looked for a good spot to shoot down on the man, and eased up on the horse.

He never saw the beauty of that long wide valley stretched out between two rolling hills blanketed by deep forests. He never looked up, never saw the brilliant fleece of cumulus clouds looking to build more thunderstorms. His vision of beauty was limited from a childhood of limited education, being shielded from the beauty and poetry of life.

When one's time is spent groveling for food, fighting for clothing, and never feeling the warmth of love, one rarely understands the concept of natural beauty or the lovely sounds of life. What Silas saw was people, objects, and wildlife out to do him in, take what little he had, or just make life difficult. There was no beauty in the natural surroundings.

There was a rocky outcrop right on the edge of the trees that gave him a wonderful view across the meadow. He estimated the shot would be more than a hundred yards but less than two hundred. Silas was good with a rifle, figured he could hit the man on horseback and was far enough away from the flank riders that they might not hear the shot with all the bawling from the cattle.

"I know that man will have at least a few biscuits and some smoked meat in his saddlebags." Silas found his mouth was watering at the thought. *I'll shoot him, and maybe that will draw another rider and I'll shoot him too.* Driven as he was by hunger, there was no such thing as common sense.

Silas tied the horse off and clambered into the rock pile, found a good spot where he could see across at the herd. The herd was moving at a steady walk and the drag rider rode calmly back and forth behind the herd, keeping them at their pace. His back was straight and he rode with the rhythm of the animal.

This was the third day of the drive and the cattle simply did what cattle do best: follow the one in front. Jeremiah Hillyer had grown up on the back of a horse, spent hundreds of hours moving cattle, and was enjoying watching the storm break up, feeling the heat of the sun as it dried his clothing. It was a good day to be in open country like this, rolling hills covered in thick grass, brush, and a forest filled with more trees than the lanky Texan had seen in years.

Silas eased the rifle snuggly into his shoulder and took a look down the long barrel, lining up the front and rear sights. He'd shot moving deer from this distance before. It was going to be a single-shot kill. The rider turned from the south to ride back toward the north, flicking his quirt from time to time, calling out for the cattle to keep moving.

Silas had a perfect shot at the man's chest and eased back on the trigger. Jeremiah Hillyer was startled by the loud explosion coming from the trees about two hundred yards to his north and caught the flanker's attention closest to him. Hillyer rode toward where the explosion was, the flanker coming on hard. *That wasn't a gunshot. What the hell did I hear?*

"My god almighty," Hillyer said, stepping down from his horse. Silas Lippincott's face was shredded and he held what was left of a rifle, the working parts a mass of exploded steel. Silas wasn't dead and as Hillyer walked toward him, he pulled his revolver and fired a shot. It missed, but hit the horse and Hillyer hung on to the reins as the horse shied back, screaming in pain.

The bullet hit the horse in the shoulder tearing a long wound along its flank but not hitting any bone. Silas crawled into a stand of brush, tried to see what was happening but blood flowing freely clouded his vision. He lost one eye when the gun blew up and the other was surrounded by cut and torn flesh. He could taste blood, knew his lips were cut bad, his face felt slack as he crawled away from the brush toward his horse.

His arms and hands were ripped and torn, bloody and painful, but Silas only had one thought: Run, boy, as fast as you can.

The barrel of the rifle was filled with mud and debris and when the powder went off, the pressure in the barrel was extreme, more than the surrounding metal could take. Working parts gave way and ripped flesh and bone.

Silas's arms, chest, and especially his face, took the brunt of the blast.

He had to crawl since his legs were torn up by shrapnel from the exploding gun. The pain hadn't fully come into focus yet but Silas was fully aware of its beginnings. He had to get away, had to find a stream, tend to his wounds. He knew that's what Pepe would want. Tend to the wounds so you can fight another day.

Jeremiah Hillyer wasn't about to let go of his horse and the horse only wanted to run in panic, away from the hurt in its shoulder. It was a couple of minutes before the flank rider rode up to where Hillyer was fighting his horse. The two of them got him calmed down and Hillyer told Jose Castro what he'd seen.

"The man's rifle blew up in his face, Jose. I've never seen anything like that in my life. I went to help him and he shot my horse. He's over there, near that big bush. Be careful." Hillyer got his canteen and was going to clean the horse's wound then help Castro.

"Tie him off," Castro said. "It's best we go after him together. I'll go on that side. You go around over there."

Jeremiah knew Jose was right, tied his horse to a tree limb and moved toward the bush. He carried the rifle fully cocked and at the ready and heard a horse run off just yards in front of him. Jeremiah raced around the brush and saw Lippincott racing through the trees, raised the rifle and fired, ripping some flesh from Silas's left arm but not knocking him from the saddle. He levered another round but Lippincott was in the trees, moving fast, and Hillyer couldn't get a second shot off.

"I never even saw him," Jose Castro said when they returned to their horses. "You think you hit him?"

"He flinched," Jeremiah said. "He's wounded bad. His face and chest are torn up from the explosion." Hillyer walked to where Lippincott dropped the rifle and picked it up. "Can't imagine this thing blowing up in my face. He'll bleed to death, Jose."

"Best that could happen," the Mexican charro said.

"Ride to the head of the herd and let Alvarado know what happened. When you come back, bring me a horse. I'll take it easy on this guy until you get back." Jeremiah washed the wound, saw it would be tender for some time but would not cripple the animal. The first few steps told him the horse would survive and be a fit worker again.

32

"JUST LOOK AT THIS, DOG-MAN," Snake said, stuffing Silas's blown-up rifle through the canvas opening at the back of the chuck. "The man lived through it. Ain't never seen nothing like this."

Dog-man turned it over and around a couple of times before saying anything. "Enough metal missing that that boy must look like a patchwork quilt about now. Are Louise and Jeannie working on him? Hope somebody's standing by with a rifle."

"No," Snake said. "That's part of what's so damn amazing. Lippincott got on his horse and rode off. He's out there bleeding bad, Dog."

Louise pulled more of the canvas back. "You got to do something, Snake. You can't let that man suffer and slowly bleed to death. I bet he ain't had nothing to eat for days, too."

"You want me to run him down and put him out of his misery? That ain't like you, darlin'."

"No, Snake. I want you to find him and bring him into camp. He needs help."

He looked a long time into her eyes and slowly smiled at her. "You are something, girl. He tried to kill you last night."

"I know. Would have if he could have. That's not the point. We aren't like him, Snake. We don't rob and steal, we don't kill people in order to take what they have. He's hurt bad, might be a wanted killer, but it ain't our way to not help someone in trouble."

Dog-man laughed right out. "What are you laughing at?" Louise demanded.

"You sound just like Snake when he's gettin' all over me for wanting to kill a bad guy. Women and children from here to Deadwood owe their lives to this man." Dog-man chuckled some more. "You've taught her right, Snake," he said.

Snake had that sheepish, ten-year-old boy look on his face again. "You're right. Both of you. I'll go find the fool and I'll try to be gentle bringing him in." He tried to hold the snicker in and failed miserably. Snake was in the saddle in minutes, riding toward the tail end of the herd. He brought one of the men with him to replace Hillyer at drag. He wanted Hillyer to ride with him as he trailed Lippincott.

Can't imagine living through a blast like that. All we've heard is just how stupid that boy is, but what did he do to jam his rifle like that? How could you jam a rifle like that and not know it? Snake's guns were his friends. He kept them cleaned and oiled, fine-tuned, he said, and would never have treated one of his as Silas did the one that blew up. The fact that Silas was aware that the rifle's barrel was full of mud would have proved to Snake just how ignorant the boy was.

"Man only has a few things that keep him alive," he muttered, "He's got to take care of them. My horse, my guns, and now, my wife. Can't be treating them bad 'cuz they are what keep you alive." He was giving his horse a lesson in life as he made the ride to the tail end of the herd.

"Jose bring you a good horse, Jeremiah?"

"Got old Lupe, Snake," Hillyer said. "She's crazy but a good worker."

"Good. Ride with me and we'll find that fool, bring him back so the women can sew him up."

"I'd rather shoot him," Hillyer said.

"His actions might bring that on, but for the time being we're gonna try to bring him back to camp mostly alive. Show me where this started."

The two Texans rode off through wet grass back toward where Silas's rifle blew up. "Nice day now that the storm's gone. Looks like we'll have more thunder and lightning tonight, though," Jeremiah said. "Cattle weren't much worried about the storm last night. Texas cattle would have started running at the first thunderclap."

"These critters have seen a bunch of them storms in their own pastures," Snake said. "Could have spooked, though. You never know what's gonna put the fear in 'em. Horses have the same attitude. I've seen a horse fight off a rattlesnake and run like hell from a butterfly."

They laughed as they rode up into the trees and Jeremiah led them to the rockfall where Silas had his trouble. "He was laying right over there, covered in blood," Jeremiah said, pointing at the stand of brush. "Must have had his horse tied off back that way."

Snake stepped down from the big stud and walked to where Silas's prints showed what he did. He spotted numerous blood spots in the mud and saw where Silas got on his horse. "Shouldn't be too hard to follow," Snake said. He walked along the trail for a few minutes, looking at the prints that were left.

"Horse is running with a bad leg, Jeremiah. Let's not walk into an ambush."

The trail showed where Silas brought his horse to a walk and the limp was more than evident. "He's still working his way right alongside where the herd passed," Snake said. They were deep in the forest and moving west. Silas let the horse make its own way and Snake and Jeremiah followed right along through the mud, around deadfalls and great stands of hardwood and evergreens.

"If my memory serves me right, we'll dip into a draw half a mile up here and cross a stream. The herd will cross it and then the trail will turn north. Alvarado will start bringing the herd toward a larger water source just a mile or more north. If Silas keeps going, he'll run right into the herd."

"Got a dollar says he'll stop at the stream. He'll need water, and might have enough sense to wash off those wounds," Jeremiah said. "We might want to come toward that water nice and quiet."

They were coming down the hillside, around trees and rocks, and heard a horse whinny below them. They stopped, Tied their horses off and began walking toward the sound. Snake motioned Jeremiah off to his right, and they used all the trees and brush to hide their movements as they eased their way down toward the creek.

Jeremiah spotted the horse standing in the middle of the creek, drinking but also coming up and looking around. *That's Castro's horse, I think. He killed that boy, but that's one smart horse. Horse knows we're here.* He caught Snake's attention and pointed toward the horse.

Snake was twenty or so yards to Jeremiah's left, couldn't see the horse but could hear the creek, and eased his way closer. As he moved around a large oak he saw the horse drinking, no more than thirty yards in front of him. *He ain't tied to nothing. What does that mean? Where's Lippincott?*

Snake moved as slowly as a man could, thanked the big storm of the night before for allowing him to be as quiet as any titmouse moving through wet leaves. He pushed through some brush and spotted what looked like a man sitting down in the mud on the creek bank but not moving.

Snake was on his haunches and slowly eased his heavy revolver out. "Don't move an inch, Lippincott," Snake called out. "There's several of us and we'll kill you dead if you do." He watched for a moment, saw no movement, and eased himself to his full height. Silas had his back to Snake and simply sat in the mud, his head hanging down so his chin was on his chest.

Jeremiah walked out from the trees, his rifle aimed at the boy's head and Snake came forward, too, each moving one slow step at a time. Was Silas dead? Was he playing dead? Each man was ready to pull the trigger at the slightest move.

Snake reached him first, pushed the end of the rifle's barrel into Silas's neck and watched the boy slowly fall over on his side. Jeremiah walked into the creek and took the reins of the hurt horse and walked him up onto the bank.

Snake dragged Silas up out of the mud and into the rocks and sand of the creek bank, and when he let him fall back to the ground heard the slightest moan. "Damned fool's alive, Jeremiah," Snake called out. "Go bring the horses."

The two men stood in amazement looking at the bloody mess that had been Silas Lippincott's face and chest not too long ago. "How it is that he's still alive is something, ain't it?" Snake said. "Ain't got any kind of what we need to help him none."

"Take him back or just leave him?" Jeremiah asked.

"Cain't do that," Snake said, knowing Louise would throw a serious fit if he did. "No, let's get him on that broken-down horse and walk our way to where the herd should be. Can't be a mile, but more north than west. They've made the turn, I'm sure."

It was difficult getting Silas on his horse and they tied him tight, not so much as a prisoner, but to keep him from falling off. Snake had Lippincott's pistol tucked in his belt and found no other weapons. With Snake right alongside. hanging on to the outlaw, and Jeremiah leading, they walked their horses along the creek toward where the herd should be.

33

"THERE THEY ARE," Pedro yelled out as he came toward the fire with a load of dry wood. "They got him, Mama."

Louise looked at this little eight-year-old boy who is now her son, and smiled. *Puttin' on weight and not the least bit afraid of hard work and just a few months ago, a skinny little kid who didn't even know how to tie his shoes or make a bow. Just a few months ago, I was just a little girl chasing wild animals and now I'm a wife and mother. Lordy, Snake, look what you've done.*

Louise jumped up and was first to reach Snake as he rode into the cow camp with Alvarado and Dawson right behind. "He alive?" Dawson asked. "Look at that mess."

"Don't rightly know why, but he is alive, George." Snake angled them to the fire and it took three men to ease Lippincott's bulk off the horse. Louise and Jeannie had blankets ready and he was laid out next to the fire. Hot water was ready, rags were clean and ready, and Dawson stood next to Snake, shaking his head.

"Look at 'em, Snake. Man tried to kill them last night and now they're gonna do everything they can to fix him up. Sometimes us that they call humans are weird. Ain't no sense to that."

"No, there ain't, George, but Dog-man says that's what makes us human. Cain't just sit and watch a man die, even if he is a real bastard like Lippincott." Snake looked at Pedro, motioned for Jeremiah and Dawson, and walked toward one of the nearby trees. He took a make-believe poke at Pedro who immediately poked back, laughing, and jumping about. Snake gathered him up and held him tight.

"Those women are gonna be busy for a while, boys, and we got a cow camp full of hungry men. Let's get the fires going, get some meat roasting, and hope we can get fed before the next round of thunderstorms." As if on cue, everyone looked into the sky and knew they'd best hurry unless they wanted to eat in the rain.

With all the activity right outside the wagon, Dog-man crawled out, found that with a little limping, he could move around, and joined the group. "Three cook-fires should do the trick," Snake said. "Jeremiah, you got one, Dawson you got one, and I'll take one. Pedro, bring wood to each, Dog-man, look at you, up and walking. Good, help with preparation, and we'll have supper ready shortly."

Teamsters were moving their animals to water first, and then into good grass, cowboys and charros not tending the herd were taking care of their animals and getting bedrolls near one of the fires, and those with the herd were moving around the tired animals, singing or just having one-way conversations with them. The fact that the man who wanted them all dead was being treated in their own camp was just something happening.

"Ain't never been on a drive quite like this one," Jeremiah Hillyer said, the slightest grin on his lean and well-tanned face. His eyes sparkled with humor as he struck some flint and got a fire going. "One man doing his best to kill all of us and us doing our best to keep him alive, and all the time driving a thousand head of cattle to market."

The men around were laughing despite their tiredness. "I think it's a lot harder to move these critters when you're spending a great deal of time looking up the hillside into the trees to see if someone is aiming a rifle at you," one of the drovers said, sparking more laughter.

"Nah, not really," another spoke up. "I just did my best to keep in with a bunch of cattle hoping they'd take the first round."

"Don't let Snake hear you say that," joshed Hillyer. "Out there riding drag and not having all that dust for protection was the worst. I ain't never gonna cuss the dust again," he laughed.

It didn't take long for kettles of beef and vegetables to be ready and tin plates were filled, sometimes twice over. Riders left out for the herd, riders came in from the herd, and more food was eaten. "Gonna sleep like a baby tonight," George Dawson said. "Not a worry in the world knowing Lippincott ain't out there trying to kill us."

"No, he ain't," Dog-man said. "He's right here in camp with us." He eased down next to the fire, rubbed a sore wound, and took the cup of coffee offered by Dawson. "Tomorrow's drive is almost straight and level, George. It will put us within about half a day from San Bernardino's stockyards. You'll make your schedule."

"I've had my doubts over these last few days. I'm sure I'm right about setting up a delivery business for this district, but what's got me worried is the total lack of law. No sheriffs patrolling the county, no marshals in the towns and villages, and outlaws just running free. Hell, I might just sell my wagons and teams and start a detective agency."

"Area's growing fast, George. Freight and people moving across the great desert from here to Arizona Territory and back, farms and ranches growing and prospering, things will settle down soon. Your warehouses and delivery service will thrive."

"What about you, Dog-man? Snake has always been the one to want to continue moving along, but I wonder if you aren't thinking about the wandering life you two had. You gonna make it as a homebody rancher?"

Dog-man chuckled as he poured more coffee. "Been wondering the same thing. Me and Snake been on the trail for a long time. Ain't seen nobody as happy as he is all settled down with a wife and kid. He's come close more than once but he ain't gonna do any more wandering. Me? I'm not the wanderer he was, George. I've been wanting to settle down for a long time."

Dog-man stretched out his wounded leg and grimaced just a bit. "No, I'm not looking to wander. I think what I'm looking for is my own kind of woman. Snake and Louise are a pair. She's the prettiest girl I've ever met and is just as rough and tough as he is. She'll fight, and hard and mean, to save his skinny butt, and he'd kill an army if they threatened her."

He sighed, took a little sip of his coffee, tried to look at the sky, and looked squarely at Dawson. "What I want is a Louise for my own. I'm not the envying type, George, but I really do envy my partner. He's more happy than I've ever known him to be."

The conversation might have gone a bit longer but rumbling thunder, close to hand, put an end to it. "Better get the lean-to up," Dawson said. Men moved quickly to stretch some canvas, get tree limbs braced and tied before the first drops of cold rain came. "Another drive through the mud tomorrow, eh?"

"I REALLY DON'T KNOW why, but he's going to live, Snake." Louise was sitting on a log by the fire, Silas Lippincott stretched out on the other side, wrapped in a wool blanket. His face had been cleaned up and the wounds were terrible to look at. The missing eye was patched, gashes were closed and roughly sutured, his nose was only about half there and ripped badly. "What you're looking at is only about a third of the problem," she said. "His chest is a real mess. You can see the rib bones where meat was torn away."

"Are we even doing the right thing?" Snake asked. "I wonder if he wouldn't be better off dead? People won't want to look at those scars."

"He's a bad man, Snake, but he is a man, not an animal. We might think about putting down a dog or horse in this condition, but a man? I know I couldn't, even if I did think it would be for the best."

Snake settled down next to her, slipped an arm around her, and kissed her cheek. "Never had to think about something like this before," he murmured so softly she almost couldn't hear him. "Where's Jeannie?"

"She's off with Wayne. She did the sewing. Good at it, too. You said we'll be at the end of the trail day after tomorrow. Will we just leave him off with the sheriff in San Bernardino?"

"If he's still alive," he said. "Has he said anything?"

"No. Moaned a couple of times when Jeannie was sewing him up. He hasn't been conscious enough to eat or drink. I'd like to move him into the wagon before the rain starts if you and a couple of men could do it. I don't think he'd have enough strength to be a threat."

"We'll move him," Snake said "But we'll tie him down, too. He's caused his last trouble as far as I'm concerned. We won't give him another chance at it." Snake got up and walked around the fire, got down on his haunches and looked at Lippincott's face, shook his head, and poked the man in the shoulder. "You awake?"

All he got in return was a slight groan. Snake poked him again. "Wake up, Lippincott. We got some talking to do." Snake looked at Louise who just shook her head slowly. "I ain't gonna hurt the man," Snake said, "but I need to know just what kind of condition he's in. He could be playing with us, you know. He's done that before."

"I know," she said. "If he does live, what kind of life would he have?"

"You mean after he gets out of prison, 'cuz that's where he's going. He's got no education, got no means of taking care of himself. Just be another drunken bum on the dirty streets of some town, I guess. Only thing he knows is how to rob and steal. Who'd hire him for anything. Maybe swamp out a saloon at closing." Snake poked Silas again, and this time got a reaction.

"Don't," Lippincott said, trying to edge away from the pointed finger. "It hurts. I hurt."

"I just bet you do," Snake said.

Louise got up and moved around to join Snake.

"I want you to try and sit up if you can. Think you're strong enough to do that?

"Hurts," is all Silas said.

"I'm gonna poke you in the ribs again if you don't try. Got hot food here, boy. Sit up so you can eat it. Got hot coffee, too." Snake reached out and poked Silas in the side and the boy reared up quickly, snarling his anger.

Louise jumped back and she saw that Snake had a doubled-up fist ready to plow Lippincott's seriously damaged face. Silas eased himself into a sitting position, glaring, first at Snake, then at Louise. "Didn't have to do that."

"Lots of things I don't have to do, boy, but it got you up. You've been more than a pest these last couple of days, and look what it got you. How is it your rifle blew up on you? Forget to clean it, did you? First rule of having one, boy."

Louise looked at Snake and smiled. *I think he's as angry at Silas not cleaning his rifle as he is about him trying to kill us. Papa said so many times that when the right man came along, I'd know it. Snake is far more than the right man. He's got values beyond being the right man.*

Louise put some stew in a bowl along with a biscuit and handed it to Snake. "You able to eat?" Snake asked.

Silas reached out for the bowl, grabbed the spoon Snake held, and started shoveling food into his busted-up mouth. Snake and Louise could see the pain the effort brought, but the pangs of hunger overrode the pain.

"Easy, boy, there's plenty," Snake said.

"The way I see it, Lippincott, you and your brother and father were looking to steal our cattle when things went wrong for you. Seems you think that's our fault. Your pa and brother paid for being stupid, and you will be payin' a price for bein' stupid for a long time. It wasn't us being wrong, boy, it was you, your brother, and your father." He poured a tin cup full of coffee and laid it on the ground next to Silas, took the almost empty bowl and refilled it.

"You cause the least bit of trouble over the next two

days and you'll join your family in hell. I'll be the one sending you off. Got it?"

Silas had a mouthful of stew, wouldn't look at either Snake or Louise, and didn't say anything. Snake's finger jabbed Silas in the ribs and the boy cried out, almost dropping the bowl of hot food. "Hurts," he said. "Don't do that."

"Answer me when I talk to you and I won't," Snake said. "You are one slow learner, boy."

George Dawson and Dog-man walked up to the fire and sat down next to Louise. "So, the little fool might live, eh?" Dawson said.

"That will depend on his attitude," Snake said. "So far, he's got a bad attitude." Snake turned his attention back to Silas. "Don't know why old man Lippincott thought they could steal our cattle, just the three of them, but this one thinks he don't have to answer our questions," and Snake poked Silas again. "Do you, boy?"

"Hurts," Silas stammered through a mouthful of stew.

"I asked if you were gonna cause anymore trouble, boy, and you haven't answered me yet." Snake gave him a fast three-count and yelled out, "Well?"

Dawson chuckled. "Mouth is too full to answer, Snake. You gonna put him in the wagon? Better tie him down. Being warm and with a full belly, this fool might just try anything."

"That's what me and Louise was talking about," Snake said. "You okay with him being in the back of the wagon with you, Dog-man?"

"No, no, no. I'll drag my bedroll under the wagon with Pedro. That boy's too sneaky for my blood. Look at him, right now, he's got his mind working on how to kill some of us and get away. He's already seen where most of the horses are picketed, probably knows where extra knives might be. No, I'll be under the wagon."

Snake knew Dog-man was right. "Yup, Dog, you're right. We're gonna have to tie him up outside the wagon where we can have a guard with him all night. Safest way, I think."

34

SILAS LIPPINCOTT TIGHTENED his muscles as tight as he could despite the pain as Snake and George Dawson tied him to a small tree. He was sitting down, hands tied behind his back, and then his body tied to the tree. He was then wrapped in blankets and a rain cover. Would it work? Would the ropes be just a little loose when he relaxed his muscles? He moaned with every move they made, crying out from time to time. Were those moans real? Did he hurt that much? Would the moans and groans have any impact on those tying him up?

These people, so proud of themselves for killing Pepe and papa, and look what they've done to me. Papa was right, these people that have everything are going to kill us all and then try to say we were outlaws. Outlaws? Taking food from the rich don't make me an outlaw. They got stuff I need. They got food and weapons and I need that. They got to die for killing my family and I'm the one to do it. All their pride ain't gonna keep 'em alive.

Those thoughts and keeping himself as taught as possible might get him out of this, Silas thought. They ain't gonna put him in jail for trying to kill the men who killed his brother and father. *I'm right. They ain't.*

"That ought to hold him," Snake said. "We need somebody sitting on the other side of that fire at all hours tonight. Two-hour shifts."

"I'll have a couple of my men," Dawson said, "if you can have a couple of yours. I think the boy is playing with us. Those wounds have to hurt, but that much? Or maybe he's just a crybaby."

That brought snickers all around and Snake called Hillyer over. "You want first watch? He might be playing opossum."

"You bet," Jeremiah said. "Rain will be coming shortly. How about we rig a lean-to?"

Canvas from the chuck was brought out and rigged so that Silas was covered and a man could sit under a flap and be near the fire but not too close to the prisoner. "If he even looks at you crossways, ring an alarm, Jeremiah. Don't have to tell you how dangerous he is."

"Don't you worry, none, Snake. The alarm will be me shooting the bastard." Hillyer looked at Lippincott, fed some wood into the fire and got busy building a pot of coffee. "You remember, I'm sure, Snake, that in Texas when we were moving cattle, it was ornery Indians we had to fight, not idiots. This is beautiful country but sure can't say the same for some of the people that live hereabouts."

Snake and Dawson were chuckling as they walked off. "That boy's gonna be with this ranch for a long time, George."

"I'll be glad when this drive's over," Dawson said. "I'll head back to Las Cruces and leave Osborn here to run things. Biggest problem we'll have is finding people for the two warehouses and teamsters to make the runs. So far all I've run into are crooks, gamblers, and killers." Dawson shook his head as he and Snake settled down near the chuck wagon fire.

"I'll be running a regular line from Prescott to Lane's Crossing and San Berdoo, and then a local express line from the warehouses to wherever the freight needs to go. I'm gonna need people, Snake and I don't see 'em so far."

"I'm gonna let that be your worry, George. Me and Dog-man got enough worries raisin' cattle and horses. Probably have to go into the Los Angeles basin to find 'em, though. Right now, old man, I'm gonna take a ride around the herd and then wrap myself in a warm blanket. See you in the morning."

SILAS LIPPINCOTT SPENT an hour pretending he was asleep, keeping a close watch on Jeremiah Hillyer and doing everything he could to get his hands loose from the tight ropes. The damage to his face and chest, and to his upper legs, hurt like the devil but it was his hands that were giving him so much trouble. They were the closest to the blast when the moving parts of his rifle blew up and the damage would be with him the rest of his life.

There were broken bones in his hands, at least one finger was missing, and the skin was torn and ripped from the blast. He wasn't able to work his fingers like he wanted to, couldn't get those ropes to do what he wanted them to do, and his frustration level was coming close to his level of hatred of Snake and Dog-man.

Hatred had been building from the moment his brother died at the hands of Dog-man, and now, after suffering the recent abuse from Snake he was ready to kill anyone who got close enough. The palms of his hands were filled with bloody wounds, those fingers he had left ached and he had a hard time holding in his cries of pain as he tried to extricate himself from the binding ropes. By relaxing as much as possible, he could feel his hands move within the binds, and he fought the piercing pain as he worked his hands free.

His hands were free, but so what? he thought. They were still behind his back and he was still tied to the tree with the ropes knotted behind the tree. Anger, pain, and frustration were mounting in waves and it was anger that seemed to need the most attention. Silas seemed to understand that thrashing about and screaming would not be to his advantage, but he also seemed to understand that he didn't have any alternative.

It took a long time to get his arms and hands back around and in front of him. All the time making those moves he kept a close eye on Jeremiah Hillyer, doing his best not to let Hillyer see his moves. The blankets and raincoat spread over him helped shield those moves. His hands were now in his lap but he was tied securely to that tree.

A wise man might work this situation a little differently. After all, Silas just had a good meal of hot meat, had plenty of fresh water, even more than one cup of coffee. Might it be better to take this opportunity to sleep for several hours, get his strength back? Wouldn't it be easier to attack that man watching him if he was not so tired, not so weak?

But Silas Lippincott was not a wise man, and he had a plan worked out that he was sure would work. Jeremiah Hillyer was sitting by the fire drinking a cup of hot coffee, keeping a close eye on his prisoner, listening to thunder off in the distance, wondering just how much longer it would be before the rains and wind arrived.

Silas Lippincott hadn't seemed to have moved since Snake left, and that was at least an hour ago, Hillyer thought. *Snake thought he was playing opossum. I wonder if he's even alive.* Hillyer got to his feet and picked up a long, thin broken limb from an oak tree, and prodded Silas with it.

Lippincott screamed out in pain and Hillyer knew the man was playing opossum. He hadn't barely nudged him. "Think you're pretty smart, eh, Lippincott? You was just hopin' I'd walk right up to you, eh? You ain't hurt none. Quit your yappin', or I'll give you something to cry about."

Jeremiah wanted to jab him again but didn't, just smiled and sat back down by the fire. He could see the flashes of lightning now, and the thunder rolled across the hillsides, much louder, much closer. He added a couple of large chunks of wood to the fire and moved under the tarp as the first cold drops of rain pelted him. It was going to be a long and cold two hours but at least he wasn't on the back of a horse taking on this coming storm, face to face.

"Gotta do my business," Silas said. Not screaming now, but his voice had an urgency to it. "Please," he said, "I gotta go."

Jeremiah had to think about this. It would mean untying him from the tree and then walking him into the trees. "Nope, ain't gonna do that," he muttered. He looked at the wounded prisoner and shook his head. "Gonna have to hold it, mister. Have to hold it until my relief comes, and then we'll take you into the trees."

"Cain't hold it," Silas cried out. "I'm gonna make a mess. Please. you gotta let me do my business."

Jeremiah stood up and looked around the cow camp and couldn't see anyone walking around. Since Lippincott was all tied up there wasn't any need for campsite guards. The only people awake were the Nighthawks riding with the herd. *Damn. Now, this is a stew. Cain't let him mess his pants, but I ain't gonna untie him either. Not when I'm alone. Dayam.*

Jeremiah walked out some from the fire and looked all around the camp. Embers were glowing at a couple of the fires but couldn't see any of the fires burning as if someone was sitting near one. The chuck fire was the closest and he knew that Snake, Louise, and Pedro would be sleeping near it but under something, out of the rain. Should he leave his prisoner and walk over and awaken Snake just so Silas could relieve himself?

That would be bold, Jeremiah decided. He looked at Silas out of the corner of his eye and found the man sitting rather serenely, not twitching about with the pains of having to go to the bathroom. *That boy's playing opossum even now.* Jeremiah chuckled softly, turned and walked up to Lippincott. "Too bad, son. Ain't nobody around to help. You'll just have to hold it until my relief shows up."

Silas cursed loud and long, cried out in pain and frustration, and when none of that seemed to do any good, sat under his covering and sulked. *You're gonna be the first one to die, you bastard. You, then Snake, and then Dog-man. But you're gonna be first.* His hands were still free, but there was no way to get his arms around to the other side of the tree to untie those ropes.

Need to cut 'em, he thought. *Don't got no knife. Ain't got nothin'.* Without being obvious, he tried to feel about where he was sitting to find a rock, something to cut the ropes. He didn't have to relieve himself, he just wanted

Jeremiah close enough to grab him, choke him to death, use his knife to get free, and then kill everyone around the camp.

He found a rock and it seemed like it might do the job. It would take a long time, but, he growled, thinking about it, he seemed to have a long time to work on those ropes.

35

"WE'RE GONNA GET WET," Wayne Nichols said as he rode up alongside Francisco Alvarado. The two had been the Nighthawks for the first two hours and were hoping to be relieved before the rains came.

Lightning bolts had been working their way across the mountains and the accompanying rains would hammer the Nighthawks and the herd soon. What was rumbling thunder off in the distance was now booming, blasting, rolling claps of thunder closer than next door. Alvarado could see the herd starting to mill about, could feel the tension building.

"Let's not worry about the rain, Mr. Nichols, let's start working on those steers. I'll go clockwise," he said, and the two riders separated, moving slowly around the jittery beeves, singing softly, reciting wild and ribald poetry, even holding calm conversations with the animals. The cattle responded, some reluctantly, but stayed together, munching on what was now wet grass.

Two men at the other end of the herd were doing the same thing as heavy rain was driven by strong winds.

Lightning blasted the nearby forests on either side of the wide valley, claps of thunder echoed back and forth across the hillsides, and one would think they might have been transported to the gates of hell.

The small creek that ran down the south edge of Buzzard Pass built quickly and was running over its banks in no time. The cattle closest to the creek moved away and Francisco Alvarado rode across to the south side, gathered half a dozen steers on that side, and moved them back into the meadow.

If this keeps up we won't be able to do that shortly. That creek's running strong now, but when this water comes down off these hills and fills that creek, it'll be a full-bore river. He didn't give his thought time to mature and rode into the cow camp and right up to where Snake and Louise were bedded under the chuck.

"I think we need the crew out there, Snake. Creek's about to be a river and the cattle seem to want to be on the other side. Need the men out there."

"Ring 'em out, Francisco," Snake said, climbing out from his bedroll. "Better get the fires lit and coffee boiling, Louise. Gonna be one of those mornings." He chuckled.

Alvarado began ringing the heavy iron triangle and sleepy cowboys, charros, and teamsters began cursing and finding trousers and boots. Within minutes, the laid-back and sleepy cow camp was alive and noisy. Alvarado rode through giving instructions, horses were saddled, and men were on the move.

Snake rode up to where Jeremiah's fire was sputtering but still lit. "How's our prisoner?"

"Still playing opossum, Snake. I'm pretty sure he's got some kind of plan to break out of here. Keeps crying out

243

to relieve himself, but I ain't untying him. He can mess his pants for all I care."

"Keep thinking that way. You won't get a relief so don't look for one. Got trouble out with the herd. Don't get near that boy unless there's someone with you."

Jeremiah watched Snake ride off into the pouring rain and tucked himself back under the flapping canvas. "You heard the man, Silas. You ain't going nowhere."

The language that came from Lippincott would burn a tree down. Jeremiah laughed, listening to him. "Better save your strength, son. Gonna be a long wet morning."

SNAKE HAD one crew and Alvarado had another, and together they kept the animals from trying to cross the now-raging water. Every little draw in the hillsides on the north and the south of Buzzard Pass were emptying into the stream and the rains were furious. The cattle were restive but not ready to bolt. they just needed to move about and weren't smart enough to keep out of the fast-running water.

The storm wasn't one of those everlasting ones and slowly died out after a couple of hours. Snake posted more Nighthawks and brought the crew back into camp. Louise and Jeannie had fires going, despite the wet, and the men got as close as they dared. The aroma of boiling coffee and drying clothing filled the air, and George Dawson chased Snake down.

"According to my watch, it's almost three o'clock, Snake. Don't see much sense in trying to go back to bed. Can you move 'em out in the dark like this?"

"I'd rather not, George, but by the time we get filled up with a hefty breakfast, it'll be coming light." He chuckled thinking about it. "Trying to move cattle in the dark usually means you'll lose a few head, and I'm not in the mood for losing beef right now. They've been moving about out there for some time already, might as well get 'em moving down the trail."

Snake grabbed a couple of men, told them the plan and to spread the word. He stopped by where Jeremiah was still guarding Lippincott. "We'll be eating breakfast first and then moving out, Mr. Hillyer. How's our number one visitor holding out?"

"He's one lucky sumbitch, Snake. Another ten minutes alone with him and he'd be a dead man. He needs to thank you for coming by just now." Snake laughed right out and walked over to where Silas was stretched out.

Lippincott seemed to be asleep as Snake approached but struck out one step early. If Snake had taken one more step, that rock would have crashed into his leg and Silas would have followed it. As it was, Silas swung the rock through empty air, Snake pulled his big revolver and smashed it into the outlaw's already beat-up head.

"Lordamighty," Jeremiah Hillyer said, racing to Snake's side. "He getcha?"

"Got lucky on this one," Snake said. "Look at that rock in his hand. He's been sawing on those ropes all night. Won't be tying him to no trees. From now on, we hog-tie this fool and if that means he'd be screaming all night, well, so be it. Damn me, but he's just one stupid fool."

Louise walked up beside Snake and gasped when she saw Silas face down in the mud, bleeding profusely from wounds in his head. "What happened? Is he still alive?"

"I'd like to think not," Snake said. "But I'm afraid he is. Cut his ropes during the night and tried to get away.

How can one man create so much trouble?" He slipped an arm around the lovely Lion Killer and snuck a quick kiss. "We'll have an early breakfast and get this herd back on the trail, darlin'."

"What about him?"

"One of our problems, dear lady, we're taking up valuable time and effort thinking about our fellow man. We will feed him and keep him alive if possible until we dump him in the sheriff's lap in San Bernardino."

She was scowling as she headed back toward the chuck. *That man had created more trouble than we've ever had. Snake can take more than I. Lippincott's lucky it's Snake's decision and not mine. feed him? Keep him warm and alive? I'd much rather feed him to the lions and bears.*

Snake bent down and tied Lippincott's hands behind his back. leaving him face down in the mud. "Ain't gonna be nice to that boy another half second," he murmured, getting back to his feet. "Drag him near the fire, Jeremiah. Tie his feet together and leave him face down. If he wakes up, shove a biscuit in his mouth, if he doesn't, too bad for him."

As Snake predicted, it was just coming light when the drovers started moving the herd down Buzzard Pass. Bright sun was already shining brightly on Buzzard Peak hundreds of feet above them. Dawson's wagons slipped in behind the chuck wagon and were surrounded by the herd of fine Andalusian horses. The herd of a thousand or so head of beef cattle were moving along, arguing loudly at the early hour.

"Well, look at you," Snake said. "How's that leg? You sure you should be out here?"

Dog-man had a grin on his face as he rode up alongside. "Never been better," he said. "Hurts like all the bees in the grass are biting, but I ain't gonna ride in that wagon and listen to that man's whining and crying another minute. Lose anything last night?"

"Only some sleep." Snake chuckled. "One more night in cow camp, and we'll be in San Bernardino tomorrow before noon. Our first herd to the sales yard, Dog. We need to send a wire to that sheriff up in Deadwood and tell him what a favor he did running us out of town like he did." He slouched way back in his saddle, reins hanging loose in his hands, and looked up at the sky.

"Been meaning to ask," Dog-man said. "What made you change your mind and bring the horses for sale instead of having a spring sale at the ranch?"

"When those fools tried to burn us out. Would have had to leave some of our people to keep an eye on the herd with so many outlaws running around. figured they'd be safer going on the drive, and we'll still come out looking good at the sale." Snake laid himself out in the saddle as he liked to do and continued.

"Up 'til we bought this place, we been on the road for some time, Dog-man. Met some awfully nice people."

"Met some real bastards, too, old man." Dog-man chuckled. "A couple of sheriffs I don't want to see again. It's been a ride, Snake, and I got a feeling it ain't over yet."

"Not by a sight, pard. The one thing we gotta do is clean up this country we live in. Run all these outlaws off, hang 'em if we have to. All these troubles we've had since we got here is because we've had almost no law enforcement. People just running loose doing whatever they feel like doing no matter who gets hurt."

"Sounding like a politician, there, Snake," Dog-man chuckled. "Damn if you ain't right, though." He turned to look back over the herd. "I'm gonna ride back and ride with Wayne Nichols for a while. He's got drag duty today."

"Come in at noon break, Dog, and we'll ride on ahead into San Bernardino to make sure the stockyards are ready for us."

"Be a good time to bring Silas Lippincott, too." Dogman rode off and Snake thought about what he said.

"He's right," Snake muttered. "Get that man as far away from this herd as possible." He knew they weren't that far out from the town and could ride in, deposit the prisoner with the sheriff, do their business at the stockyards, and still be back in cow camp before dark. Where the herd might make eight miles in a day, a rider can make fifty or sixty without too much trouble.

This fine Andalusian stud I'm riding? The condition he's in? I'm gonna enjoy riding into town. Let him stretch it out some, so fast and quick I'll be reaching for the saddle horn. He laughed right out, hurrahing some of the closest steers, keeping them moving.

36

LOUISE AND JEANNIE NICHOLS were waiting for him as Snake rode into where the ladies were set up for noon break. *Those two look angry enough to bite somebody's head off. Hope it ain't mine they're after.* He stepped down and Pedro ran up and took the reins to tie the big horse off.

"This don't look like a friendly camp, Pedro. What's been going on?"

"That man's been screaming all morning. Mama said she was either going to shoot him or shoot you if you don't do something about it. She wouldn't really shoot you, would she?" His big brown eyes got all watery, his lips were quivering, and Snake had to hold a chuckle back.

"No, Pedrito, she wouldn't, but she might find some way to get even that we wouldn't like. Let's you and me go make her happy, eh?" They feigned taking punches at each other, laughing and running into where the fires were burning.

"Me and Dog-man are gonna take old Silas into San Berdoo after our dinner, Louise. That should make you feel a bit at ease. I know he's been a pain, but like you said earlier, we ain't the kind to just kill a man 'cuz he's a pest."

She smiled, threw him a kiss and poured a mug of coffee for the long Texan. "You're timing couldn't be better, Snake. Me and Jeannie would have had his meat stripped out and under the smoke in another hour." She looked at him kinda sideways. "Just the two of you? Like it used to be?"

She had a questioning look on her face. "You are coming back, right?"

Snake reached out and grabbed her, pulled her close, cast an eye about for those who might be watching, and gave her bottom a little pat. "It's you and me, my lady, for the rest of our lives. I've always been afraid of this kind of commitment, but I ain't afraid of nothin' anymore."

"You're afraid of Mama," Pedro said. "You said so."

"Little scamp," Snake said, grabbing up the boy. "There are some things that are just between us men. Things the women don't need to know." They were laughing, and Louise had to laugh, too, thinking that Snake might just be a little bit afraid of her.

"ABOUT TEN, MAYBE TWELVE MILES?" Dog-man settled into the saddle and handed the lead rope to Snake. It was attached to the horse Silas Lippincott was tied to.

"Be there in about three hours, Dog. What a pleasure to drop this fool off. You sure that leg of yours is up to this? That was a mean-looking wound."

"Ain't no infection, don't hurt much unless I bang it on something. I need this ride."

Snake gave a long look at his partner and nodded.

Maybe it is that we both need this ride, he thought. *Our first drive to market with our own cattle and horses and it should be a wonderful time. Ten years down the road we should be able to look back on this as something more than pleasurable. Instead, we've been putting up with a stupid young man who wants to kill us because his family is nothing but outlaws. He has come close to destroying a most wonderful experience.*

"You're right, Dog. We need this ride." Snake led off with Silas following and Dog-man trailing. They rode further down Buzzard Pass and turned north where the trail split. It was a broad trail, used often by heavy wagons, herds, smaller than those of Snake and Dog-man, and an easy ride. The day was pleasant, all the smells of fresh fallen rain in the forests and grasses, lots of blue sky, and conclusion to a serious problem tied to a horse being trailed.

Dog-man was enchanted by the scenery. Large trees of every kind, ground, black and rich in places, red with clay in others, and thick underbrush just off the trail. "Could have used some of this greenery and timber at that mine of ours," he said. "Some of those beeves we're moving, too."

"That was dry country, Dog. Don't miss it none. Wouldn't mind finding a ledge of gold like that again, but in kinder country."

"Where are you taking me?" Silas demanded. The soft friendly air the boys were riding through turned sour at his comment. "You got no right to hold me. Got no right taking me someplace."

"What we got is every right to kill your ugly butt," Snake growled. "Taking you to the sheriff, sonny boy, and with a little luck, he's gonna hang you from a high oak tree."

"Ain't done nothing to you," Silas whimpered.

"Killed one of our men, you did. Shot Dog-man you did. Stole one of our horses, you did. Tried to kill others. Best be quiet now, or we'll just pull off this main highway we're on, find a decent tree, and hang you ourselves."

Dog-man had to chuckle listening to Snake but understood the anger in his voice. *This has been a most interesting trail drive. Some of the most beautiful country to ride through and some of the most dangerous and ugly men to fight off. The beauty of one doesn't eliminate the ugly of the other, I'm afraid.*

Dog-man let his mind drift back to that first day when he sat his horse on a high ridge watching the large herd move out. The noise, the dust, and sheer beauty of the scene almost brought water to the man's eyes. That all of this belonged to him and Snake was overwhelming and he had to stop for just a moment and collect himself.

"I don't know how we did this Snake, but it's the most wonderful feeling in the world that I'm having. Even the vile Silas Lippincott can't take any of this from us."

"He come mighty close, Dog-man. Too close for me to want to think about. I knew you was chasing him, heard that shot, and damn me if my heart didn't just stop."

"You really felt that way?"

"Couldn't help myself. Figured you got yourself all shot up so's I would have to do all the work around the place. You was gettin' even, sort of."

Dog-man laughed right out but cussed at Snake too. "You had me goin' for a minute there," he called out.

They rode in silence for another hour or so, enjoying the beauty of the landscape, the rolling hills, deep green forests, and bright blue sky. "Be coming close to town soon," Snake said. "Didn't much care for the town when we were here before."

"Nope, me too," Dog-man said. "Best part of town was the stockyards. Right now, the best part is gonna be the sheriff's office."

They crested a ridge and looked down on San Bernardino, spread out across some fine grazing land, dotted with orchards, and sprinkled with groups of houses and business buildings. "Gonna be a real city one day, I'm afraid," Snake said. "It's people that ruins good country, Dog."

"We're people, Snake."

"Well, we're different," Snake said, not bothering to add anything else. They rode into the town, saw the sheriff's sign hanging in the breeze and rode up to the tie rack. The sheriff, Jake Anthony was sitting on a bench enjoying the mid-day sun. They stepped down and tied the horses off.

"Got a customer for you, sheriff. My name's Snake, this here is my partner, Dog-man, and that piece of ugly outlaw is Silas Lippincott."

"Lippincott, eh?" Anthony said. "Well, bring him on in and tell me all about it. Been looking forward to having a Lippincott in my jail." The sheriff was a tall, thin, almost skinny man of about thirty-five years. His weathered face seemed to have a permanent sneer, scowl, spread across it. It probably had as many stories to tell as there were lines to see. "Silas Lippincott, eh? Couldn't get Wally or that bastard kid, Pepe, eh? I got bullets set aside for them."

"Wally and Pepe made the mistake of trying to rustle our herd, which is just a few miles south of here and coming on hard," Snake said. "Had to bury 'em. This one killed one of our men, stole a horse, and has been working to kill us for the last three days. Glad to give him to you, Sheriff."

"Glad to take him, Snake," the sheriff said with a genuine chuckle. His eyes were squeezed in a grin as he helped get the prisoner untied and off the horse. Silas was hurt, stupid, and did the wrong thing at the wrong time. He made a grab for the sheriff's sidearm. Jake Anthony knocked the hand aside, pulled a big Remington and slammed it across the side of Lippincott's already bruised and bloody head.

"Well, just damn me," Anthony said, kicking the inert figure in the head, twice. "Just don't cotton to that behavior in my prisoners, boy." Snake and Dog-man both stood with their mouths open, watching the sheriff physically abuse the prisoner.

"I think you've got him pretty much calmed down, Sheriff," Dog-man said. "Want some help gettin' him inside?"

Sheriff Anthony slipped the pistol back in its holster, bent down and grabbed Silas by the boots, and dragged him face down up the two steps to the boardwalk in front of his office, across the walkway, and into the office. "Judge will see him in the morning. I'll need statements from you two before then."

"We've got business at the stockyards, Sheriff, but we'll be back and have those for you," Snake said. "Just so you know, the kid's wily and stupid at the same time."

"I kinda got that figured out when he went for my gun. I'll be right here when you get back," Anthony said.

———

THEY WERE WALKING their horses toward the stockyards right down the middle of the main street, past hardware stores, millinery shops, gun and ammunition dealers, and blacksmiths. "I think I could handle a cold beer before we hit the stockyards," Snake said. "Sheriff's a tough old bastard, eh?"

"Cold beer sounds good. Don't think I've ever seen anything like that." Dog-man chuckled.

"Almost felt sorry for old Silas there," Snake continued. "'Course that don't mean I didn't have it in mind myself, you understand. I have a little bit more control of my responses to idiots than the sheriff."

Dog-man motioned for the barman as they found room at the long oaken plank. The Golden Palace Saloon was not golden, surely was not a palace, but the beer was cold and tasty, and the boys decided a second one would be perfect.

"You boys brought a lot of dust in with you," the barman said. "Whatcha been doin' to get so dusty and sweaty? Don't know if I got enough beer to cool you off."

"Bringing in a herd from Lane's Crossing," Dog-man said. "The cattle and the rest of the crew will be here tomorrow. Had to bring a feller in to see the sheriff."

"Hope he lives through it. Sheriff ain't known for bringing prisoners before the judge."

"That so?" Snake gave Dog-man a long look and nodded his head. "Got a real tough lawman hereabouts, eh? We could use one at Lane's Crossing."

"Wouldn't want Anthony. He killed Jed Hopkins yesterday and all the fool did was accidentally break a window at the hardware store. Man's not got that kind of right just because he wears a badge. You boys be careful dealing with the man."

"Nice talking with you. We better get to the stockyards," Dog-man said. They tossed off the last of the beer and walked out the door in time to hear two shots fired. "Sounds like they came from the sheriff's office, Snake."

"Did indeed," Snake said. "Stockyards right down the block here. Let's just keep walking."

Dog-man didn't want to but something told him that Snake was right. Stay the hell out of this problem, let Anthony work it out himself. The pens at the stockyards were busy with riders moving critters about. Sales would be going on all week long, buyers from more than half a dozen slaughterhouses were on hand and cash was flowing. Every man was sunburned, dusty, and well-armed.

"I seen half a dozen badges, Dog-man, but they ain't deputy sheriff badges. Cattlemen's association enforcers are here for herd and money protection. Good to see. I don't think I'd want Sheriff Anthony's protection."

It took less than an hour to make the arrangements for their herd's arrival and the two made their way back to the sheriff's office. "No need for your statements, gentlemen," Anthony said. "That fool Lippincott made another grab for my gun and I had to kill him. Go on back to your herd, his case is closed."

Anthony scratched his beard, looked at Snake, and continued. You got Mexican working that herd?"

"Some of the best," Snake said. "Real charros. Why you ask?"

"Don't much care for them beaners myself. Keep a close eye on 'em. I don't put up with no nonsense."

"Good day to you, then," Snake said. "We'll get back to our camp." They walked back to their horses, stepped into the saddles and rode out of San Bernardino at a solid trot. "I don't put up with his kind of nonsense, neither, Dog-man. Will all of this stupidity end? My godamigty, the sheriff don't like Mexicans? Does he even know that this was Mexico just a few years ago? What the hell is wrong with people?"

"People are scared of things they don't know nothing about and too ignorant to learn, Snake. We got to make sure that Francisco and the others are fully aware of this situation. One little word, action, and we will have us a war. Right now, let's just ride to camp. I could eat a whole steer."

"I can already taste the steaks that Louise will have ready for us," Snake said. They kept the horses at a good trot for at least half an hour before letting them settle into a walk. "Can't get away from that town fast enough," Snake grumbled.

"That man ain't no better than any murderer he's had in his jail," Dog-man said. "Well, they elected him, they got to live with him."

"Unfortunately, so do we. I bet they made some good time with the herd after their dinner, Dog. We might be mighty close to camp."

Those well-bred Andalusian stock horses made excellent time and the few miles back to cow camp were eaten up by the long legs and deep chests. "Smell that?" Snake asked, didn't wait for an answer, just touched the side of the horse with his spurs, and the race was on. They were head and head coming into cow camp, bringing the horses to a skidding stop just yards from the main cook-fire.

"You boys were almost late. Another ten minutes and there wouldn't have been any food left for you." Louise laughed, watching the two act like they were ten years old again. "Two steaks coming up. Pedro, grab their horses, will you?"

37

THE FIRES WERE BURNING BRIGHT, the stars were shining for the first night in the last several. Snake and Dog-man had the crew settled in with coffee, maybe a flask or two, for a long talk about San Bernardino and Sheriff Anthony.

"We're riding into a most dangerous situation," Snake said. He went on to describe what had taken place with Silas Lippincott and the conversation they had about Mexicans. There were some loud words spat out from several areas and Snake let them continue, didn't hold anyone back.

"I've run into this up the valley," Francisco said. "It dates back to when the gold seekers came. This was Mexico, there was little law, mostly the communities were under church rule, or those that held the land grants. The Americans swarmed the countryside, Snake, and treated everyone as second class. Still do in some cases."

"Well," Dog-man said, "we didn't bring our herd in to change the social order of San Bernardino. The sheriff will be on the prod and his answer seems to be to kill first and you won't have to answer any questions. I'd like for us to bring the herd in, make the sales, and ride out, all of us."

"Run into men like him," George Dawson said. "Maybe there needs to be a change in the social order, Dog-man. From what you said, it seems the people elected a hard case and don't know what to do about it."

"Ain't our job, George, as much as I'd like to shoot the bastard myself," Snake said. "I'm figuring we're just a few miles out and will be putting these critters in the stock-yard just after midday. It's important to remember the sheriff's attitude. It's wrong, but we ain't there to make things right. We need to sell the herd and make tracks back for Lane's Crossing."

"How long do you think it will take?" Francisco Alvarado looked at the men sitting around the fire. Half a dozen Americans and half a dozen Mexicans. Two women and a child, as well.

"We'll be able to ride out the day after, I think," Snake said. *The first thing me and Dog-man did was head for the saloon for a cold beer. These men have that coming and more. That sheriff is going to depend on that and sure as hell will prod somebody into a fight.*

Snake shook his head. "Don't nobody go off alone for a cold beer. Anthony will look for that. Go in threes or more if you can and don't let that fool prod you. He is the kind to shoot first, maybe even in the back."

"Me and my boys will be in town for several days, weeks even, Snake. I'll be pulling away from the herd when we hit town, but we'll try to keep an eye on things." Dawson looked at his teamsters and then around at the others around the fire. "Damndest ride I've ever been on."

"Is there a better time of the day than sunrise?" Snake was pulling his boots on, Louise and Pedro were getting the fire and coffee going, and the sky was just beginning to move from night to shades of gray, which would soon explode with color. The air had a chill to it and Snake held his hands over the warm fire looking across the wide expanse of beautiful early morning mountains.

Activity was taking place throughout the cow camp with teamsters swilling coffee while untangling harness leather, cowboys and charros tending to tack while not spilling their coffee. Soon the aroma of sizzling side meat filled the air and it wasn't but just a few minutes after that that the clarion voice of Francisco Alvarado rang out.

"Saddle 'em up, boys, it's time to head 'em out. Let's move now. Sun's halfway to noon." Some grumbling, a few nasty comments, and horses were saddled, mules were harnessed, and Louise, Pedro, and Jeannie Nichols in the chuck led the great herd from the good grass. Voices echoed through the forest, urging on a thousand head of fine cattle, several hundred horses, and let's not forget George Dawson's wagons, loaded with gold ore and hides.

Only one horse balked at having to go to work, put on a fine demonstration, the charro cheered on by all. Sun-fishing, whirling, kicking, and flaying hooves finally quieted down and the young Alvino "Gordo" Garcia got a good hand from all.

"Almost there, Snake. Our first drive and sale. Sure hope we meet that sheriff in Deadwood someday. Like to shake his hand and tell him thankee. Done us a big favor, runnin' us off like he did." Dog-man was laughing and his horse was doing its own little dance.

Snake chuckled, looking back over his shoulder. They were reaching the high spot on the trail. Everything would be downhill now and into San Bernardino. "Hell of a sight, Dog. Ground's wet enough that all of that ain't covered in dust." He spread his arms wide. "How are we gonna protect our boys when the sale is over."

"Been thinking about that," Dog-man said. "It ain't law but it sure is tradition to pay 'em off after the sale, let 'em kick up their heels before heading back to the ranch, but that sheriff knows that, too. He's got blood in his eyes, Snake."

"We got to pay 'em, and after that, it's gonna be up to them to protect themselves. We can't do any more than what we done. Warn 'em. That's it."

The two were well out in front of the herd and were enjoying the sounds of the men calling out to the cattle to keep 'em moving, the loud and boisterous yowling of the cattle, and the wonderful song of the mules from time to time. "Been wanting to hear all this for a long time, Snake." Dog-man spent as much time looking forward as he did wrenched around looking at the herd coming down behind them.

It was a full half day's ride before Snake, Dog-man, and the chuck led the great drive down the main street of San Bernardino and to the open and welcoming gates of the stockyards. People lined the streets, some waving and hollering their hellos, some cursing a blue streak at all the dust and leavings of a thousand head of cattle, and kids, mostly young boys, trying to be cowboys, hazing the cattle along.

Sheriff Jake Anthony was standing at the open door

to the jail as they passed by. Snake nodded his hello and it wasn't returned. Instead, Anthony turned and stepped into the office, closing the door. "Friendly bastard, ain't he," Snake growled.

"Went in to count his bullets." Dog-man laughed.

It was a chore but all the cattle were in various pens, horses separated and penned, and the tally-men got together to add up the numbers. Losses on the drive were common, but on a short drive like this, despite the weather, there were few. Snake and Dog-man nodded to buyers who lined the way and the noise slowly came down to a mild roar.

SNAKE AND DOG-MAN, covered in dust and sweat made their way into the stockyard offices to meet with the tally-man. "We did it, Snake. We made our first drive, and I'm ready for our first sale."

"There were times I didn't think we'd make it," Snake said. "Well, look who's here. Howdy, Gordy. Didn't think you spent much time in stockyards."

County Commissioner Gordy Whitman, sunburned despite the several days of thunderstorms, stuck out his hand. "They've called for special meetings of the commission so I've had to come in from my new mining property. Heard you and Dog-man were bringing in your herd and wanted to see the show."

"Like the show, did you? A thousand head, Gordy," Dog-man said. "What's the special meeting about?"

"Trying to get a sheriff for south county. We need one in Lane's Crossing as you boys well know. I think we have the answer, though. The San Bernardino County

Sheriff will appoint a South County Sheriff. We'll have someone on the job soon, now."

Snake stood still for a moment, slowly shook his head before saying anything. "We met Sheriff Anthony. Don't think much of the man, Gordy. He ain't nothing but a killer with a badge."

Whitman smiled and wagged his head, too. "Problem is, Snake, he's elected. We don't much cotton to his ways, either, but can't fire an elected official. You be very careful around him. He's killed some good people, and this county needs people like you and Dog-man. The problem is, when the lawman is worse than the criminal, it's the lawman who's wrong. The people unfortunately believe Anthony when he says he's cleaning up the town."

Whitman wiped some sweat from his forehead and tried to smile. "The idea of the sheriff appointing a deputy for Lane's Crossing is the right one even if the current sheriff isn't right for the county. that's our next problem, eh?"

"Kill off people you don't like ain't cleaning up the town," Dog-man said. "Will you have anything to say about who might get appointed as deputy for Lane's Crossing?"

Before Gordy Whitman could answer, Snake spoke up. It wasn't like him to edge Dog-man out like that and Dog-man stood mute for a moment. After hearing Snake, he understood.

"We got some paperwork to take care of, Gordy. Glad you saw the show. When Anthony appoints a sheriff for Lane's Crossing do the commissioners get to approve or disapprove?"

"Part of the deal, Snake. You fellers have a good day,

make lots of money, and maybe we can get together for a drink this evening. At the Golden Palace?"

"Yes sir, that's our plan," Dog-man chuckled. "Make sure you yourself approves of the new lawman." He smiled at both the commissioner and his partner. "The sale is tomorrow so we won't be up late. Have our camp just out of town. Anthony told us he don't like our hands. Too bad for him."

38

FRANCISCO ALVARADO HAD the crew working with the stockyard riders and got the cattle separated into age and weight divisions, got the horses put together for the sale and met with Snake and Dog-man at the little camp on the edge of town. A creek was nearby and most of the men found time to shed filthy clothing, take a needed bath, and dress for the evening meal.

Steaks were cooking over open fires, beans were boiling in huge cast iron dutch ovens, and the aroma of coffee was in the air as well. "The stockyard people want our hands to work with their riders during the sale, Snake. I said that would be fine," Alvarado said.

"It is," Snake said. "You take care of that end of things, and me and Dog-man will be inside watching the sale." He sat quiet for a minute, looked at Dog-man, looked at Louise, and took a long sip of coffee.

Ain't never done nothing like this, he thought. *These are our cattle, our beeves. Growed 'em up ourselves, we did and now we're gonna sell 'em.* He looked again at Louise, sitting at the fire, stirring a pot of beans. Her buckskins carried stains from more than one encounter with something big and mean, her face as soft and tender as a fresh blade of grass, and her eyes looked right back at him. *She was hurt so bad when Dog-man found her. I ain't worthy of all that love she pours over me. Just ain't.*

It was Jeannie Nichols who broke the reverie, ringing the big bell. "Let's eat, boys. Don't let it get cold. Grab your pans and get in line," she hollered out in her broken English, a huge Paiute smile on her face. "Clean your pans, and we'll have some apple pie afterward." Snake wondered if she might have a whole barrel of apples stowed away somewhere?

A round of hollering and the stampede was underway. "Boys are hungry, Snake. We never did stop for dinner today. They haven't had anything to eat since sunrise." Louise was laughing watching the men try to be first in line at the two big fires. She let them do their own beans and served them the steaks they pointed out on the grill. Each man had his own idea of which one was the best.

"Glad we did this," Snake said, "but don't want to do it again for at least a year down the road."

"No spring sale?" Louise teased.

"Never," Snake tried to growl, but he was too happy to pull it off. "I'm glad I changed my mind about the horses. Imagine, Louise, with all the nonsense we've put up with on this little drive if I was worrying all day and every night about the horses back at the ranch?" He had to laugh and Louise frowned thinking about what he said.

Pedro brought Snake his tin plate full of steak and beans, went back for his own, and sat down next to him. "You'll be riding with the boys at next year's drive, son.

I'm gonna like that. You and me, driving cattle. I'm gonna like that."

Maybe it was, maybe it wasn't, but Snake was aware that the smile never left his face the rest of the night. "I ain't one to get all melancholy," he said to Louise as they slipped under bedroll blankets, "but tonight is just about as grand as it's ever gonna be. I ain't never been this much at peace with the world, never."

She wrapped her arms around him and pulled him to her. "I think I know how to make us both even more at peace," she whispered in his ear.

———

MORNING CAME TOO EARLY, and the growling could be heard in every corner of the cow camp. "Up and at 'em, boys, we got beeves to sell," Alvarado said, ringing the triangle as he walked among the bedrolls. It was gray dawn, no crimson or purple to be seen yet and the men slowly rolled out.

It was the first morning they didn't have to fight mud and rain. The threat of thunderstorms was with them all evening but never happened. they slept under stars, not heavy rain and flashing lightning.

At breakfast, Snake again went over the potential problem of the sheriff when the sale was over. "Want you back at the ranch, boys. Don't want you dead or in jail. Let's saddle up and give 'em a show."

It soon became a hot and dry, rather dusty day, and the auctioneer's song was loud and lively, money flowed across the bookkeeper's desk, and the day finally came to an end. Men with association badges and big guns were as visible as they could make themselves, and the man from the bank wrote out the deposit slips and took charge of most of the money.

Snake found it most interesting that neither the sheriff nor his deputies had been seen. *Seems to me if he was the least bit interested in keeping the law that he would be here protecting what might could very well be stolen. He's trying to build himself a reputation as a gun-slinging killer. Probably plannin' his first bank job right now.*

"Gather around, boys," Dog-man said, standing in the middle of one of the empty corrals. "This is the part you've been waiting for. A quick word before Snake hands it out. You did a fantastic job bringing this herd in, fighting off a madman, and challenging the gods of bad weather. You've earned every dime of this. Snake, go ahead and hand out the purses, and boys, me and Snake will be at the Golden Palace shortly. The first drink's on us."

There was a great howl went up and Snake had buckskin purses filled with gold coins for each man. There were smiles, handshakes, and some shoulder slapping as each man took his purse. Louise had tanned the leather, designed, and made the simple draw-string purses for each hand.

"Me and Jeannie will take Pedro back to camp, Snake. Try not to get in trouble, okay?" Louise smiled up at the tall Texan. "But if you have to kill that man, make sure you're in the right."

"Ain't in the mood for killing, darlin'," he said. "We won't be long. Let's plan on pullin' out early in the morning. Need to be back on the ranch."

"I can feel the pull." She smiled, trying to wrap her arms around him. "I miss sitting on that porch in the morning."

268

THE GOLDEN PALACE was filled and then some when Snake and Dog-man eased their way in. Men from the stockyards, buyers, and cowboys were standing two and three deep at the bar, gold and silver coins were seen flashing, and laughter filled the air.

"Best take a table, Snake. Ain't gonna fight my way through all that."

"There's Gordy Whitman sitting with George Dawson. Let's join 'em."

Dawson was wearing a big smile when the boys made their way to the table. A bar-maid was right behind them with two pitchers of cold beer and two big mugs to be filled. "Just signed the deal on my first warehouse in San Berdoo, boys. I'm in business."

"Great news," Dog-man said. "You have something to do with that, Gordy?"

Whitman just sat and smiled right along with Dawson. "As a matter of fact, I do believe that Mr. Dawson and I have just become partners in a couple of businesses, eh George?"

"Indeed we have. Warehousing to serve local businesses along with direct connections with the soon-to-be arriving railroad for incoming and our manufacturers. We got us a plan, boys."

George Dawson had more to say but the four of them noticed how quiet it had become in the large saloon and gambling hall. Dawson, sitting so as to see the front doors, nodded toward them and Snake and Dog-man turned in time to see Sheriff Jake Anthony and two of his deputies push their way through the crowd.

"Trouble," Gordy Whitman murmured. "He ain't here to celebrate your first sale, Snake."

"Wasn't anywhere around the stockyards, either," Snake said. "Is this his way of a show of force? Come into a full saloon with two deputies?" Snake looked over to Dog-man. "Keep an eye on our boys."

"He's dressed to put on a show," Dog-man said. "He ain't wearing a simple shirt and canvas pants, Snake, and that ain't just a big Remington tucked in his waist. Them's wool pants, a fine linen shirt, and that's a special gun belt and holster he's got strapped on. He's not here to keep the peace."

Snake got up slowly, looked up and down the long bar and found where Alvarado and Hillyer were standing along with several of the hands. He moved through the crowd and edged up alongside Jeremiah Hillyer. "Sheriff just came in, boys. Let's do everything we can to keep this nice and peaceful."

Alvarado motioned for a couple of the Mexican hands to turn so as to face behind the bar and Snake did the same with Hillyer and the others. The noise level in the Golden Palace had dropped considerably with the arrival of Anthony and Snake watched the lawman shove his way through the crowd on a direct route to where he was standing.

"You always drink with Mexicans, Snake?" Anthony said, loud enough for many around them to hear.

"Often as possible, Sheriff. Some fine hands here," he said, looking at his crew. "Join us for a snort or two?"

"I don't drink with Mexicans," Anthony said. "In fact, I don't like 'em to be in the same saloon I'm in."

"I'd suggest you leave then," Snake said, "since we're staying."

There were a few gasps at the comment and more than one guffaw could be heard. Snake smiled and watched the barman move back and away from the area, saw the two deputies spread out on both sides of the sheriff, but also saw Dog-man, George Dawson, and Gordy Whitman move in closer to the action. They arranged themselves so if gunfire erupted they wouldn't be in the line of fire, as the barman did.

The quiet was in anticipation of death and Snake watched men flash money, make soft comments and wondered just what the odds were on his death at the moment. Those on the floor had seen the sheriff in action. No one had seen Snake draw and shoot.

Anthony stiffened at the comment, and Snake watched the sheriff's hand slowly move toward the big revolver at his side. "Now, you ain't gonna shoot me for tellin' the truth, are you, Sheriff? Why, my goodness, it is a free country. Have a drink with me and my Mexican hands, my fine Texas compatriot, there, and my Spanish foreman. We'd love to get to know you better."

The reaction varied among those in the gaudy saloon, from outright fear to absolute silence. In between the two was a mix of gasps and laughter. Dog-man coughed right out, Dawson bellowed a laugh, and Gordy Whitman knew that bullets would be flying in seconds.

Anthony looked at his deputies and nodded. "Get them beaners out of here," he said. "Snake, you're under arrest." He pulled the Remmie and screamed in pain when the short bullwhip Jeremiah Hillyer carried snapped across his wrist. The gun, fully cocked, went flying through the air and crashed to the floor without going off. Anthony was bent over, holding his wrist, cussing loud and long.

The deputies saw six men, three of them Mexican, holding guns and they were pointed right at them. Anthony, holding his bleeding wrist dove for the gun, rolled away and came up with the gun in his left hand.

Snake was faster, far more accurate, and Sheriff Jake Anthony's body jerked twice before he was able to pull the trigger.

"I assume you boys have eyes to see the world and its happenings?" Snake said softly to the deputies. "I'm sure you saw your boss, the late Sheriff Anthony, pull a gun on me, and I'm also positive that both of you will swear to that in written reports. Right now, you need to get that body to the undertaker."

Snake was standing with a still-smoking revolver, facing the two lawmen. The gun was pointed at the filthy saloon floor, and the two men would never forget just how fast that tall cowboy had been, killing the sheriff. They nodded and moved to carry Anthony's body out the door.

"Glad I was here to see that," County Commissioner Gordy Whitman said. "I don't think either of those deputies will try to avenge the killing, Snake, but to be safe, I'm going to file a report with the justice of the peace. I'd suggest you write one, as well."

"Good idea," Snake said, tucking the revolver back in its leather. He turned to his crew. "Thank you for not getting involved, boys." He looked at Hillyer. "Wondered why you always carried that quirt. Never saw you flick your horse with it, though."

"Ain't for horses, Snake," Hillyer said, showing the slightest smile. He flicked his boot with the tightly braided quirt and turned to the bar, nodding at the barman for another cold beer.

"Get us all one, pard. This has been one hell of a cattle drive," Snake said.

SNAKE AND LOUISE were wrapped in each other's arms tucked under a wool point blanket under the chuck wagon. "It had to rain, eh?" Snake growled. "Ain't no other way for this drive of ours to end but with a crashing, smashing thunderstorm and drenching rain. Didn't even get to finish my story."

"We're finishing it now," Louise purred. "And nobody but us can hear it."

ABOUT THE AUTHOR

Reno, Nevada novelist, Johnny Gunn, is retired from a long career in journalism. He has worked in print, broadcast, and Internet, including a stint as publisher and editor of the Virginia City Legend. These days, Gunn spends most of his time writing novel length fiction, concentrating on the western genre. Or, you can find him down by the Truckee River with a fly rod in hand.

"It's been a wonderful life. I was born in Santa Cruz, California, on the north shore of fabled Monterey Bay. When I was fourteen, that would have been 1953, we moved to Guam and I went through my high school years living in a tropical paradise. I learned to scuba dive from a WWII Navy Frogman, learned to fly from a WWII combat pilot (by dad), but I knew how to fish long before I moved to Guam.

I spent time on the Island of Truk, which during WWII was a huge Japanese naval base, and dived in the lagoon. Massive U.S. air strikes sunk thousands of tons of Japanese naval craft, and it was more than exciting to dive on those wrecks. In the Palau Islands, near Koror, I also dived on Japanese aircraft that had been shot down into the lagoons.

My own service time consisted of my defending you from Puerto Rico during the Cuban Missile Crisis. Seems as though I couldn't get away from tropical paradise. The diving was good but the fishing was splendid.

I've been living in Nevada since 1963, following my service time with the army. You'd have to hunt hard and long to find a spot in the Silver State that I haven't visited, and you'll find many of those spots in my stories. I've caught ten and eleven pound trout at Pyramid Lake and caught ten inch brook trout that were fully mature and would take you arm right out of the socket with their strikes.

Besides Virginia City, home of the fabled Comstock Lode, I've lived in Manhattan, Nevada. There were 120 of us at the time. I spent some time in Silver Peak, another very small community, and our home now is in an area called Cold Springs. There's a casino here called Border Town. The state line separating Nevada and California runs right through it. We can ride our horse a few hundred yards and be in California, right along the eastern flank of the Sierra Nevada.

We have a small hobby farm and raise a considerable amount of our own food. Cold Springs is about twenty miles north of Reno. We raise chickens for meat and eggs, and large New Zealand White rabbits for their meat. We raise the standard New Zealand which are large, but there are also Giant New Zealand rabbits. We haven't gotten into them. The goat provides milk and young ones for their meat.

My lovely wife says the little hobby farm keeps me out of trouble, and then snickers and says, maybe not. If you're in our area, stop in, I always need help cleaning corrals."